TRUSTING DREW

BURLAP AND BARBED WIRE #5

SHIRLEY PENICK

Cover Photo by Jean Woodfin Photography
Cover Models: Tionna Petramalo & Tyler Smith King
Editing by Carol Tietsworth
Formatting by Cora Cade

Contact me:
www.shirleypenick.com
www.facebook.com/ShirleyPenickAuthor

To sign up for Shirley's New Release Newsletter, send email to shirleypenick@outlook.com, subject newsletter.

To those who put their lives on the line to protect us. Thank you.

CHAPTER 1

*D*rew Kipling took a deep breath of the chilly morning air, he loved the early winter days in his mountain home. The day was not quite cold enough to see his breath, but instead was crisp and clear, with a slight breeze. The sky a brilliant blue as it often was at this altitude. He was happy to walk past his extended cab truck to the barn, where his horse waited. He had the next two days off and the first thing he was going to do was go out on his horse for an hour, or four. He'd been working for ten straight days, they'd been shorthanded due to the damn flu.

Nearly everyone in the Spirit Lake Sheriff's department had contracted it on the same day, when they'd found a hiker half out of his mind from fever, walking around on the edge of the lake. The guy was a huge mountain of a man and had put up a fight. The sheriff was forced to call in reinforcements to get the guy subdued. All the men piled into two patrol vehicles to accompany the tourist, to make sure once they got to the urgent care, which was just about forty minutes away, they would be able to muscle him inside. The doc had listened to the tale, taken a look at the hiker, and told the rest of them they were contaminated and to go straight home. He didn't want them beginning an epidemic.

That was the last time he'd had a day off. He and one of the other guys on the night shift had missed the flu party, since they'd missed the call for help. They'd discussed calling in a couple of officers from one of the neighboring towns, but they'd decided not to, when they heard several of those towns were shorthanded, too. Instead, the two of them had been working twelve-hour days, for ten damn days, while the rest of the crew hit their beds.

At least now, everyone was on the mend and were no longer deemed contagious, so he'd gotten to sleep late this morning and was now going to take his horse on a long ride across the family ranch. When he entered the barn, his horse shook his head to let Drew know it was about time he'd shown up. Drew quickly saddled the animal, and they headed out into the sunshine. The Colorado Rockies loomed in the distance as he rode across the acres his family owned. The cattle were in the southern fields, so he headed north. He didn't mind working the herd on his day off, but he needed some time to chill first. A ride up into the National Forest would be just what the doctor ordered.

He had his ever-present badge and pistol in his saddle bag, along with a first aid kit, and some lunch. One of the rifles that the whole family carried with them when they were out was strapped to the saddle. Early winter could pose problems for animals not having their readily available food source. They'd had a couple of snowfalls, but not enough to send the animals into hibernation. The snow up at the higher elevations made the evergreens stand out in stark contrast, God he loved this time of year. Cold, crisp, and gorgeous. The air was clean and pure. He filled his lungs with it, as he gloried in the day.

As he rode nearer to the National Forest at the top of the

ranch, there was something down on the ground, so he spurred his horse into a run, to check it out. When he got closer he realized it was a person, a woman. Blood covered the ground and her hair. He quickly got off his horse and dropped the reins on the ground, to signal his horse to stay put.

Grabbing the saddle bag which had the first aid kit, he rushed over to the woman. She wasn't dressed for the weather, wearing only a thin pair of slacks and what used to be a silk shirt but now was in tatters. No coat, no shoes. Her long brown hair was a tangled mess with twigs and dirt and blood matting it. What in the hell was going on?

"Miss, are you all right?"

She groaned and tried to open her eyes. "Head hurts."

He knelt down beside her, keeping his weapon behind him and the first aid kit by his side. He pushed the hair back on her forehead and saw the gash that had been causing the bleeding. It wasn't deep, but head wounds always bled like a mother.

"You've got a small cut on your forehead."

She groaned, still not opening her eyes. "No, hurts in back."

He rolled her slightly and found a knot on the back of her head, easily the size of a baseball. "Oh yeah, you've got a knot."

She shivered, so he pulled off his coat to wrap around her. He needed to get her somewhere warm, her skin was cold to the touch, and she'd lost blood. He wondered how long she'd been out in the cold. At this altitude and with the breeze it wouldn't take long for her to get hypothermia. Drew weighed the cold against her head injury and the cold won. They were a long way from the house, he'd been riding close to an hour, but one of the cabins they had for temporary winter housing was close by.

"There's a cabin not too far from here. Can I try to get you there? It's got a fireplace, wood burning stove, blankets, and maybe something hot to drink."

Her eyes, when she finally opened them, were startling blue, and filled with fear, nearly terror. "I don't know you."

He reached back and pulled out his badge, "I'm Deputy Drew Kipling, my family owns this land."

She took the badge and looked it over carefully, her fingers running over the surface. "You're a cop?"

"Yes, ma'am."

Relief filled her eyes and her body relaxed. "Thank God. All I could think, as I was running, was that I needed a cop."

He was surprised by that, what had happened to this woman to have her running through the forest wanting a cop. Was someone after her? They would be a whole lot safer in the cabin instead of out here in the wide-open spaces. "Well you've got one, but let's get you up and moving. I'll get you to the cabin, check your wounds, and get you warm. Then we can talk about the rest."

"I think I twisted my ankle, that's when I fell."

Glad she was lucid and answering his questions, he asked. "Does it hurt anywhere else?"

"No, just my left leg and head."

He took his saddle bags down to her feet, letting her continue to hold his badge. His mind thinking through the various options to get her warm and safe. Hoping whoever she was running from wasn't following her. He didn't want to take the time to wait for one of the ranch vehicles. His horse would be the best option at this point.

Her leg didn't feel broken, but her ankle was swelling, and her feet were bleeding. Probably from running through the forest with no shoes. Where in the hell were her shoes? Drew pulled an ace bandage from his first aid kit and quickly wrapped it around her ankle.

4

"I can carry you over to my horse and we can get to the cabin."

She said in almost a whisper, "Okay."

He lifted her, she was short but curvy, not heavy, so he carried her over to his horse. With a spoken command his horse knelt on the ground, which made it easier to climb up onto his back with his burden. He didn't want to jar the woman, but he didn't want to take too long to get to the cabin. He gave his horse the command to rise and with his knees nudged him into a gentle lope.

SHE WAS content to let this man carry her to the cabin. She didn't know why, but she trusted him. He'd wrapped his long coat around her, still warm from his body heat, and something else around her ankle that kept it secure from hurting with each step the horse made.

They were heading away from the forest, which caused her to relax even more, something was not good in there. The land was flat with scattered pine trees. It only took a few minutes before two buildings came into view—a cabin and an even larger barn. The cabin was single a single-story structure made out of logs, it wasn't large, but it did look welcoming. The barn was a more modern-looking construction.

When they got to the cabin, he carried her into the unlocked building and laid her on the couch in front of a fireplace. He left for a moment and returned with blankets, that he piled on her. Was she cold? She didn't really feel cold. After the blankets were carefully spread over her he turned to the fireplace and lit the already laid fire with a single match.

This was a very odd place. It looked like no one lived

here, but the door was unlocked and there was a ready-made fire in the fireplace and also the woodburning stove. He lit the stove with a single match, also.

"I'll be right back. I'm going to put my horse in the barn, and then get a basin of water to clean up your forehead and feet."

Her feet? What was wrong with her feet? She didn't feel any soreness on her feet, but then she realized she didn't feel them at all. Her ankle still throbbed though, as did her head.

She noticed she still held his badge in her hands and laid it on the coffee table near the couch.

After he'd put a cold pack wrapped in a cloth under her head and another one on her ankle, he began washing the blood from her face and cleaning the cut on her forehead.

"I told you my name is Drew, right?" He started making small talk. "What's yours?"

"My name is…" Her name? What was her name? She couldn't remember. At all, which was ridiculous. How could she not know her own name? She gasped. "I, I don't know. I can't remember."

He looked sharply at her and then shrugged it off. "It's probably just from that bump on your head, don't worry."

But as he cleaned her head and then examined her feet, that's exactly what she did. She tried as hard as she could to remember her name, but there was nothing there. It made her head ache to think so hard.

"So why were you running through the forest, with no shoes, and no coat, wanting a cop?" he asked casually.

"No shoes? I don't have shoes on?"

"No, and your feet are torn up a bit. I think maybe I should call my brother. He's not far away and is a veterinarian. It might be better to have him look at your feet until we can get you into town."

Fear raced through her at the mention of town. "I can't go to town. They could find me there."

"Who? Who can find you there?"

Her mind was blank again. Where were her memories? This was getting annoying and if she was honest a little scary. "I have no idea. I don't like this. Why can't I remember? All I know is I can't go to town."

"Okay, no town, but how about bringing in my brother or his wife? They are both vets, with good medical training."

She didn't feel any fear at the idea of them coming. She supposed it would be all right. If her feet were torn up it would be good to get them treated. She couldn't wear her heels with torn up feet. Heels? That was her worry? That she wouldn't be able to wear her heels? What a stupid thought, but it stayed there, not going anywhere.

Drew waited for her response, so she pushed her dumb thought about shoes to the back of her mind. "That would be fine."

She was a little surprised when he didn't leave to go call his brother, but stayed right beside her. She continued to search her mind for clues, but there were big holes where her memories should be, and that scared her a lot more than a veterinarian looking at her feet. Then the shivering set in.

She heard someone answer the phone and say something.

Drew shook his head. "Change of plans. Can you bring a complete first aid kit out to cabin two? I found someone who needs some help."

Drew paused then said, "Yes, you or Alyssa would be great."

Another pause. "Cut on her head, feet are torn up from running through the woods in only stockings, a huge egg on the back of her head, maybe amnesia, and I think hypothermia."

"They're on the way," he said, as he pushed end.

Her body was suddenly shaking so hard that even her teeth were clacking. "W-w-w-hy, a-a-m I sh-sh-shiver-er-ering?"

"I think you have hypothermia, so you didn't feel the cold, but now that you're warming up, your body is reacting. Would you like some coffee? Or something hot to drink?"

Mmm, coffee sounded wonderful, but for some reason she couldn't fathom, she managed to stutter out, "Do you have any tea? Herbal tea?"

Drew shrugged. "I can look. I know we have black tea, coffee and even hot chocolate packets."

Hot chocolate also sounded like heaven on earth, but she said. "Black or green would be fine, if you don't have herbal."

Drew nodded and went across the room to rummage around in the kitchen area.

Why was she asking for tea when she could have coffee or hot chocolate, was she on some kind of diet? Did she belong to some strange religious sect?

That didn't sound right, if her first thoughts were about wearing high heels. Didn't religions that wouldn't drink coffee or hot chocolate, frown on vanity, which would include fancy shoes? Maybe she was losing her mind or had already lost it. But, the thoughts of her heels that were not plain pumps, no they were sky high killer heels. That her... Brother? Boyfriend? Dad?... some male she knew, called 'hooker shoes' or even 'come-fuck-me stilettos'.

That certainly didn't sound like talk that would go along with some religious sect.

Drew brought her a steaming mug of something with a tea bag tag hanging out of it and a towel wrapped around it. He also brought a sugar bowl and spoon, a small plate with a snack pack of cheese and crackers and another package of nuts and dried fruit. He helped her sit up, tucked a bed pillow behind her back, then gave her the mug. Her cold hands loved the warmth, but she was glad for the towel insulating it. Her hands were shaking, and she was afraid she might spill.

"I found some green tea. Do you want sugar?"

"N-no."

"Your hands are still shaking, let me take the tea bag out." He dragged it out of the cup and plopped it on the plate. "Do you know when you ate last?"

She shook her head, she had no idea. Did she feel hungry? Maybe a little, but she didn't think she could manage food, until she had some idea about what was going on. It might not sit well in her churning stomach. She was happy with the tea for now. It was still too hot to drink, but the warmth rising from it felt wonderful. She was content to hold it while it cooled.

CHAPTER 2

*W*here the hell were Beau and Alyssa? Drew paced to the window and back to the couch. She was shaking like a leaf, he was certain her feet were going to thaw out soon, and she would begin feeling the pain from the lacerations. He wanted the medical professionals here when they did. Sure, he'd had some training with the sheriff's department, but Beau and Alyssa knew a whole lot more than he did.

He wondered if the cabin had any Epsom salts in it and if he should be having her soak her feet. Should he go look, or should he wait? He threw a couple more logs on the fire, he wanted it nice and toasty for her, even if she *was* buried under a pile of blankets.

Where the hell was Beau?

It couldn't hurt to have her soak her feet, it would help soften the tissue and maybe some of the blood that was probably making her stockings stick to the wounds. She was sipping the tea now, so that would help warm her from the inside.

"I'm going to see if we have any Epsom salts to soak your

feet in. We'll need to get your stockings off. There might also be some clothes you could wear, too."

She looked up at him and just nodded, like she didn't understand what he was saying or was deep in thought. He quickly went to the bathroom, and sure enough, under the sink was a plastic basin and a carton of salts.

Then he rifled through the clothes that were in the bedrooms and found the smallest set of sweats he could find. Most of the ranch hands kept a set of clothes in each of the three cabins, so that if they got stranded, they could have something to wear while they washed their jeans. But none of them were even close to the size of this girl. She was so petite, what he found would probably still envelope her, but they would be warmer than what she had on and not ripped to shreds. He didn't think she'd noticed yet that her shirt was in tatters and the pants not much better. Maybe she was in shock, did hypothermia create memory loss? No that was probably from the huge egg on the back of her head.

Finally, he heard the vet truck pull up outside. He put everything he'd found on a chair and hurried to the door. "It's about damn time you got here. She's shaking like a leaf."

His sister in law, Alyssa, answered, "Oh good, that's excellent, that means she only has mild hypothermia. If she wasn't shaking it would be worse."

"Glad to hear it, but I don't know what to do, for sure, to help. I got her some blankets, and am heating up the cabin, and made her some tea." Now he wished he'd though to have them grab some of Alyssa's clothes, she and this girl were about the same size. If he had to guess, he thought they might also be about the same age, early to mid-twenties.

Beau slapped him on the back. "Perfect, let's have a look at our patient." Beau noticed the basin and Epsom salts. "Great idea, get some warm water in that with a handful of salts. Warm, Drew, not hot. Just barely warm, lukewarm just a little above body temp."

Alyssa was already talking in soothing tones to the woman. She drew back a little when Beau approached but Alyssa explained that Beau was her husband and a very good vet and the two of them wanted to help her feel better. She relaxed and said that would be fine.

Beau let Alyssa take point and he acted as her assistant.

Drew went about filling the basin with barely warm water and salts, then took it over to where they were gathered. Alyssa checked the cut on her forehead and said nothing else needed to be done there. The ankle appeared to be sprained, but if it didn't get better in a day or two, it would be good to have it x-rayed, after the swelling went down some.

Alyssa eased the woman's feet into the basin after having looked them over. "Soaking them will help. Until you get your memory back, we need to call you something. Let's talk about that, while your feet soak."

RONALD STOMPED AROUND in the forest. Where in the hell could she be? He'd only been away an hour and she was gone. Nowhere to be seen. Dammit, he had to find that stupid bitch, before his employers found out he'd lost her. She couldn't just disappear. She had to be nearby. But which direction would she go? He had no fucking idea.

Of course, she could get lost in this damn wilderness and die. She didn't have any shoes or a coat or her phone or purse. He'd thought that would be deterrent enough to make her stay in the cabin. It was winter for God's sake and they were in the mountains of fucking Colorado. Where did she think she was going?

He'd even had her tied to the bed, not that he was that great at knots or anything; he wasn't a damn boy scout. And maybe he'd been gone two hours, but still, it hadn't been that long. He'd gone into the rat hole of a town and gotten some booze. He was sick to death of hearing her talk and whine and complain about every damn thing. She didn't like the food. She needed to work out to keep in shape. Her family was going to be worried. Blah, blah, blah, bitch, bitch, bitch, moan, moan, moan.

For fuck's sake, he was tired of hearing it. He'd thought this was going to be an easy gig, when they'd approached him. Seduce little Miss Montana, get her to trust him. He'd even gone so far as to propose to the pain in the ass. And she'd bought it hook, line, and sinker. That part had been fun and easy, he'd even managed to get into her virginal panties a time or two. Not often. She was a damn prude.

But this part of the plan sucked big time. Keep her holed up in some remote location until the stupid pageant was over and she'd lost. He'd just needed an hour of silence. He'd even brought back some healthier fucking food for her, and now she was gone. The ungrateful bitch.

He decided to keep searching until it was close to dark, and then he'd come back and see if she returned when the temps dropped. If she didn't, he just hoped to hell she froze to death or was eaten by a bear. He didn't know what he was going to tell them. Fuck, what a mess.

LISA, she'd settled on Lisa. They'd gone name after name, until her head pounded and she begged them to stop, saying the one that she felt most comfortable with was Lisa. She'd still not thought it was quite right, but was happy to be called that for now.

14

They were working on her feet now. During the naming game she'd started to feel more comfortable with Beau, so he was working on one foot and Alyssa the other. He was actually a little more gentle than Alyssa, so she was glad he was helping.

It took a couple of soakings to get her stockings off and then the cuts cleaned out. She'd only needed a few stitches, so that was encouraging. There was one deep gash on her left foot which had been the worst. They were currently wrapping her feet, and she needed to pee in the worst way.

Lisa said, "I, um, kind of need to pee. I think the two gallons of tea Drew made me is making itself known."

Alyssa cocked her head. "That and the hypothermia. That's a really good sign. But you can't walk on your feet yet."

Beau said, "I can carry her in there if you can help her, honey."

Drew, who had been watching, but not participating much said, "No I'll carry her, but Alyssa you're still going to need to assist. Maybe you can help get her into the sweats I found."

She was glad Drew had volunteered. She felt more comfortable with the cute cop than she did Beau. She was shocked by her thoughts, Drew certainly was cute, but it still surprised her to think that, and she had no idea why.

The simple act of emptying her bladder turned into a monumental feat. But she and Alyssa managed to get it done. She didn't feel any embarrassment with Alyssa helping her get undressed or seeing her practically nude, as she helped her into the enormous sweats. Thank goodness the pants had a drawstring at the waist or they would have never stayed on.

Alyssa laughed, "When you come up to the big house, one of us girls can loan you some that might come closer to fitting."

Lisa felt her heart race. "Do I have to leave here? I don't

really want to see a lot of people until I get my memory back, you said it should only take a day or two. Can I stay in the cabin? Can Drew stay with me?"

Alyssa nodded. "That would probably be fine. I can imagine it would be weird to meet people, when you can't remember your own self. I think Drew is off tomorrow, too."

Lisa felt relief at that and Alyssa called out the door. "Drew, your services are needed."

When they got back to the living room they all talked about the idea of Lisa and Drew staying in the cabin. It had two rooms with bunk beds, and the couch also folded out into a bed, so there was plenty of sleeping space.

Drew confirmed that he had tomorrow free and called into his boss to take the rest of the week off. Since everyone else was feeling better after ten days flat on their backs, they were eager for the work.

Alyssa said, "I'll come in the morning and bring you some sweats that you won't drown in and some food, too. There is plenty of canned and freezer food, but maybe something fresh would be good."

Lisa thought about that, what would she want to eat. "Salad would be great and maybe some hard-boiled eggs, if you have them. I *am* feeling a little hungry."

Drew said, "Well let's see what we've got here to cook. The cabin should be pretty well stocked as we are heading into winter."

He began asking her about the different foods they had on hand and although some of them sounded delicious, she couldn't bring herself to eat them. She could tell Drew was getting upset with her.

Alyssa took her hand. "Lisa, are you on some kind of diet? Are you diabetic or something?"

Lisa could feel her eyes fill with tears of frustration. "I don't know. Some of the things he's mentioned sound delicious, but then I think of all the carbs in them, and I just can't."

Alyssa patted her hand. "What about a nice steak? I'll bet there are some of Meg's green beans in the freezer, too."

"That sounds wonderful. I could maybe have half a baked potato, too."

"Perfect. You heard the woman, Drew, get a couple of steaks out and put them in some cold water to thaw, pick one of the thinner cuts, so it doesn't take too long."

Drew relaxed, and a smile covered his face. "Will do. Got it, no carbs, or very few carbs, anyway." He pulled some food from the fridge and started water running in the sink.

Alyssa stood. "I'll bring out some more things tomorrow."

Suddenly Lisa grasped that Beau and Alyssa were going to leave. She wasn't at all apprehensive about being alone with Drew, but she didn't want anyone else to know she was here. "Beau, Alyssa, can you keep it quiet that I'm here? At least until I can remember who I'm running away from?"

Beau and Alyssa exchanged a look. Alyssa said, "We can do that, but there might be other people looking for you too. People you *want* to find you."

That surprised Lisa but as she thought about it she agreed that Alyssa was right, there would be people looking for her. But she had a very odd sensation that she might not know the good ones from the bad ones. She nodded. "That's probably true, but it won't hurt for a day or two." Lisa stopped and wondered if that statement was true. There did seem to be some kind of urgency about the situation. She sighed. "At least I don't think it will."

Beau shrugged. "We won't say anything tonight. Maybe by tomorrow you'll have your memory back."

"I hope you're right, Beau. I don't like the uncertainty."

Drew who had been quiet during the exchange, spoke up.

"You know we should probably have Thomas take a look and see if he can find where she came from."

Beau agreed, "Yeah, we aren't expecting any weather tonight, so tomorrow would probably be as good as today, since it's getting late. Easier to track in the daylight. Plus, he's on the opposite end of the ranch today. I'll have him come by first thing in the morning."

Lisa asked, "Who's Thomas?"

Drew probably heard the hesitation in her voice, because he sat near her and took her hand. "He's one of our ranch hands and has worked for us his whole life, so whoever you're running from he'll not have been a part of it. And he lives on the ranch, so he won't be spreading any tales. Thomas can probably follow the trail you left through the woods, back to wherever you started, and might be able to find some clues as to what's going on. Don't worry though, he's as good at staying concealed as he is at tracking. He won't be seen, if whoever you're running from is still around."

She thought that over and decided to trust Drew's opinion. She squeezed the hand holding hers and looked over at Beau and Alyssa. "All right, let's have him go look in the morning."

Beau nodded. "I'll send him out first thing. And Alyssa will come out to check out your injuries, bring some clothes that fit, and some food you'll be happy eating."

Lisa felt the first spark of hope and happiness she'd felt since Drew had found her laying on the cold ground. She smiled at all of them. It felt good to know she was being taken care of, and there might even be some progress tomorrow. She hoped she would have some memories to go with it in the morning.

Drew let go of her hand and stood. "I'm gonna get that food cooking for you."

"I'll be happy to eat it. I *am* hungry."

Beau and Alyssa left, and she was alone with the cowboy cop. It was a pleasant homey feeling, she was warm and safe and a little drowsy. She tipped over on the couch to shut her eyes for a minute or two while he cooked.

CHAPTER 3

$\mathcal{L}$isa had laid down on the couch. Beau had told him that she would be feeling drowsy but not to let her sleep too long in one stretch, in case she had a concussion. She could sleep while he made her some dinner, it was about three in the afternoon. How had the day gone by so fast? He'd found her first thing in the morning.

He chuckled at himself, well first thing after he'd slept late and had eaten a huge rancher's breakfast. He'd been subsisting on quick meals and little sleep for the last ten days. They didn't have a super busy department, but with only two of them on duty for over a week he'd been kept hopping. Not only taking all the day calls but then writing up reports after the twelve-hour shift.

Hanging out with the pretty little miss would be nearly a vacation. He wondered if she was married or engaged, there was a slight indent on her ring finger. Nothing like his mother had, after decades of wearing a ring, but there was something there.

He'd been floored by the smile from a few minutes earlier

and had needed to move out of the immediate vicinity of that smile. It was like liquid sunshine, warm and happy, and entirely too enticing. She'd been a good patient so far, and not quite as crazy as he thought he would be, if he couldn't remember his own name, or why he'd been running away from something like she had been.

She'd either been terrified to run out without shoes or a coat into the Colorado mountains in the winter, or was a strong-willed person who wasn't about to let a little thing like cold and pain stop her. Based on her very firm resolutions about food, he was betting on the later. She had certainly exhibited some fear but nothing on the scale of terror that would warrant what she'd been through.

Drew thought about calling his boss to ask him to keep an eye out for anyone unusual in town, but with hunting season in full force that would be a silly request. All the tourists would be unusual to some degree or another. Although a tourist in clothes similar to hers would stand out. She wasn't exactly dressed as a hunter, in her black slacks and silk blouse.

He'd give her until tomorrow, just as Beau and Alyssa had promised. Hopefully, her memory would be back by then. Beau had said this type of amnesia was very rare and usually short-lived.

For now, he would broil her a steak, sauté the green beans that were almost thawed, and bake her a potato. He should make her something to drink, maybe iced tea. He put water on to boil. It was too late in the day to make sun tea. He put some bottled water into the fridge to cool, too. They always kept a couple of cases of bottled water on hand in the cabins.

By the time he'd made the iced tea and baked the potato the steaks were thawed and ready to be put under the grill. He'd not asked how she liked hers, so he decided on medium, which would only take a few minutes. After putting the steaks in the oven, he dropped the green beans into a skillet with a tiny bit of butter, since she'd mentioned only carbs he hoped a little fat would be all right. He let them cook for a moment while he flipped the steaks.

Drew turned off the flame under the beans, seasoned them and put the lid on to keep them warm while he pulled out the steaks. Making up a lap tray for her, he took it over to the coffee table to wake her up.

"Lisa, I have dinner for you. Lisa."

She mumbled, "Lily." And then sat up and looked at him. She frowned like she didn't know who she was, and then smiled that killer smile again.

"Lily, my name is Lily, not Lisa."

What a pretty name for the lovely woman, with the smile that made his heart speed up. "Is your memory back?"

She frowned then shook her head. "No. I still can't remember anything else. If I hadn't been asleep I might not have remembered my name, but since you woke me with the wrong one, my instincts took over. Yay, I know my name. Well my first name at least."

Drew helped her sit up, and put the tray over her lap. If he had her last name he could run a search on her, but Lily wasn't quite unique enough for that.

"Oh, my goodness it smells and looks delicious, I'm starving."

She dug right in eating and Drew watched in appreciation of her enthusiasm for his cooking, until she asked, "Aren't you going to eat too?"

He quickly stood and went to get his plate. He didn't want to look like some freak staring at her. "Yes, I was just making sure you were happy with the meal."

She waved her fork at him that had a large bite of the steak on it. "It's perfect. This is delicious beef, and I know my beef."

He grinned at her, no one knew beef like a rancher did, and he could admit pride in the cattle they raised. "The cattle were born and raised right here on the ranch."

"I wondered what kind of ranchers you were. You never said."

"We're cattle ranchers, Lily. Welcome to the Rockin' K ranch in Grand County Colorado."

She was just watching him as she chewed her steak. Finally, she said, "Colorado? I had no idea. There were mountains out there when you brought me in. So where is Grand County?"

He got out his phone and pulled up a map of the state, taking his plate he went over to the couch and sat next to her to show her the app, and point out where they were.

"Oh, we're right by Rocky Mountain National Park."

Drew nodded. "Yes, we're on one side and Estes Park is the town on the other side."

She took another bite of steak, and his phone from his hand, and zoomed in on the map looking all around as she ate. Drew was happy to let her look. She finished with the map and started scrolling through his pictures when she must have realized what she was doing.

Her cheeks flamed, and she handed him his phone, like it was a bomb about to go off. "Sorry I just… That was really rude of me."

He laughed. "It's okay, there is nothing top secret on the phone. Just pictures of my family or friends. Maybe an old crime scene, if you scroll far enough."

"Or a girlfriend, or wife."

He looked at where she'd stopped in his pictures and grinned. "Sister and nephew. No girlfriend, no wife." He turned the phone back, showing her the screen. "Emma, the youngest of my siblings. I'm second to the last. Beau is second to the oldest."

Drew flipped through until he found a picture of Adam. "Adam the oldest, is getting married to Alyssa's best friend, Rachel, in January, in Hawaii of all places." He flipped through a few more pics before he found one of the twins and their girls. My twin brothers, Chase and Cade. They decided to marry their ladies here at the ranch in December, in a joint ceremony. They said they'd done everything else in their life at the same time so why would they want to change that? Plus, the girls are great friends."

Lily laughed at his expression. "So, marriages popping up all over the place. I suppose you're next in line."

"Not for a long time for me, I've got plenty of time before I succumb to the wedding bug. Emma isn't married either, maybe she can be next."

"Oh, but she has… never mind, just ignore my nosiness." Her cheeks flamed again.

"No worries, she had Tony out of wedlock. Some drifter knocked her up and went on his merry way. It's not a secret and we all love both of them. If the guy ever comes back to town he might leave with a few broken bones, however. She was still in high school, a senior, but still."

"Wow, that was brave of her to keep him."

"It was, and she's a great mom. Tony is a rascal, that is loved on by all of us, and if truth be told we all spoil him rotten."

Lily shook her head. "Loving doesn't spoil a child. So, the six of you?"

"Plus, mom and dad and Grandpa K."

"Do you all live on the ranch?"

"Yeah, Beau and Adam's houses are built, and Chase and Cade are working on theirs. Emma and I both have a parcel of land, for when we want to build. But the house we all grew up in is plenty big enough for all of us. And we have the bunk house and these cabins. There are four of them, almost all exactly the same as this one."

Lily nodded, then squirmed in her seat.

He tensed at her movement, hoping she wasn't in pain. "What's wrong? You look uncomfortable."

"I could use a trip to the bathroom. This hypothermia thing is getting annoying."

He could understand that, but so much better than a severe case and a trip to the hospital. "Of course. Your wish is my command."

As she used the facilities, which was a bit of a challenge, Lily thought about all he had revealed, and wondered what her own story was. Did she have siblings? Were her parents still alive? Where was she from? Why had she said that about knowing beef?

She washed her hands and frowned at the slight indentation on her ring finger. Was she married or engaged? She'd noticed when they were working on her feet that she had a perfect pedicure and other than what looked like recent damage she had a manicure also. And those clothes she'd had on felt confusing. A silk shirt just didn't seem quite right.

Even though they were enormous on her, she felt like the sweats fit her better. But if she really thought about it, jeans seemed like the most natural clothing for her. She had no idea why all these things felt a little off, but they did. She hoped she got her memory back soon.

Lily looked at the ring indention again. When Drew had carried her to the bathroom, he'd smelled wonderful, like outdoors, leather, and man. She'd felt a small zing of attraction and not really any guilt, which didn't seem right if she was in a relationship with someone.

Maybe… No, she needed to stop the speculation it wasn't getting her anywhere, and it only caused more confusion. Dammit, she needed her memory back. Now!

She called out to Drew and he came in to carry her back into the living room. He put her down on the couch and then looked around the room. His hand rubbed the back of his neck as he turned toward her. "So, what do you want to do now?"

She shrugged. It was too early for bed and the nap she'd had while he'd cooked had revived her. There wasn't a TV but there were lots of old paperbacks in the bookshelves.

"We have some books, or we could play cards, or…" He trailed off and she could see he was at a loss for ideas.

"Cards would be fine. Poker?"

A slow smile slid across his face. "Poker is one of the family favorites. Let me see what we can find to bet with."

Her body tingled and her mind went down a very naughty path at that statement, so she was glad he'd gone into the kitchen to rifle through the cupboard, that way he didn't see the blush that she could feel on her face.

He came back with a couple of bags. "We have M&Ms. pretzels or peanuts."

She wanted the chocolate but heard herself say, "Peanuts."

Her responses always denied her desires. But even as she pondered that, she could almost hear herself saying it was only for a short time longer. What that meant, she had no idea.

Drew put the cards, peanuts and some drink refills on the table. Then he scooped her up and deposited her in one of the chairs, lifted her feet and pushed another chair under her legs. "Might as well keep them elevated to avoid swelling. Do you remember how to play poker?"

She nodded, "I do. I can't remember my name, or where I live, or anything about my family, but I can remember how to play poker. This memory thing is really odd. It's like the food choices, I know I like to eat those other things, like chocolate and coffee, but there's some reason not to eat them."

"Maybe food allergies or something like that? Do you think the peanuts are safe? Lots of people are allergic to them."

"No, I think peanuts are fine. It feels like there is a short-term reason why I'm not supposed to eat the carbs and caffeine. For instance, I wanted the M&Ms, but felt like I needed to pick the protein. Even as I picked it though it was like I was telling myself it's only for a short time. It's really weird."

"When your memory returns, you'll know why."

"At first I thought I was in some kind of religious organization. But some of my other thoughts didn't line up with that."

"Like what?"

Lily wasn't about to tell him about the idea of playing strip poker. "Well when you said my feet needed attention, my first thought was that I needed to get them fixed so I could wear heels."

"You were dressed professionally, so pumps—"

She cut him off. "No, not pumps, sky-high killer heels, that's what came to mind."

His eyebrows shot up nearly to his hairline. "Well, yes, that wouldn't go with the religious idea."

She picked up the cards and was shuffling them like a pro. She looked down at her hands. "And I clearly know how to play poker so that wouldn't fit either."

Drew looked at her hands and then back up into her eyes. "You've got a slight ring indent. Do you think you're married? Or engaged?"

Lily shook her head. "I wondered the same thing. I don't

feel married, but I can't say for sure. There isn't a tan line, so I don't think if I am, it's been very long, which would point more to engaged, not married. But even then, I can't say for sure. I don't feel like I'm missing anyone. The only thing I feel about people is to avoid them."

She frowned and shook her head, her hands still expertly shuffling the cards. "But I also feel like there's a clock ticking. Like there is something I need to do at a specific time and place."

"Well, let's hope you remember what that is. But for now, what you need to do is deal the very well shuffled cards and ante up."

She looked at her hands that held the cards and grinned. "I can do that."

They played for a couple of hours and she won more than she lost. Drew teased her about being a card shark.

When she lost three hands in a row, Drew said, "I think you're getting tired. Let's stop for tonight."

Lily yawned. "I think you're right, my brain does feel a little fuzzy."

"Do you want something else to eat?"

"No. I ate plenty of my winnings."

"Yeah, our 'chips' have dwindled. I'll take you into the bathroom, there should be a spare toothbrush in there."

"Alyssa got me out one and even found a new hairbrush in the back of the cupboard. She said the cabins are used by anyone that needs them, so those kinds of things were stocked."

"Yep. You never know who's going to stumble out of the woods and need shelter. Normally it's hunters or one of our hands that are rounding up cattle that use the place. Not pretty ladies with no shoes."

Lily laughed. "Yeah, I suppose I'm an anomaly. Clearly, I was not hunting. The question is, what *was* I doing?"

Drew shook his head. "That's the million-dollar question, isn't it?" He stood, scooped her up like she weighed nothing, and carried her into the bathroom. "While you get ready for bed I'm going to get you a bottle of water and some ibuprofen. Do you want an ice pack for your head?"

"Yeah, it might be good to ice it for a bit, it's starting to pound again."

"Beau and Alyssa said to wake you a couple of times in the night, to make sure you don't sleep too hard. We can get more ice then, too, if you want."

She readied herself for bed and even found a hair tie to contain her heavy locks. She hoped that Alyssa could help her take a bath tomorrow and wash her hair. They'd tried to get all the blood out, but it still felt stiff and yucky.

When Drew carried her into the bedroom, she was stunned at the care he'd taken to put anything she might want close at hand. He was a very caring man, nothing at all like Ronald. Wait! Who was Ronald? She tried to remember but the thought was gone. She sighed in frustration.

"What's wrong? Is there something else you need?"

She grimaced. "No. I almost had a memory, but it didn't fully form."

"Even though that's frustrating, I think you should take it as a good sign that your memories are coming closer." He set her down on the bed and backed up a step.

Lily laughed at him. "All right, Pollyanna, I will endeavor to think like that."

Drew grinned at her. "It's not often I get called Pollyanna, not in my line of work."

She'd forgotten all about him being a police officer. Now if she could only remember what she'd wanted a law enforcement person for. What good did it do to have one, if she couldn't recall why she wanted one? Other than for protection, that was a nice bonus. But who did she need protection from?

Lily yawned, and Drew turned to the door. "I'll be back in a few hours to wake you and see if you need anything."

She was asleep before her head hit the pillow.

CHAPTER 4

*D*rew set his phone to go off in four hours. It was early still, so he wasn't all that tired. He'd slept in this morning. But he had Lily to take care of, so he shouldn't stay up too late. Maybe he would read for a while, but first he wanted to check Facebook and maybe see if there was any news about a missing person.

He scrolled through all the news channels but didn't find anything. Then he went out and looked at Facebook, some of the girls he knew were talking about some Beauty Pageant that was coming up in a week in New York. Not something he was interested in, it seemed to him that women who participated in things like that were kind of plastic.

Not like Lily, who'd run through the forest barefooted, with a gash on her forehead and a lump on the back of her head. Her feet and clothes torn to shreds, and if she hadn't twisted her ankle he was certain she would have kept going. There certainly wasn't anything plastic about her. He had to admire her fortitude, and strength.

She was gorgeous, and had a sweet temperament, anyone else in her circumstances would be raving mad and probably freaking out. She couldn't be much over five feet tall and was curvy in all the right places. What did people call girls like her, a pocket Venus, that was it. He'd always thought it was a stupid label, but she fit the term perfectly.

Drew wondered again if she was engaged or married, something had caused that indention. He needed to stop obsessing about that and turn his mind to helping her. Hopefully Thomas would be able to trace her path and they would find some clues. Or she would regain her memory. Beau had said it would likely be only a day or two.

Once they had something to go on he would call in his boss to help. Her only being able to remember that she needed a cop indicated something illegal had taken place. His mind was going around and around in circles and it wasn't getting him anywhere.

Drew pulled up the reading app on his phone, and settled in to read the thriller he'd been wanting to read for over a week. He finally wasn't exhausted and had the time.

His phone was beeping madly, Drew wanted to throw it across the room, it was pitch black in the room except for the damn phone flashing. He turned off the alarm, looked at the time, and nearly went back to sleep, when his fuzzy brain remembered that he was supposed to check on Lily, which was why his phone was going crazy.

He got up and dragged on his jeans. He'd left a t-shirt on, so he was presentable. This was the second and final time he needed to check on her before morning. The first time she'd woken easily and had known who he was and what she was doing in the cabin. Her memories had not returned but she wasn't sleeping too hard.

He figured this time would be the same, but as he pushed open the door, and before he could call out her name he knew this time was different. She seemed to be dreaming and the dreams weren't the pleasant sort. She was thrashing around in the bed.

Drew softly called out her name and she whimpered. He moved closer, but he didn't want to startle her.

She mumbled, "No, stop. What are you doing?"

He called out her name again. "Lily, wake up, it's just a dream. Wake up now, Lily."

She frowned, still fully asleep. "Why are you doing this, Ronald?"

Drew said a little more forcefully, "Lily, it's Drew, wake up now."

She stilled and then opened her eyes. "Drew? The cop, Drew?"

"Well deputy sheriff, but yes, that's me. You were dreaming."

She nodded and winced. "I was, and now my head hurts again. Can I have some more ice? And maybe some pain killer?"

"Of course, I'll be right back with ice and a cold bottle of water to take the ibuprofen with."

When he got back to the room with the supplies, she was sitting up in bed frowning. "I was trying to remember my dream. But I can't remember much more than feeling confused and frustrated."

Drew unscrewed the top and handed her the water bottle, she already had the pain killers in her hand. She quickly swallowed them and drank about half the water.

"I brought you some crackers, so the ibuprofen doesn't upset your stomach."

She smiled at him and took one. "I don't really think I need them, but I'll nibble on one, just in case."

While she ate, he dragged a chair over to sit by the bed. "You were talking in your sleep."

She stopped eating. "What did I say?"

"You were asking someone named Ronald why he was doing this."

Drew noticed her run her thumb over the side of her ring finger, like people do, and wondered how this Ronald was involved. Was he her fiancé? Was Lily running away from him and if so, then why?

"I still can't remember." She sighed and went back to nibbling on the cracker.

"Just give it time." He laid the bag of ice on the bedside table. "I'll let you get some sleep, see you in the morning."

"Drew, thanks for taking care of me."

He turned back. "You're welcome, Lily."

LILY WATCHED him go and wondered about the tension she'd felt from him just then, like he was holding something back. She couldn't begin to guess, although earlier she had noticed a shadow of maybe sadness in his eyes when she'd been teasing him about getting married next. She'd been too busy trying to remember what was going on in her own life to think about it then, but she had noticed it.

She wriggled around to lay back down in the bed and put the ice on the knot at the back of her head. Drew was very kind and considerate. Beau and Alyssa had been too, but they were medical professionals. Drew was in law enforcement and she didn't normally think of people in that profession as being kind.

Not that she thought of them as jerks, but they always seemed a little aloof, a little stand-offish. He didn't seem that way. But maybe that was because he was in his home and not on duty.

Lily snuggled down into her pillow, the pain killers were starting to take effect. She hoped everything would heal quickly she didn't have much time. As she drifted off to sleep she wondered why she'd thought that, what was the urgency she felt, even though she couldn't remember.

The light was peeking in the corners of the window. It was morning, the light wasn't strong, so it was either early or cloudy. She had no way of knowing. She hoped early, so it didn't rain. Rain would wash away her trail and Thomas wouldn't be able to give them any more insight.

It seemed like Beau and Alyssa had mentioned it was supposed to be nice for the next couple of days, cold but clear, just like it was yesterday. Had it only been one day? It seemed like a lot longer.

Lily sat up and scooted to the edge of the bed, she wanted to see if she could put any weight on her feet. She needed a bathroom break and she didn't want to have to rely on Drew to carry her everywhere, if she could do it herself. Lily also knew she had to let her feet heal and not cause the healing process to slow down.

She would have to walk in heels soon. Why she needed to do that, she had no idea. Lily just knew it was imperative. Sliding her feet to the floor she put a tiny bit of pressure on them. The pain ratcheted up and she knew it was too soon, she didn't want to pull the stitches open.

Drew knocked quietly on the door. Lily was thrilled with his timing and called out. "Come in."

He pulled the door open and saw her on the edge of the bed. "I thought you might be wanting a potty break."

"I do, you have perfect timing."

He smiled at her and her heart skipped a beat, strange but true.

"Thanks. I expect Thomas and Alyssa any time, and I thought you would want to be up and about, to meet with them."

She nodded, for having known each other only one day

they seemed to be in sync about things. Which was nice but surprising, she had no idea why it was surprising, only that it was. "You thought correctly."

"Any other memories surface?"

She sighed with frustration at all the half thoughts she was having. "No, but I do feel an urgency to get back on my feet. I have the strangest notion that I need to wear heels soon."

Drew chuckled. "I gotta admit that's not what I think would be foremost in your mind."

Lily shrugged. "Right? I mean it is kind of a weird thought. But it doesn't feel wrong, it feels important."

"Hmm, well let's get you into the bathroom and we'll see what Alyssa has to say about getting those feet healed up quickly."

He scooped her off the bed and into his strong, safe arms. She wanted to roll her eyes at herself, what was this total confidence in a man she'd not even known twenty-four hours. It was a conundrum. "I hope she can help me take a bath, the blood in my hair is itchy."

Drew stilled, and she wondered what he was thinking. It didn't last long before he was carrying her into the bathroom.

She was glad the bathroom was tiny, so she could sit on the toilet and still reach the sink. She brushed her teeth and splashed her face with cool water and felt almost human. Drew answered her call and carried her into the living room, where there was already a mug of tea on the table, bless him. He got her all settled as a knock sounded on the door.

At the door were two men she'd never seen before. Drew brought them in and introduced her to them. The tall thin one was Thomas, the 'famous' tracker and next to him was another younger guy. Both of them were dressed in cowboy gear with warm coats over the top, both had taken off their hats when they'd entered the building.

Thomas said, "I hope you don't mind that I brought Jimmy-boy here. I've been working with him to teach him all that I know. I thought this would be a good test for him, since even I don't know where we're going or what we will find."

Lily nodded at his glance. He turned back to the men. "Not a problem, Thomas. But we do need to know whatever you find as quickly as possible."

"Yes, sir, Drew, we won't draw it out. With two sets of eyes, I think it will go quicker."

Drew specifically told them where he'd found her.

Thomas came over to look at her feet size. "No shoes? You were a determined lady. Not just everyone would run out of the woods barefoot with no coat on a cold winter day."

Drew showed them the clothing she'd had on, so they could look for any bits of them on branches or the ground.

"That shirt is torn to shreds, as are the stockings, and the pants aren't much better. I imagine we'll find the trail easily." Thomas said. "Do you mind if we take a swatch of each to compare? Not that I think we're going to find a lot of shredded clothing in the woods, but I would rather be certain."

Lily nodded. "Feel free, I'm not going to be wearing them again."

Drew frowned, thinking about something. "Yeah, go ahead and take a bit, but she might need the rest for evidence."

Lily's breath caught in her throat. She'd never once thought of needing evidence. She'd never really considered why she was running and looking for a cop. But it did indicate there was some kind of law being broken.

As the men cut small swatches out of her clothes she

pushed hard to try to remember why she'd wanted a cop, but all there was to find was a big blank spot. Alyssa and Beau had both said it would only be a day or two and she realized she'd been counting on it being *this* morning.

She forced herself to smile when the trackers took their leave. It wasn't their fault she couldn't remember, and they might find out something important.

Drew came over and took her hand. "I'm sorry. I noticed that what I said about evidence upset you."

"No, it's all right. I mostly was just trying to remember. I guess I had put all my hope into remembering this morning, so I'm frustrated that I can't."

"I can fully understand that and sympathize with you. Do you want some breakfast? I'm not sure what exactly, since we don't have any eggs or produce."

She didn't really feel hungry, the tea was nice, but food did not appeal. Plus, she hoped Alyssa would bring something better for her diet. She looked at her body and didn't see any reason to be on a diet, she just knew she was. When was her darn memory going to return anyway? "No, let's wait until we see what Alyssa brings with her. I don't think I'm an eat-first-thing-in-the-morning person, anyway."

"Fair enough. I had a toaster strudel when I first got up, so I'm good for a little while."

"How long were you up before you came to get me?"

"Long enough to make coffee, have a strudel, and then take care of my horse."

She'd forgotten all about his horse. "Of course. So, is the barn stocked as well as the cabin?"

He laughed. "Better. We gotta take care of our animals, and sometimes we need to bring some of the cattle into the enclosure, to tend to them."

She grinned at him. "Makes sense."

There was another knock on the door and Alyssa called out. "Drew come get the door, my hands are full."

Drew rushed to the door and pulled it open. Alyssa handed three bags to Drew and went back to her vehicle for more.

Drew brought everything in to set on the table. "Looks like she brought enough food and clothes for a week. Not sure what else she's getting out of the truck."

Alyssa bustled in just as he said that, and lifted the medical kit, and another bag with more. "First aid stuff."

Alyssa came over and looked at the knot on her head. "The swelling has gone down some, keep icing it. Your forehead looks fine, for all that blood there really should have been a bigger wound. Now let's look at those feet."

Drew said, "Tell Alyssa about your foot concern."

Lily could feel her face heat, it seemed like such a vain concern to be having. Alyssa had knelt at her feet and was starting to unwrap the bandages. She looked up. "Tell me."

God, she didn't want to sound like some prima donna. She grimaced. "It's going to sound stupid… I keep worrying about getting my feet into high heels. I don't know why, but I just have this overwhelming need to get my feet healed up as quickly as possible, so I can wear heels." She shrugged and soldiered on, "And not just pumps, but sky-high killer heels. Some man in my life calls them 'hooker shoes'."

Alyssa's eyebrows had shot up.

Lily said, "Not that I'm a hooker, at least I don't think I am, but for some reason I need to wear those shoes soon. That need keeps coming back. It's right up there with my desire to stay away from the carbs."

Lily vaguely waved her hand at her body. "I'm vain, but I don't see why I am on such a strict diet. But the idea of carbs, while enticing, just feels wrong, but only for a little while longer. Something is clearly happening soon where I need to wear high heels and keep my body as shredded as possible."

Alyssa looked closely at her. "You're not tall enough to be a runway model."

Lilly laughed. "Yeah I'm a good eight inches too short for that."

"Maybe another kind of model though, like for advertisements or romance book covers?" Alyssa guessed.

That didn't sound right either, besides that, her face on advertisements or even book covers would be obvious. "But then wouldn't I be recognized? By one of you?"

Drew interjected, "Maybe that beauty pageant coming up next week."

Both she and Alyssa turned their heads to look at him. Then they both laughed. That was a silly idea. Her in a beauty pageant? But as Alyssa checked her feet and then helped her bathe and wash her hair the idea prickled.

After she was clean and in women's sweats with her feet rebandaged, Alyssa said, "Now, your feet will heal faster if you take some mega doses of vitamin C, morning, noon, and early evening, none at bedtime. Stay off them at least one more day, two would be better. You're healing well, there isn't any inflammation or redness to indicate infection. I'll come back in the morning to redress them and check the healing."

Lily was grateful for the advice and some concrete instructions. Whatever it took to get her back on her feet and in those heels was welcome. "Thanks, Alyssa. I appreciate everything you've done, and especially the clothes that fit."

Alyssa laughed. "Yeah, those sweats were huge on you." She turned to Beau. "Is Thomas out tracking?"

Drew nodded, "Thomas and Jimmy."

"Jimmy?"

Drew raised one shoulder in a half shrug. "Yeah, Thomas

has been teaching him, I guess, and thought the two of them would do better than just one. Since timing is of the essence, I didn't complain."

"I had no idea. Well I'm out of here, got some young'uns to check on this morning. See you tomorrow."

CHAPTER 5

*R*onald needed to move. Lily hadn't come back in the night and he didn't want to be anywhere near this place, in case someone came looking. He couldn't imagine that she had gotten out of this God forsaken wilderness. Even with the car's GPS he damn near got lost every time he came up here. The road in was more of a footpath than anything and it wound around and around, it would take hours to walk the damn thing, to get out to the highway. But he would keep his eyes open as he drove it, just in case.

He wasn't going to take any of the food he'd bought, the car was a rental and he would turn it in as soon as he got to Denver. But what should he do with her shoes and purse and stuff. He'd rented the cabin under an assumed name, so should he just leave them here?

If she had managed to make it to the police, he didn't really want the evidence on him. Could he find somewhere to ditch it? He was going to keep the ring, so he could return it, but he didn't want anything else. Maybe if he set everything neatly in the cabin it would look like she was crazy running off into the woods.

Could he convince her of something like that? She was a gullible little thing, so it might be possible if he could think up a good enough story. Like her being delirious, food poisoning maybe? Drugs? He would think about it on the long drive back to the airport.

Ronald felt something was closing in on him, so he just decided to leave everything, but the ring. He quickly hung the coat in the closet, put her shoes underneath it with the bag she'd brought with her. They'd only planned on a weekend escape so there weren't a lot of clothes to scatter around. The skimpy nighty was interesting, maybe he should have delayed telling her his plans a little. Oh well, too late. He left her purse with the phone in it next to the couch.

He locked the door and left the keys as the owner requested and hurried to the rental car. An overwhelming feeling of panic engulfed him, so he tore off in a cloud of dust. He didn't relax until he hit the town of Granby and highway forty that would take him to the interstate highway leading to Denver.

DREW DIDN'T EXACTLY KNOW what to do with Lily. He'd fed her breakfast and then lunch from the food Alyssa had brought and they had chatted for a while, but as the day wore on and both of them lapsed into silence, he realized she was as anxious to hear back from Thomas as he was.

Drew was pretty certain she'd only been out in the wilderness a couple of hours before he'd found her, so he didn't think she'd gone too far. He couldn't think of anything that would keep his attention as they waited.

When Alyssa came rushing in the door, both he and Lily were startled by her return.

Drew said, "I thought—"

Alyssa cut him off, "I know, but I have news. I was watching TV while eating a sad solitary lunch, since it took me the rest of the morning to check on the younger stock as I mentioned. Well you won't believe it but coverage of the beauty pageant coming up next week came on. I thought about switching channels, but then decided after our conversation this morning to watch, still not expecting anything."

She looked at Lily. "You *are* a contestant; your full name is Lily Smith and you are Ms. Montana."

Drew was beyond shocked at that announcement and Lily looked the same. Her mouth had dropped open and a frown had covered her features. "Are you sure? That doesn't really feel right to me."

Alyssa nodded, "You could have knocked me over with a feather, but I saw your face. They were just listing all the contestants, so it was really quick, but I am certain it was you. I had to eat the rest of my lunch in the truck on the way here, to give you the news."

Drew said, "You could have called."

"Oh no, this was too important for a mere phone call." Alyssa patted her pockets and frowned. "Pull up the pageant website on your phone, Drew. They should have the contestants listed."

He did as he was told and could barely scroll through the information with Alyssa hopping from foot to foot next to him. When he got to the M-states Alyssa pointed, nearly knocking the phone from his hand. "See! Right there, it's her, I know it is."

Drew zoomed into the picture and he had to admit it looked just like her. He handed the phone to Lily. "It is me. But I can't believe it. It still doesn't seem right."

Alyssa said, "The internet doesn't lie." Then she frowned. "Well at least it doesn't *always* lie."

Lily muttered, "Lily Smith. Do you mind if I do a search on that name?"

Drew waved his hand in her direction; a search was a great idea. He was still shocked to find out that Lily was a beauty pageant contestant. She certainly had the looks to be one, but she didn't fuss over her appearance, at all. It would explain the strange diet with the pageant being next week. It also explained the concern about her feet healing. But it still felt so out of character.

Lily sighed, "It's too common of a last name, there is a couple of articles about the pageant, but besides that there, is just a lot of other listings. Even with Lily being more unique there are too many."

She handed his phone back to him just as a knock sounded on the door. Maybe it was Thomas with news. He pulled the door open and sure enough it was. Both he and Jimmy were loaded down with stuff.

He opened the door wide for the men to come in with their burdens. Thomas had a small rolling suitcase and a woman's coat. Jimmy looked to be carrying bags of groceries. They deposited everything, and the men went to gather around Lily.

Thomas handed Lily a purse. "The trail led us directly to a cabin in the National Forest. We got to the cabin a little after the owner, who had received a call saying that the cabin was empty. There were no people there, but all of that, had been left behind, the guy had already started making a pile of what had been left. I told the owner that we thought there might need to be some police investigation, but he said he had some new people coming in and he had to get it ready for them. Since he'd already moved everything, rather than argue and bring more attention to the issue that you wanted kept quiet, we just gathered up what he didn't want, and brought it here."

Lily was looking through the purse, at the ID and credit cards, all of which looked to be hers. She pulled out her phone, but it had no power. "It looks like it must be my bag. Was there a charger in the suitcase?"

Jimmy nodded. "Yes, there was, do you want me to get it for you?"

"Please, in fact can you bring the bag over and show me what is in it?"

Jimmy's ears turned pink. "Maybe Alyssa can help with that."

Lily wanted to roll her eyes, she was sure there was some underwear and maybe a night gown in there, but nothing too racy. But the guy wasn't very old, several years younger than she was, probably, so maybe he'd not been around women much. "That's great, thanks so much for helping to find my stuff."

Drew said, "Anything else you can tell us about the cabin?"

Thomas shifted from foot to foot. "The strange thing about it was that there didn't seem to be anything amiss. It didn't look like anyone else had been there. Nothing seemed out of place. It was almost as if you'd just gone out for some fresh air."

Lily frowned, but only nodded. Drew was watching her closely and knew she didn't think that felt right. She had clearly been running and her first words were about finding a cop. Something just wasn't adding up in his mind, or hers apparently.

The trackers took their leave and he left the women to look through the suitcase while he put the food away. There was herbal tea and lots of protein snacks and low carb food. But there was also some food that he knew Lily would not want to be eating. So that made him wonder who that food was for. It certainly pointed to a second person, to him.

≈

ALYSSA HELPED LILY GO through the suitcase. There weren't a lot of things, just a couple of outfits and a sexy nightgown, which was kind of a surprise. It wasn't a comfortable looking nightgown, more like seduction wear. She guessed this was what had made Jimmy's ears turn pink, because everything else was pretty normal looking. None of it looked dirty or worn, however. The slacks and tops were in a similar vein to the shredded outfit she'd been found in, but there were no creases to indicate wearing. There was a laundry bag too, that had nothing in it.

Had she run out of the cabin within the first few minutes of arriving? That didn't make sense, most check-ins were in the late afternoon, but Drew had found her in the morning. Late morning, yes, but still morning. So, if she'd spent the night, she'd gotten up and put on the same clothes, including underwear, that seemed very odd indeed.

Alyssa said, "There are no dirty clothes."

Lily nodded. "I was just noticing that. It seems strange, doesn't it?"

"Yes, it does. Drew, didn't you find Lily in the morning?"

"Yep. Why?"

"There are no dirty clothes."

He rolled his eyes. "So, she ran off before she changed them?"

"But most cabins don't check people in until later in the afternoon. So, if she spent the night she got up and put on the same clothes."

He shrugged.

Alyssa continued. "Including underwear."

It finally sunk in and Drew looked up. "That's not normal."

Alyssa crossed her arms. "No, it's not."

He looked back toward the kitchen. "None of the foods she would like have been opened, not even the tea. But the foods she wouldn't like, are open."

Drew came into the room and sat in the chair. Lily and Drew watched Alyssa repack the bag to take to the bedroom. The sexy nighty caused his eyebrows to raise, but he didn't mention it.

Alyssa got the charger and the phone and plugged them in. She opened the front of the bag and found shoes. A pair of worn sneakers and two pairs of fancy high heels. "All right, well we have certainly confirmed the sky-high heels question. You do have them, but the most worn ones are the sneakers. The heels look pretty new. That could be due to the fact that after you wear these killer heels your feet need comfort, which they would find in the sneakers."

Lily agreed with that statement, just looking at those shoes made her feet hurt.

"I'll leave the sneakers out, since your healing feet will be better in them. I'm going to go put the suitcase and clothes in the room you're staying in. Unless you're ready to face the world."

Lily shook her head, no, she didn't feel up to others, yet. "Maybe tomorrow. After my phone charges I want to look through it. It will most certainly have clues."

"Sounds reasonable. I'll put these things away then. Taking the rest of the day to heal would be best anyway."

CHAPTER 6

*D*rew was alarmed at the disappointment he felt knowing Lily had planned a getaway with someone, that included seduction wear. Clearly, she was involved with someone, and that sucked. He'd not really realized that he was feeling drawn to her in a sexual way. He knew he wanted to help her, but the level of disappointment he was feeling went far beyond normal.

This was the first time since high school that he'd been attracted to a woman. He was glad to know that part of him hadn't died with Monica, but couldn't he have felt it for someone not already taken?

"So, what do you want to do while you wait for your phone to charge? We've got books, or we could play cards."

"If you don't mind I just want to lay down here on the couch for a few minutes and think about things, if I don't fall asleep that is. It's been a lot of revelations and maybe if I just let my mind mull them over, my memories will return."

"Fair enough. I'm going to go check on my horse, I'll be back in a little bit."

Drew went out into the fresh air, where he could think

better, too. He needed to see how all the pieces fit together. His horse greeted him, and Drew took a brush down and started grooming.

Lily had clearly been in that cabin with someone else, even though that person had cleared out. Why would someone leave her like that? Unless they'd done something wrong and didn't want to get caught. Lily running away without her shoes or coat didn't make sense either, since they were in the cabin, again unless something untoward had been going on.

Had someone threatened both her and her boyfriend? So, Lily had run one way and he'd gone the other? But if that had happened, his clothes would have been in the cabin too, unless he'd snuck back to get them. But then why had he left Lily's clothes behind?

None of this made much sense. And her having no dirty clothes was also a mystery, had she slept in the clothes she'd had on? They hadn't looked very comfortable for that. Maybe the two of them had arrived really late or early in the morning and they'd simply crashed rather than getting undressed. He supposed that was possible.

But then why was some of the food opened? This was the strangest set of circumstances he'd ever run across. Maybe he needed a fresh perspective. He wondered if he should call in the sheriff.

Drew filled the water trough with fresh water and gave his horse both hay and grain, then walked out to lean against the fence post. His brain whirled with all the clues he had, but he didn't get any closer to a reasonable explanation.

Lily needed her memories back. They both needed to get on with their lives.

He'd seen movies about people losing their memory and wondered how much of what they showed was true. Movies showed people regaining their memory instantly when something triggered it and wondered if that really could happen or if it was more subtle than that. If he took Lily to see the cabin, would if help?

Thomas had gotten a card from the owner of the cabin. Drew decided to call the owner to ask about taking Lily to see the space. After a quick phone call, it was confirmed that Drew could take Lily in two days. The people currently staying in the cabin where only there for a short time, if Lily's memory was not back in two days he would drive her out to the cabin.

He still probably needed to bring the sheriff in on it. There was a reason she'd been running and maybe with two heads it would be easier to figure out. His mom, dad and Grandpa K could be counted on for good ideas, too. He would broach the subject with dinner and see if she was ready to move to the big house.

That would also bring a close to the intimacy of the cabin and help him get his head on straight. She was taken, and having more people around would help him to remember that.

LILY DOZED FITFULLY on the couch while her mind ran around and around with the information she'd just heard. Being a contestant in a beauty pageant just flat seemed odd to her. But even odder was the scantiness of the nightgown she'd packed. It was clearly not made for sleeping.

With the slight indent on her finger it appeared she was with someone, which made her attraction for the hunky cop off limits. A total bummer. Maybe they should move to his parents' house as he'd suggested. It would put more people in their path and keep her from getting too close to the man. Maybe tomorrow.

She could rest the remainder of today and keep off her feet, then after Alyssa came to check on her they could all go together.

Lily also needed to check her phone and see what interesting information that might bring to her mind. There certainly should be pictures and phone numbers of friends, maybe even a calendar of events. Emails would give her itineraries for the pageant, which was supposed to be next weekend.

When she drifted off, she had weird thoughts, they weren't quite dreams, because she wasn't fully asleep. Her mind wouldn't let her relax enough to sleep, it was thinking too much. But she wanted to give her phone enough charge, so she didn't have to sit right by the wall.

She'd decided to leave it plugged in until Drew came back in. He was such a nice man and she felt safe with him. Who was this guy she was with, was he a nice man? She didn't feel very favorably towards him and that made her wonder. Why would she have that scanty nighty if she didn't feel positive towards him? Maybe they'd had a fight. But her running out of the cabin in her bare feet seemed a little extreme for a fight. She sighed, nothing made sense.

When she heard Drew come back in the door she sat up. He'd brought fresh air in with him and his hair was tousled. "Is it windy out?"

"No, actually it's very pleasant."

Lily sighed.

"Are you feeling cooped up?"

"A little, or maybe it's just restlessness, wanting to know what's going on. Nothing makes any sense to me."

"I was thinking about that. It might be a good idea to bring in a few more people to help us figure that out. Unless your phone reveals all."

Lily nodded. "I was thinking the same thing, maybe

tomorrow after Alyssa checks on me we should go to your parents' house."

"Yeah, talking things over with mom, dad and Grandpa K would be good. We could also have the sheriff come out to the house. He's one of my dad's buddies."

It all sounded like a good idea, but she would miss this little cabin and having Drew all to herself. She cleared her throat from the lump that was forming. "That's probably a good idea. Do you think my phone is charged enough?"

"Most likely." He unplugged it and brought it to her. The lock screen showed her with a guy. Lily wondered if she would remember her password, but as she took it from him, she realized she had biometrics programmed in because it immediately unlocked.

He sat in the chair to the right of the couch and pulled out his own phone. She started with the pictures. She flipped through a few of them, but without context they were no help. She had apps for both Facebook and Instagram. She pulled up Facebook, rather than look at the feed she went to her profile and started with her own posts.

There was a post about her taking a few days off to go to an undisclosed location for the weekend. It was going to be a surprise and she'd been excited about it.

When she got to the post where a guy named Ronald Duvall had proposed she'd felt an irrational anger and had actually wanted to throw her phone across the room. She resisted doing that and looked carefully at the post and all the comments. She'd been happy at the time. Lots of hearts and happy faces. What had changed?

She must have made some noise because Drew looked up from his phone. "What's wrong?"

"I just don't know. I'm looking at Facebook and I came across a post where a guy named Ronald Duvall asked me to marry him. The post is all happy, with smileys and hearts, but when I saw it, I wanted to throw my phone across the room and scream."

Drew was taken aback by that. "Not what one would expect looking at that kind of post."

"Right? So, what changed?"

"The million-dollar question. Do you feel fear when you look at him?"

"No, actually I don't, but I am totally pissed off when I look at his ugly lying face."

Drew snorted. "If he's the same guy on your lock screen, he's not ugly. As to the lying comment, I can't say."

She still felt like the guy was a weasel. "Well he looks like a lying rat in sheep's clothing to me."

"Do you feel like you were running away from him when I found you?"

Lily looked back at the picture of Ronald on her phone. Was she running away from him? She didn't feel fear, she only felt anger, so if she had been running away, then why? Dammit only more questions. "Maybe, but I don't know why, I really don't feel any fear looking at him."

"Do you want me to run him?"

Like through the criminal database? She didn't think he would find anything, but it wouldn't hurt to know. She looked back at the engagement post and noticed it had only been a few weeks ago. So that's why there wasn't much of an indention on her finger and why she didn't feel engaged. "Sure, go ahead."

While he did that, she continued to scroll back through her profile posts. Prior to about a year ago there was no mention of any pageantry. In fact, there wasn't much of anything, she was not a very avid poster. She did see a post where she had shared that a friend of hers had begged her to join the pageant, but she couldn't see why.

She clicked over to that friend's profile and there was

nothing at all on it recently, that didn't sound good, because that friend had been an avid poster prior to asking Lily to join the pageant. Then she just kind of faded away. It made Lily shiver.

Drew huffed, which thankfully pulled her attention from Facebook. "Nothing, at all. It's too empty."

"Are you saying it's a fake name?"

Drew rubbed his hand around the back of his neck. "I suppose that is a possibility. But why?"

Lily glanced back at her phone. "This is not helping as much as I had hoped. I'm just finding more questions."

"Maybe leave where you are and check email or your calendar. If you're in a pageant next week, we need to know about it."

Hopefully she would have more luck with that. She clicked over to her email and found a folder labeled Pageant. There was a ton of information in that folder. The most pressing was that she needed to be in New York on Wednesday next week. Her flight was out of Billings, Tuesday afternoon, which gave her eight days to get her feet healed, her memory back, and her butt home and then to Billings.

Lily glanced through a few more emails in the folder and then decided she knew enough about that for now. She went back to her inbox and didn't see anything significant. So, she opened up her text messages and saw a bunch of messages waiting from "Mom".

Scrolling down to the first unread one she started there and read going forward in time. The first one just mentioned having a good weekend with Ronald, then there was some about her pageant dresses being back from the seamstress and that her mom was looking forward to having her try them on when she got back.

The most recent mentioned that her mom and dad would

pick her up at the airport tonight, since Ronald was going on to New York. Knowing they would worry when she didn't get off the plane, a phone call was in order, but she didn't even remember her mother, what would she say? "I need to call my mom, she thinks she's picking me up at the airport tonight."

Drew looked up. "Want me to leave so you can talk?"

Did she? No, not at all. "No need, you know as much about this as I do."

She scrolled through her contacts to find the one that said mom and pushed send. A woman answered the phone. "Hi honey, are you boarding your flight?"

Lily said, "Mom?"

"Well of course, what's wrong, honey?"

Lily didn't exactly recognize her mother's voice, but she did recognize the feelings it gave her. Comfort and security and love. Her throat closed up and tears threatened. She tried to speak through her tears, "Everything mom, everything is wrong."

"What? What's happened, Lily?"

She started to cry harder and looked at Drew. He was instantly by her side, wrapped one arm around her, and took the phone. He pushed speaker, so they could both hear. "Mrs. Smith? This is Drew Kipling, I'm a sheriff's deputy in Spirit Lake Colorado."

They both heard her mother gasp.

Drew hurried on, "Now don't worry, ma'am. Lily is fine, nothing a couple of days won't cure."

Her mom shrieked, "What?"

Shit, he was making things worse, but Lily was still sobbing too hard to help.

"Now don't worry, ma'am. Lily has had a few challenges, but really, she is fine. Just a bump on her head and a couple of stitches in one foot. But well, she also lost her memory, my brother says it's probably from the bump and once the swelling goes down she'll remember everything. It only happened yesterday."

Her mom harrumphed. "Why am I talking to you? Instead of Lily?"

"Lily was overcome when she heard your voice and started crying. She's been very stoic up until now."

Lily was finally starting to calm down, when she heard her mom yell out. "Howard, start packing, we're going to Colorado."

Lily choked out, "No, wait mom, you don't need to do that."

"It's only a ten-hour drive to Denver. We'll be there tomorrow. Drew was it? Where is Spirit Lake?"

Drew said, "It's two hours west of Denver in the mountains, when you hit interstate seventy turn west and follow the signs to Rocky Mountain National park, our town is right before you get to the park. Call when you hit the town and we'll guide you to the ranch. The Rockin' K ranch."

"Very good. Lily honey, we'll talk when we get there. I have to go help your father, now. We'll see you tomorrow."

Lily sighed, she hated having her parents drive so far, but she needed her mom and her dad. She said, "All right mommy, drive carefully. Don't drive straight through, there is no emergency, I'm fine."

Her mom harrumphed again, but said, "Don't worry. We'll stop in Casper for the night. Love you, see you soon."

"Bye." Drew pushed end and Lily put her head on his shoulder and sucked in his warmth and strength. He curled his arm tighter around her and she felt safe and protected.

CHAPTER 7

*D*rew held Lily for a long time. He thought she was still crying. Not the wracking sobs from before but quiet, cleansing tears. There was nothing wrong with that, so he didn't say anything just held her close and let his hand draw circles on her arm. He enjoyed the closeness, and the idea that he was bringing her comfort, it had been a long time since he'd felt this way.

Since before Monica had died, they had been to prom and it was just a few weeks until graduation. He'd thought about asking her to marry him, but they were both going away to college. She was going to be a nurse and he was going for a business degree. He'd planned to use that for the ranch. Her crazy mother had ruined their 'after the prom' plans with a single text. Monica had been devastated that she hadn't been accepted into the college she'd wanted to go to, so he'd held her, much like he was holding Lily.

Monica had let all her frustration and sadness pour out of her while he held her and spoke soothingly. Then she'd been tired, so had decided to go home rather than spend the night like they'd planned. He didn't mind, not too much anyway.

So, she'd given him a goodnight kiss and that was the last time he'd ever seen her.

A drunk driver had T-boned her car pushing her into the side of a mountain. The dumb ass was so wasted he never even took his foot off the gas just kept right on going forward. He'd been in a huge truck and Monica's little car hadn't had a chance and neither had Monica.

That's when he'd changed his mind and had gone into law enforcement. Hopefully to keep drunk assholes off the roads. He'd gone to the police academy after high school graduation and took classes at night to get his degree. He'd been so focused, he'd finished his four-year degree in three and a half years. He'd not been interested in doing anything but getting his degree. He'd helped at the ranch as needed, but that had been the extent of his life.

Lily sighed, sat up and grabbed a handful of tissues from the box he'd left on the table from her first night there. "What are you thinking about?"

He put his stoic face back on, so she wouldn't see his vulnerabilities. "Life, the universe and everything."

"The answer is forty-two."

Drew guffawed at that, not many people his age knew that reference and even fewer of those were female. "So, who's the geek in your family?"

Her eyes shuttered, and she murmured, "I have no idea."

Dammit, he was an idiot. "We can ask your mom and dad when they get here."

Excitement filled her face and then it faded. "What if I don't remember them?"

"What if you do?"

Lily's eyes locked on his, she asked, "Do you think I will?"

"I think it's entirely possible. It will have been two days then since you hit your head, so the swelling will have eased. Beau and Alyssa said the amnesia probably wouldn't last long. And it's your parents, so they would be your most deep-seated memory."

Lily nodded. "Them and my bossy sister." She gasped and looked at him, a glorious smile covering her face. "I have a sister! I can't remember what she looks like or her name, but I know I have a sister and she bosses me around. So, she must be older."

"There you go. Your memory is returning, just slowly and in bits and pieces. Nothing to worry about." He hoped he wasn't talking out of his ass.

But her smile didn't dim, which caused a very strange effect on his heart. But he didn't dwell on that, because he still didn't know if she was engaged. Clearly, she had been, but wanting to throw the phone across the room at seeing her engagement picture, did not bode well for Ronald Duvall, or whatever his name was.

He didn't want to think about that, he was just some hick cop, the way she'd been dressed and the whole beauty pageant thing indicated she came from money and sophistication. They weren't poor by any means, their ranch had nearly always done well, but sophistication meant wearing your good boots instead of your riding boots, new jeans, along with a solid colored shirt and maybe a string tie. Nope, they were from completely different orbits.

Which meant it was better to stay away from futile imaginings. It would be entirely too easy to visualize. He cleared his throat and stood. "Are you hungry?"

"Yes. All this drama and revelation has worked up an appetite."

"Great, maybe you should keep looking through your phone to see what else you can discover while I make you a salad with lots of protein on top."

"And maybe a few croutons, I think I love croutons."

"Yes, ma'am, croutons coming up." He saluted which

made her laugh. He felt like a hero getting a good strong laugh out of her. It was a deep throaty laugh that punched him in the chest and caused warmth to suffuse his body.

He double-timed it into the kitchen. It would be best to get out of that little cabin and in with some other people where there would be a buffer between them. He didn't need to lose his head or his heart to someone in a totally different world than he was in, let alone the geography. Montana didn't really seem to fit her though, although he supposed in Helena or Billings there would be more sophistication, but still it didn't quite fit her, to his idea anyway.

Changing the subject in his mind to stop the craziness, he made a mental list of who he needed to call for tomorrow. Alyssa, so she could bring the truck, rather than riding out, that way Lily could ride back with her. Drake, so he could join in the brain-storming, he'd been the sheriff Drew's whole life, so probably had some good thoughts. Hopefully his boss didn't tear him a new one for not calling sooner. He also needed to call his parents, so they could get a room ready for Lily and her parents, and arrange for a confab around the kitchen table.

He couldn't take Lily to the other cabin until the day after tomorrow. That was probably just fine because after all that was going to go down tomorrow, he didn't believe there would be time to go out to the cabin anyway. Just thinking about all of it, made his head hurt, and he hoped it wouldn't overwhelm Lily.

He put the food on the table and went to get Lily. She was consumed by her phone and didn't even notice him. "Lily, lunch is ready."

She finally looked up at him. "I think my sister's name is Rose. There is a Rose Brown that comments on everything I post, and the personal messages are bossy, just like I said. Plus, I think she kind of looks like me, don't you?"

She handed him her phone and there was a very pretty woman in the picture. Not as pretty as Lily, but there was a resemblance. "Yes, there is a likeness between you, but you're a lot prettier."

Shit, he didn't mean to blurt that out, but she just smiled as she took her phone back. "Well thank you, kind sir."

~

Lily savored the feel of Drew's arms around her as he carried her to the table. Tomorrow everything would change, and they wouldn't have their little cabin in the woods, and the closeness that brought. She could only imagine what might happen tomorrow but even if her memories didn't return, she would have a lot more information.

She knew her parents being there would be good for her and her stability. But she liked the intimacy that being alone with Drew brought. She already knew she was going to miss that, miss him. It couldn't be helped, she had to get back to her real life, whatever that was, but she was determined to enjoy the man while she still could.

She breathed deep to draw in his scent, of outdoors and man with just a hint of leather and horse. It was delicious. She sighed as he set her down.

"What's wrong?"

She ducked her head not wanting to admit she liked him holding her. "Nothing, just so much happening. Tomorrow will be very different. I'm not sure I'm ready for it."

He took the statement as she'd intended. "It will be all right. I'm sure your parents are fine people, and I know mine are. Everyone will be great, and maybe you'll get your memory back."

He took her hand and squeezed it encouragingly. "Now

eat this gourmet salad I made for you, and look there's even a bowl of extra croutons, in case I didn't give you enough."

She looked at her salad which nearly had more croutons than salad and laughed as he'd wanted her to. "I think you gave me plenty. Is there any salad under that mound of croutons?"

"Yes. There is. But I did bring an extra plate in case you need to move some croutons aside to get to it." He had a sparkle in his eyes that indicated he was teasing her. She loved it.

"Now what would be the fun in that? Most of the joy of croutons is testing your salad-eating skills to see if you can eat the salad without avalanching the crunchy goodness." She turned her salad this way and that, with a slow perusal. Teasing him in return as she pretended to find the best place to start.

When she'd lulled him into the proper state, she stabbed her fork right into the middle causing a cascade of salad onto the larger plate beneath it. She took the huge bite that was speared by her fork and shoved it into her mouth. The salad dressing got on her face as she chewed in delight.

Drew nearly fell out of his chair he was laughing so hard, which is exactly what she was going for. She managed to swallow the bite before joining him in gales of laughter.

He sputtered out between guffaws. "I thought… you were going… to be all… dainty…and then you stabbed…and salad flew everywhere. I nearly peed my pants."

She said as she wiped tears of laughter from her cheeks. "You should have seen your face when I stabbed it."

"Everything exploded."

"It did, I surprised the hell out of you."

"Yes, you definitely did that. I can't wait to tell my sister, Emma, she'll love it."

Lily grinned at him and she saw his expression change from laughter to... was it yearning?

"You've got some salad dressing..." he took his napkin and wiped her upper lip with it.

The atmosphere in the room changed as he touched her so intimately. And she knew, that whether he felt it or not, she definitely felt yearning.

He pulled back and blinked. Then he cleared his throat, but his words still came out rough. "I got it."

Lily gathered her wits that had exploded all around her in a much bigger mess than her salad had made. She murmured, "Thanks" and looked back to her salad.

Which caused both of them to chuckle one more time and that cleared the air, so they could eat.

They talked about inconsequential things as they ate, and she managed to keep up her end of the conversation, but part of her mind was puzzling over that moment. If she truly was engaged, why had she felt that sizzling attraction and overwhelming yearning?

She didn't really feel like she was someone who would cheat. Plus, she'd been so angry to see the engagement photo, she'd wanted to yell out 'liar'. She and Ronald had been dressed to the nines and at a very fancy restaurant. The ring had been enormous and if truth be told she thought it had looked gaudy, it had overpowered the size of her hand. Lily had posted a picture of the food and she had no idea what it even was, but it had been heavy with cream sauce. She actually couldn't imagine eating it. And there had been champagne, did she like champagne?

Drew had stopped talking so she looked up. "Sorry, just trying to remember. It didn't help." She shrugged.

Drew blew out a breath. "It's got to be hard, I'm so sorry."

Lily said, "So, changing the subject. If my feet heal quick

enough and we don't have to leave immediately, any chance I could ride one of your horses?"

"Do you ride?"

His eyebrows had gone up in surprise, which made her want to laugh. "I don't really know for sure, but yes, I think I do."

Drew grinned at her. "If it works out, by all means, you are welcome to have a ride. If it doesn't work out this time, you can always come back."

Lily's breath caught at the idea of coming back, and that yearning filled her again. She looked down at her plate, so he couldn't see it. "That would be fun."

"It would be, and the invitation is open ended. You can come back in a few weeks or when you're old and gray."

He was teasing her, and she liked it, she liked it a lot.

CHAPTER 8

*R*onald's phone rang. He picked it up and looked at it in horror as he recognized the phone number. Shit, he didn't want to talk to them. He didn't have a choice though, they'd planned to call him every few days. If he didn't answer they would get suspicious. He just didn't know if he had it in him to lie. Oh, he'd lied to that gullible twit, but that was a whole different ball game.

He slapped a smile on his face, so he wouldn't sound tense and swiped the green button. "This is Ronald."

"Good to know. How's your little package doing this morning?"

"Just fine." He hoped she'd either been eaten by a bear or was lost in the wilderness.

"Has she realized that she isn't going to be in the competition, so she doesn't need to complain about the food?"

"No, still bitching and moaning."

"You could always put her out of your misery. Smother her with a pillow for instance, or take her out into the forest and let a wild animal have her for a snack."

The joy on the other end of the line when these things

were said, turned Ronald's stomach. He wasn't a violent person. Choking back his horror, he said, "Thanks for the advice. I'll keep it in mind."

"You do realize when this is over, if she's still breathing, she's going to go straight to the police?"

Ronald had thought about that and wasn't sure how to stay out of jail, if she'd stayed put. But now he could make his getaway. "I hope to be far away when that happens."

"Her not breathing would be better all around, but I'll leave that up to you. Talk to you in a few days."

DREW DRAGGED his ass out of bed. He'd not slept worth shit, thinking about all the changes today would bring. He'd really enjoyed spending this few days with Lily, she was brave and funny and so damn beautiful his heart hurt at the idea of her leaving. But she was most likely engaged and clearly from a different social circle than he was from. He could never fit into that life.

He'd pulled up her Facebook profile after she'd gone to bed. It was clearly her pageant profile, so open to the public, and it showed her in fancy restaurants with Ronald the Suit. Which is what he'd dubbed her fiancé, the guy wasn't in one picture without a three-piece suit. Not only that but it was always perfectly set, no jacket off, no loosened tie, no rolled up sleeves.

Drew knew he would suffocate dressed like that day in and day out. Did the guy never chill? There had even been pictures of a barbeque they had attended, and he was still perfectly turned out, Lily had been in a pretty sun dress with fancy sandals, but Ronald the Suit was in his suit and tie.

He couldn't see what Lily saw in him, but then again maybe it was the class thing. He was just a cowboy cop, what did he know about big city life? Although, there had been other guys at the barbeque, and they'd looked normal.

Enough, his mind had gone over and over this last night. He needed to get moving. Alyssa was going to be there in two hours and then they would all head up to his parents' house. His mom had quickly assured him that three more people would be no problem at all and not to worry.

He hadn't exactly been worried, just wanted to give them time to prepare. Lily hadn't turned her nose up at the cabin and his parents' house was warm and inviting, but it was definitely lived in. He and his five siblings probably hadn't been easy on the house or it's furnishings. Funny how he'd never even thought about that until Lily had come along.

He shook his head at his foolishness and went to take care of his horse. He needed to pack up the fresh food and change the sheets and prepare the cabin for the next time it was needed. When his horse was settled in with his breakfast he hopped into the shower.

After his shower he looked in on Lily and found her awake and dressed. Still in the sweats she'd borrowed, rather than her own fancy clothes. He didn't know what that meant. "You're up. You could have slept a while longer."

"I'm too nervous. I'm going to meet all your family and the sheriff and even my own parents. I feel like throwing up."

"No throwing up. My family are just normal folks, you've already met some of them, the rest are no different. The sheriff is my dad's best friend, so nothing to worry about there either. And your parents love you, it wouldn't surprise me if they beat us to the house."

She gasped. "They said they would spend the night in Casper."

Drew nodded. "Yep, so we're talking a six-hour drive. I imagine they are worried about you and didn't sleep easily. I

73

can see them on the road by five or six which means they could drive in by eleven or noon easily. If not earlier."

"You told them to call when they get to town."

"I did, but I also told them the name of the ranch, so it wouldn't be hard to get directions, either by GPS or asking in town."

"I hadn't thought about that."

"Well let's get busy, as my Grandpa K would say, we're burning daylight."

She laughed and let him carry her to the bathroom where she could freshen up. While she did that he stripped the beds and put clean sheets on them. Putting the dirty ones in the washer. He noticed her sheets had her scent on them and was almost sorry to wash them. He shook his head at his own foolishness and went to get her from the bathroom.

It might be one of the last times he got to carry her around. When Alyssa came she might declare Lily's feet healed enough to walk on, at least short distances, like to the bathroom. He set her down at the kitchen table. "What do you feel like for breakfast?"

"Not a lot, my stomach has butterflies flying like crazy. I was almost serious about throwing up."

"Hmm, in that case tea and toast, with maybe a slice of cheese to go with it?"

"We can give it a shot."

As he made the food for her, and then an enormous bowl of cereal for himself, he tried to think about how to distract her, so she could at least eat a little bit. He couldn't think of a darn thing, that wouldn't remind her of everything. Darn it, there had to be something.

He let out a sigh when Lily herself came up with a topic to talk about. "So, do you rodeo or did you in the past?"

"I don't too much anymore, I did in high school. I have a friend that's a professional. He's going for all-around cowboy this year. One of my brothers is a mighty fine roper, but the rest of us just played with it. My sister was good at barrels and she was right up there in roping, too. She and Cade made a great team for team roping."

"What event did you do?"

"Saddle bronc riding mostly, some bareback, did some bullfighting for a while for the riders. Mostly to keep my best friend from getting stomped." He shrugged like it had been no big deal.

"The fighting is just as dangerous as the riding."

"Can be, if you aren't quick on your feet." He'd had a time or two where he'd needed some healing after a rodeo, but he wasn't going to go into it.

"Well I'm glad you don't do it anymore, at least the bull-fighting."

He wasn't a bit sad to have left the rodeo in his past. He still helped out on the ranch, so he didn't have to turn in his cowboy card. "Yeah, I'm good, no need to prove anything."

"What did you have to prove?"

He chuckled at the typical female comment. "I'm the youngest of five boys. I had to prove everything. Or at least that's what I thought."

"Not anymore?"

"No, I finally realized all five of us, plus Emma, are each our own person. Our parents never did play any one of us against the other. Each of us have our own strengths and weaknesses. So, I can be myself and the rest of them can be who they are. One thing our parents did stress was that we could be and do whatever we set our minds to and worked hard at."

Lily nodded, but he could see her looking inward. He wondered about the same thing she probably was thinking about. What her parents had been like, during her growing up. Finally, she said, "They were very wise."

"I like to think so." He put her food down in front of her and she didn't hesitate to eat it, so maybe the talk had helped her forget her anxiety.

He sat down across from her with his cereal and started shoveling it in.

"That's the biggest bowl of cereal I've ever seen, you could have cooked yourself something better to eat."

Drew shook his head. "No, this is perfect, by the time Alyssa gets here and looks at your feet and we get back to the house, my mother will have prepared a feast. That will be about the same time this wears off."

Lily rolled her eyes at him. "That's enough cereal for three people."

He just grinned at her. "I have a high metabolism." And he went right back to shoveling it into his mouth, while Lily nibbled on toast and cheese.

When they were finished eating he carried Lily to the couch and set her down on it. He needed to get moving. He suspected Alyssa would be here at any moment and he needed to get the sheets in the dryer and pack up all the food. He really did believe her parents would be knocking on the door any time.

Alyssa showed up while he was in the laundry room, so he left the women to their tasks and got busy with his own. He could come back later today or tomorrow to get the sheets and towels out of the dryer or send one of the ranch hands out to take care of it.

LILY WATCHED as Alyssa examined her, from head to toe. "Everything is healing nicely. The knot on your head has shrunk and your forehead scrape is hardly noticeable. Your ankle sprain seems to be fine, no swelling there. Let's see how your feet are doing, they are going to be the most crucial part for your pageant."

Knowing that was true, Lily held her breath as Alyssa removed the bandages. She poked and prodded and then looked up with a big smile. "They are looking a lot better than I had hoped."

Lily let out a huge sigh of relief.

"You should still stay off of them as much as possible, but if we wrap them up well, you should be able to walk to the bathroom."

While Lily was glad to hear her feet were healing she also knew she was going to miss having Drew carry her around. She'd felt very special with his arms wrapped around her.

"Well, at least Drew won't have to cart me around all the time. That should be a relief."

His deep voice spoke from behind her. "On the contrary, carrying you around has been one of the highlights of our cabin-in-the-woods experience." He walked into the living room with a teasing smile on his face.

She giggled. "I'll keep that in mind, if I ever need another personal transportation slave."

He laughed with her, but she sensed something from him. Was he disappointed for their time to end, like she was, or was it merely wishful thinking on her part?

Alyssa was busily bandaging up her feet when Lily's phone chimed with an incoming text. She read it and then looked up. "Mom says they just got to Granby."

Drew nodded. "Just as I thought. We've got maybe forty minutes."

Alyssa anchored the last part of the wrap and stood. "Well we better get a move on then. Lily, try standing and let me know if you feel any pain or pulling on the stitches."

They each took a hand and helped her stand, keeping her hands in theirs to anchor and steady her. "I don't feel any real pain, some twinges maybe, but nothing I can't live with."

Alyssa smiled. "Excellent, let me get those sneakers I saw in your luggage and see if we can get them on if we let out the laces. They will help protect your feet, too."

Drew said, "I'll get the food out to the truck."

"Even if we do get the shoes on her, I'll want you to carry her to the truck and then into the house. Her shuffling around to use the bathroom or whatever is not the same as walking outside."

Drew saluted and went off to gather up what shouldn't stay in the cabin. They might not need it again for weeks or even longer.

When Alyssa brought the shoes out, Lily said, "While I get these on, can you go pack up my clothes for me? Drew gave me a trash bag for the dirty ones, but I haven't worn much more than your sweats."

"Of course. I'll be right back."

Lily didn't want to be weird about it, but Drew packing up her clothes felt too intimate. Especially with that naughty nighty. She was nearly tempted to throw that in the trash, but couldn't bring herself to do it.

She unlaced her shoes and then got them on her feet, they were tight, but she figured that was better than nothing at all. The soles would keep her from hurting the cuts down there. She stood up by herself just as Drew came back for another load to take out to the truck Alyssa had driven.

He said, "Look at you all up and walking in your tennies."

"I got them on, they are a little tight but not too bad. They look older than dirt, so I imagine they were stretched out."

"Most likely. Where's Alyssa?"

Lily ducked her head. "Packing up my clothes."

"Perfect, then I think we're ready to roll." He yelled out to Alyssa. "Gonna carry Lily out."

Alyssa yelled back, "Right behind you."

Lily was swooped up into Drew's arms where she kind of wanted to stay forever. When they got outside Lily looked up at the brilliant blue sky above her. "It's so blue."

"It is, it's the lack of pollution and atmosphere up here that makes it that color. Plus, the fact you've been trapped inside the cabin for days."

Lily laughed from pure joy and looked all around. "It's gorgeous here."

Drew had gone still, she looked up at him and saw a flash of something in his eyes, before he covered it with a blank expression. Then he looked around like he'd never been here before. "It's a great place to live."

Alyssa bustled out of the cabin with Lily's suitcase. "Why are you standing in the yard?"

"Lily's been trapped in the cabin, she's enjoying our blue skies and mountains."

"That makes sense, but if we want to get back to the house before her parents arrive we need to go. Lily can look while I drive, get her in the truck."

"Yes, commander bossy, as you say." Drew saluted.

Lily laughed at their playfulness as Drew settled her into the front seat of an enormous extended cab pickup truck. Drew went off to get his horse and Lily asked. "Is this your truck?"

"No, it's Beau's. I brought some supplies to replenish what Beau's horse ate, while he was here." The truck roared to life when Alyssa turned the key and they drove off.

Lily nodded. "Oh, that makes sense. I noticed Drew refilled the firewood stacks in the cabin, too. And he washed all the sheets and towels and the dishes. He's very handy."

"They all are, everyone knows that being prepared this far out, can be the difference between life and death, for both man and beast, so nobody takes it for granted."

"Well other than taking the things out of the dryer I think it's ready."

"Someone will be back out today to finish it up."

Lily swallowed. "I'm a little nervous about meeting everyone."

Alyssa glanced her way. "You don't need to be. The Kipling's are some of the nicest folks on the planet. I don't know who all will be gathered together to meet you, but it might be the whole crowd. But don't worry, no one will treat you badly. The family is wonderful and the women the guys are engaged to are great."

Alyssa grinned. "One of them, is my best friend, she's marrying the oldest in January. We're all going to Hawaii for that, because Rachel, that's my friend, sold her first photography book for a fortune and has several more commissioned."

"That's amazing. I'll bet you're so proud of her."

"I am, she's always been hesitant to show her work. I dragged her into our town art gallery, at one point, to trick her into letting them see her work. They, of course, immediately put it on display. So, she got over me tricking her pretty quickly."

"Yeah, Drew has told me some stories about you."

Alyssa looked at her in surprise. So, she relented. "And everyone else too. Since I couldn't remember anything he kept me entertained with stories of all of you."

Alyssa relaxed. "That does make sense. I can't imagine not remembering anything. Have any memories returned?"

"Just bits and pieces. I know I have an older sister that's very bossy. After I remembered that I looked her up on Facebook, her name is Rose. And the family pics I found also have a man in them that looks several years younger, so I assume I have a brother."

"Facebook would be handy for things like that, as long as you can sort out who is who."

"Yeah, it took me a while. My sister is married with two kids, so I had to dig to see if she really is my sister, but I'm pretty sure she is."

Lily was silent for a minute and then blurted out the most confusing part. "I found engagement photos of me and a man named Ronald Duvall. There are hearts and smileys all around it, even from me, but when I saw it I wanted to throw my phone across the room and scream."

Alyssa's eyebrows had risen nearly to her hairline. "That's not a normal reaction to an engagement photo. I've only been married a few months, but I still go all mushy seeing pictures of Beau and myself."

"Exactly, so what is it with my violent tendencies?"

"I have no idea, but I think you can trust it. I don't suppose we'll know for sure until your memory returns."

Lily sighed and hoped that would happen soon. She was tired of all the unknowns. Tired of all the questions. Tired of trying to guess.

Alyssa patted her arm. "Don't worry, it will come back to you."

Lily muttered, "I hope you're right."

"Of course, I am. Drew did tell you what a know-it-all I am, right?"

She turned to watch the woman driving, speculating on what she'd heard. "He told me some pretty funny tales along those lines."

Alyssa laughed, and the sound filled the truck. "I'm certain they are all true and not even close to the whole truth. I was quite precocious as a child and I am not the least bit shy as an adult."

They pulled up in front of a large house and Lily saw

Drew walking out of an even larger barn. "How did he beat us?"

"He came the direct route. We had to follow the road. Well, we didn't have to, but I did, so we didn't bounce all over the place. I don't see any extra cars or trucks, so I assume your parents haven't made it yet. Good, let's get you settled, and you can meet the family, before yours get here."

Drew pulled open her door and lifted her into his arms. "Let's get you inside before your folks show up. We don't want to worry your mom by her seeing me carry you."

Lily hadn't even thought about that. "Good idea, we don't need her freaking out... if she does freak out... I'm so tired of not knowing."

"Maybe you do know," he said. "Go with your gut feeling and don't think about it too hard."

Not a bad idea. "In that case hurry, so she doesn't freak out."

He chuckled and carried her right into the house to set her at the huge table filled with people. The only one that looked familiar was Beau who smiled and tipped his head toward her.

Drew said into the silence that had struck the moment he'd set her down. "Everyone this is Lily Smith. Lily, this is my family. I need to go carry in stuff from the truck, can you all introduce yourself to Lily. Mom, you start."

Drew walked out leaving Lily with a whole room full of strangers, but then his mother laughed and said, "Lily, my son is an idiot, but we are very happy to have you in our home. I'm Meg Kipling."

Meg Kipling was a pretty woman with laughing eyes and a warm smile. Lily said, "Thank you for having me. Your son has been very helpful and good to me. You did a fine job raising him."

An older version of Drew said, "I helped with some of that. I'm Travis Kipling, welcome to our home."

The rest of the family introduced themselves and Lily was very glad Drew had talked about each one, so she could keep them all straight. Even the twins, because although they looked alike, their personalities were very different, so it wasn't hard to tell them apart. Chase was the more serious of the two and Cade was clearly the jokester of the family. She saw some teasing in Grandpa K's eyes too, although with him being the patriarch of the family she noticed everyone was very respectful toward him.

When the adults were finished introducing themselves. Little Tony spoke up. He was such a cutie. "I am Tony and I just turned five." He held up five fingers. "Now that I'm five, I get to go to school and ride the school bus."

Lily smiled at the little guy. "Do you like school?"

Tony shrugged like she'd seen Drew do, with only one shoulder. "Most of the time. I don't like having to hold hands with a girl when we go to lunch. But my teacher says it's to keep us all together and make sure everyone is there. I don't know why the boys can't walk side by side and the girls too."

Lily's smile had grown as Tony had complained about holding a girl's hand. She nodded solemnly and said, "Teachers sometimes do strange things." She looked up and saw identical expressions of restrained mirth on the other faces in the room.

Drew went over and ruffled Tony's hair. "Are you still complaining about having to hold Cindy's hand? You're going to have to get over that, buddy."

"Why? You don't have to hold some girl's hand all the time like the rest of the family. Neither does Grandpa K."

Grandpa K said quietly, "I would give anything I have, to hold my sweetheart's hand one more time." Then he said more forcefully, "And one of these days I think you'll see Drew holding hands with a girl again."

Tony looked at Drew with wide eyes. "Not you too, Uncle D."

Drew laughed and ruffled Tony's hair one more time. "You can never tell Tony, it could happen."

Lily was wondering what Grandpa K had meant by saying, again. That Drew would once again, someday, hold a girl's hand. It was a puzzle. There was a knock on the door and since Drew was still standing he went to answer it.

When Drew brought the two people into the room Lily said, "Momma, daddy." She pushed back from the table and her parents enclosed her in hugs.

Her father's voice was rough when he said, "Lily-bug, what's this I hear about you losing your memory?"

All her memories slid back into place. "Oh daddy, the memories came back when I saw you and mom, and you called me Lily-bug."

She heard Drew say, "They did?"

But she couldn't respond, she was so glad to have her parents with her and her memories back, she was over-whelmed. She didn't want to break down in front of all the family, so she pulled back and asked Drew, "Bathroom?"

"Down the hall, first door on the right."

She said to her mom and dad, "Meet the family. I'll be right back."

Her parents nodded, and she hobbled away.

CHAPTER 9

$\mathcal{D}$rew was torn between following Lily and being the host. He looked at Lily's mom who said, "She'll be all right, she just needs a minute to calm down. She doesn't like to cry in front of others."

That actually didn't help much, because he wanted to soothe her, but decided to comply. He sucked in a deep breath and said, "Mr. and Mrs. Smith, this is my family."

Lily's mom stopped him, "Elaine and Howard will be just fine, no need to stand on formalities. You and your family have been taking care of our girl, so that makes you our family, too."

"All right. As I said at the door, I'm Drew, and I found Lily and took her to our cabin that was nearby. We have extra cabins to tend to the animals, in the winter."

That statement didn't seem to raise any questions, so he went on to introduce the rest of the family. Including that Beau and Alyssa had tended to Lily's injuries. He was a little surprised they hadn't questioned the fact that they were veterinarians and not doctors. He'd thought they might balk at that. But they didn't even bat an eye.

85

Lily came out of the bathroom; her eyes were red from crying but she had a smile on her face. She looked at him and said, "I remember everything. There is a lot you need to know, but I think the sheriff should hear it too. When is he coming?"

Travis looked at his watch. "Ten minutes."

"Perfect."

Elaine said, "Lily, we brought all your things with us."

"What things, mom?"

"Well, some of your regular clothes, and some of your 'Ronald clothes', and everything you might need for the pageant. We didn't know what to bring, so we brought it all."

Drew wondered what the hell 'Ronald clothes' meant.

Lily made a rude noise. "The Ronald clothes can be burned, as far as I'm concerned, that is over with a capital O. The rat fink lying... bastard."

Drew noticed Howard and Elaine exchange a glance and then Howard sat back in the chair he'd taken and folded his arms like he was perfectly pleased with that statement. Drew had not heard Lily utter a swear word, even through her entire ordeal, so he knew her statement was a big deal.

Lily's mom glanced at her hand. "Where's the ring?"

Lily said with clenched teeth, "He took it back."

Elaine nodded. "It didn't fit your hand anyway. It was too big and ostentatious."

That got a giggle out of Lily. "It was hideous, wasn't it?"

"I didn't want to say anything, but yes, it did not suit you at all. It did suit Ronald. But then I never really felt like you and he meshed."

Lily sighed. "We didn't. If he hadn't given me the full court press, I would have never picked him. But he was persistent and I... well I gave in. And now I know why."

The room tingled with expectancy and then Drake

walked in. He was introduced to Lily and her family, while Meg put some food on the table for everyone to munch on, because clearly this was not going to be a short meeting.

When everyone had plates of food and a beverage of their choice Lily started speaking. "We'll start with the pageant because that's what started this whole adventure. My best friend since kindergarten always dreamt of being in a beauty pageant. She was very pretty and certainly had the personality for it."

Her breath hitched for a moment and Drew dwelt on the word *was* pretty. Lily soldiered on. "We would play pretend pageant for days on end. Her mom got us fancy dresses and found a dime store tiara somewhere. We practiced walking in heels and strutting out swimsuits. We made sashes out of everything from towels to bed sheets."

"When we got old enough, Olivia did join some local contests and did well, but she never won. So, she nagged her mom into getting her voice lessons and whatever else she could think of. In high school she worked hard at the gym to have a killer body, that she was certain would help her win the next pageant. She'd stopped participating in all the smaller ones and had set her sights on the biggest of them all, deciding she would compete when she turned twenty-two."

Lily stopped speaking and she looked down at her hands. Her mother reached over and held them. Elaine continued the story. "Olivia started feeling weak and was having trouble at the gym. At first, she decided it was because she wasn't eating enough carbs or maybe protein. She tried a few different things, and vitamins. Eventually she went to the doctor and they started running tests. They finally found it was Leukemia, of all things. She underwent aggressive treatment, but after three years she lost the battle."

Lily looked up, her eyes both shattered and determined.

"She begged me, on her death bed, to enter and win the pageant. It wasn't something I wanted to do, at all. But, I couldn't tell her no."

Drew saw the women wipe their eyes with their napkins and several of the men were blinking, the rest lifted their drinks and swallowed hard.

His mother finally broke the silence. "Of course, you couldn't. So that's why you're a contestant, but how did you get here?"

At that question Lily's eyes blazed with fury. "Someone doesn't want me to win, or even participate. I have no idea who that is or why they are so determined. But Ronald the rat in sheep's clothing told me as much. He was paid to seduce me. To get close to me, so he could whisk me away right before the pageant and then make sure I didn't make it back in time."

Elaine gasped. "What?"

"Oh yes, all that 'I love you', 'you're so beautiful', 'I can't live without you', was all an act." Someone paid him, and they even gave him the money for that ugly ring. And paid for all our dates and for him to fly back and forth to Montana from New York, or wherever the rock he climbed out from under is located."

"That's a lot of money." Her father said.

She nodded. "He told me all about it as soon as we got to that cabin in the forest, here in Colorado. The minute we walked in the door; all his suave pretense dropped. He took my shoes, purse, phone, suitcase and coat and locked it in the trunk of the rental car. Then he tied me sloppily to the bed and laughed while he told me all about how he'd duped me and couldn't wait to try it again with some other woman. At first, I was mortified, and then I got pissed."

"That's my girl." Howard said, but Drew could see the banked rage in the man's eyes.

"So, I started nagging and bitching and moaning about everything. The pageant was almost two weeks away, so I thought maybe he would get tired of me and let me go."

Elaine whispered, "He could have killed you."

Lily shook her head. "No, Ronald the rat, bragged about the plan he'd come up with. Said he wasn't a killer, that his employers would have been fine with that, but he wasn't going to become a murderer over some stupid beauty pageant."

"Anyway, I complained that all the food he'd brought with him I couldn't eat. I could of course, but I was trying to drive him crazy. The next morning when he told me he was going to go get me some food, so I would shut the heck up, I decided to make a run for it. He was a city boy and wouldn't know uphill from down, but I'm not so stupid, I knew I could find my way out of the woods."

Howard rolled his eyes. "Of course."

She grinned at her dad. "You taught me well. After Ronald the rat left me alone, I untied the rope. He had my left hand tied to the bed."

At that the entire room scoffed. Her left hand? The guy was dumb as a box of rocks.

Lily grinned at them. "Right? Plus, Tony here could have untied the rope, the man did not know how to tie a knot to save himself."

Tony said, "I'm good at knots. Grandpa K teaches me."

Cade pouted and whined, "What about me?"

"You teach me about knots too, Uncle Cade, but I like the ropin' practice better."

Cade preened at that and his twin brother whacked him on the back of his head. "Quiet, let the girl talk."

"It took me less than a minute to untie the rope, but then I realized I didn't have shoes or a coat. I searched the cabin, but there was nothing. He'd even taken the towels and blankets. But there was no way I was going to sit there meekly and wait for his return. He obviously didn't know me at all. I grabbed some of the snacks and crap he'd brought to the cabin and headed out and down the mountain. I didn't want to take the road because it wound around so much it would take forever. I assume that's because it has to bypass your ranch."

Travis affirmed that. "Yeah, the family homesteaded this land before anyone thought about making that land a National Forest."

"Anyway, I headed downhill as fast as I could go barefoot, eventually the cold made my feet numb, but I wasn't stopping. My feet slipped out from under me and I whacked my head on a boulder."

Beau interjected, "Probably slick from the blood."

"Most likely, after that I was feeling woozy, but I just kept on, thinking I needed a cop and to stay out of sight so no one from the pageant knew I was on the loose. Then I twisted my ankle and fell down, I might have lost consciousness, because the next thing I remember was Drew."

She looked up at him and he picked up the narrative.

LILY BREATHED a sigh of relief when Drew started talking. She took a drink of her tea, still warm since it was in a mug rather than a tea cup and decided to eat while Drew talked. Now that she had her memories back, her stomach had settled right down.

She marveled that all she needed to hear was her father's pet name for her, and all her memories had flooded back. It had overwhelmed her, but it hadn't taken too long in the bathroom to settle. She was glad no one had followed her.

Although she did like the feel of Drew's arms around her when she felt lost.

He was such a good man, nothing like Ronald the rat. How she could have ever bought his slick lies and settled for someone like that, she couldn't begin to fathom. She'd even dressed the part, wearing slacks and silk shirts. She would have to dress up for the pageant, but then it was back to jeans, for this girl.

As she listened to his narrative about their days together she realized he glossed over all he'd done for her. It wasn't like she expected him to tell about every cup of tea he'd made her, but he'd single handedly cared for her every need, from the moment he found her face down on the ground until he'd carried her into this house.

When he finished with his side of the story, Lily spoke up. "Drew took care of me every minute of every day and I couldn't have asked for a more compassionate, considerate helper. Plus, he's a great cook."

Drew started to look embarrassed at her praise but then laughed. "You hardly eat a thing; how would you know if I'm a good cook?"

Her mother shook her head. "Yes, well this pageant has her eating like a bird, but normally she does enjoy food."

A grin covered Drew's face that pulled Lily in, and then he winked at her. "Good to know."

Sheriff Drake, who had been silent throughout the entire recitation, cleared his throat. "All right so now on to the next steps. What is the timeline for the pageant?"

Lily's mom took over. "The pageant is next weekend. Lily needs to be in New York on Wednesday. There are a couple of sightseeing excursions and time to let the contestants get to know each other. There are also going to be photo shoots and practice runs for the actual event, since some of it is televised, they want the girls to all know where they are going and what they are doing."

"Makes sense. What is Ronald's full name? I want to run him, since this is his first time, it's likely he used his own name."

Lily gave the Sheriff the name and address for Ronald. When Sheriff Drake was finished typing in the information he looked back up again. "So, when do you need to be back in Montana to collect your pageant clothes and stuff?"

Elaine said, "We brought it all with us, just in case."

Her dad shrugged. "We decided rather to be safe than sorry, especially if it gives Lily-bug an extra day or two to recover from her ordeal."

"Excellent. Since no one knows Lily is here at the Rockin' K, I think she'll be safest if she stays put until right before the event."

Lily was startled by that statement. Was she in danger? Her dad immediately agreed and so did Drew, so clearly the men thought she might be. She wasn't so sure that was the case, but what did she know about it?

Her mom said, "They told us that the contestants could bring an assistant with them or a bodyguard if they wanted to. We laughed at it when we got the notification, but I don't see it quite as funny now."

Everyone started discussing the implications of the notification. Had there been others, or was it standard procedure? She had no idea. Should she drop out of the pageant? That was not an option she felt comfortable with, she'd not only made a death bed promise, but she didn't like the idea of some bad guys winning. She looked up and straight into Drew's eyes.

What she read there was support, he had her back regardless of what she decided. That helped calm her, so she could think more clearly. She knew her parents would, too. Her older sister Rose had always thought it was a foolish idea. Her younger brother, William, teased her about it, but was supportive.

The sheriff spoke loudly, "We need to make some decisions here, folks."

When everyone had quieted he asked her, "Do you still plan to compete?"

She raised her head and squared her shoulders. "Yes, I'm not breaking my promise. And I refuse to let these guys win."

"I'm not surprised by that, you seem to be a very strong young woman." He glanced at her parents and then turned to Drew.

Drew glanced at his parents and then said to the sheriff, "I'll need to take my vacation next week."

Sheriff Drake shook his head. "Nope, you'll be on the clock. In New York."

Lily gasped. "What?"

Drew shrugged like it was obvious. "I'll be your bodyguard for the pageant."

She caught her mother's sigh and out of the corner of her eye thought she saw her father's body relax also. She looked into Drew's eyes. "I can't complain about that. Thank you."

Drake got their attention again. "Now that that's settled. Can you tell me one more time exactly what Ronald said about his employers? And I'd like to record it if it's all right with you."

Lily nodded and carefully relayed everything she could remember. When she was done Sheriff Drake and Drew asked her some questions, so she clarified those points. Some of the questions helped spur her memories of nuances, she might not have noticed without the inquiry.

The Kipling family and her own parents had been silent and still, during the questioning. When Sheriff Drake turned off the mini recorder he'd pulled from his pocket everyone started talking at once.

She was shocked at what they had discovered from her words. Clearly, she wasn't cut out to be a police officer or detective. She hadn't come to any of the conclusions or opinions they all had.

CHAPTER 10

*D*rew was glad that Lily was happy to take his help as her bodyguard. It sounded to him by the way she'd talked that this wasn't a lone individual, that that dipshit Ronald had gotten involved with. Something bigger was at stake and he wasn't about to leave Lily unprotected.

The question that was still stirring in his brain was why Lily? Had some of the other contestants been threatened too? He would be amazed if she was the only one, but whoever this was, couldn't get rid of all the other contestants, that would be a little too obvious. So why Lily?

The second question was just as hard to answer and that was why. Why? Was there some huge award? Was one of the other contestants desperate to win? Why? It just didn't make sense.

As everyone at the table talked about these same questions, Lily was starting to droop. He went over to her chair. "It would be fine if you took a rest, you're still healing, and you've had a big day."

"I should stay, but a nap sounds wonderful."

He scooped her up into his arms and the room quieted. "Lily needs to rest for a bit, she's still recovering, and it's been a busy morning." Then he walked out of the room and carried Lily up the stairs, to the room his mom had gotten ready for her.

"Just your stuff from the cabin is in the room. It's got a bathroom that attaches to the bedroom your parents will be in, so the three of you will be nice and cozy. I imagine the summit going on downstairs will go on for a bit longer, which gives you some alone time."

She'd rested her head on his chest. "Thanks, I was trying to stay alert, but I'm exhausted."

"You'll feel better after you take a nap. We've got plenty of time to sort everything else out."

He took her in and set her down on the bed and helped get her shoes off.

Before she laid down Lily said, "Thanks for going with me to the pageant. I will feel safer with you there."

He stood and kissed her on top of her head. "It will be my pleasure to be by your side. Now rest."

As he walked to the door he pulled the shades down on the windows and noticed she was already nearly asleep when he pulled the door closed.

The room quieted when he walked back into the kitchen.

"Lily told me she didn't sleep well last night, so I wasn't surprised to see her flagging. A nap will revive her."

Lily's mom had tears in her eyes. "Thank you so much for finding and taking such good care of our girl. Tell us what she was really like when you found her. You both glossed over that, we need to know." She looked at her husband and he nodded.

He looked at Beau and Alyssa, but they just waved him on. "All right. When I first saw her she'd fallen, from the sprained ankle."

Drew went on to explain the best he could her condition and what all she'd said when he'd found her. When he finished Alyssa continued with her examination, with Beau interjecting as needed. Alyssa finished by saying, "All in all she wasn't that bad off. If she'd stayed on that cold ground any longer than she did, that might not have been the case. But her flight had kept her warm enough until then."

Elaine thanked them both for explaining, then looked around the table. "Would you all mind if we brought in our things and settled in? I could use a nap myself. We didn't sleep much either."

His mother said, "By all means."

The twins lept to their feet. "Let us help you with that."

Drake motioned to Drew and he followed his boss into the office. "Let's talk strategy for keeping Lily safe."

"Fine with me. What do you think about all of it?"

Drake huffed out a breath. "It all seems preposterous to me. But we can't just ignore Lily's testimony, something is going on. What that something is, I have no idea. But it doesn't sound like an individual. Ronald kept mentioning bosses, plural not singular."

"Yeah, I noticed that too. Do you suppose Lily was singled out, or do you think more than one contestant was targeted?"

Drake folded his arms. "No idea, just Lily seems odd, what good would that do with all the others? I guess you'll find out when everyone shows up. If there are other missing contestants, you might need to bring in other authorities or the pageant organizers."

Drew would have to figure out the inner workings of the pageant to know who to approach, and also to know who might be missing. "Hopefully the organizers aren't the ones behind it."

"Right. I'm sure you can discover a lot on the internet about other contestants."

He had seen quite a bit of information about the pageant and the women on the different social media sites as well as some newscasts. Maybe he could have Emma or one of his future sister-in-laws' help him gather that info. "You don't really need to keep me on the clock. I can take vacation."

"No, you'll need that vacation for all the weddings coming up. She was found in our district, so she's one of ours now. It will just be your normal hours, no overtime, although I think you'll be on duty the whole time."

Drew shrugged. "You got that right. Any idea what I need to do to carry a weapon on a plane?"

"Nope, guess that's your first order of business. I'm going to head out. Don't let your heart rule your head."

Drew looked at his boss. "What did you say?"

"You've clearly grown fond of her and she's certainly a sweet young woman, but you'll need to keep your head clear to protect her. Leave the romance until after the pageant."

What the hell? He didn't have romance in mind. Sure, he liked Lily and admired her and there was some sort of chemistry between them. But certainly not what Drake was inferring. "Who said anything about romance?"

"Nothing needed to be said. Just keep your head on your shoulders. That's all I'm saying, women, especially beautiful women, can be distracting."

Then Drake left him standing in the middle of the office. What the hell was that all about? He didn't feel like he was distracted by her. He was attentive, but would that be a distraction? Did Drake see something he hadn't yet seen himself?

Shit, it was entirely possible. He had to admit, at least to himself, that he was tuned into her more than any other woman he'd ever known, even Monica. Drew rubbed a hand over the back of his neck, he couldn't ever remember worrying about Monica being tired.

Maybe it was just because Lily was injured, and he'd been tending to her. Yeah that had to be it. Didn't it? Hell, he had no damn idea, he'd not been with a woman in so long he wouldn't know attraction if it bit him in the ass.

LILY WOKE from her nap feeling fully restored. She'd been silly last night, not sleeping and worrying about everything this morning. It couldn't have gone any better if she'd scripted it. She still needed to talk with her parents. Drew had said they were on the other side of the bathroom. So, she hobbled that direction and was glad to hear them talking in low voices.

She rapped once on the door and then opened it a bit. "Mind if I come in?"

"Not at all, come right in, Lily-bug," her dad called out.

She tried not to hobble as she went into their room but by their worried faces she hadn't quite succeeded. Limping over to her mom, who was on the bed, she saw their room was the mirror image of hers. Her dad sat in the chair he'd pulled up next to the bed.

Her mom frowned. "Just how bad are your feet, Lily?"

She didn't want her mom to worry. "Not that bad according to Alyssa, but it's only been a couple of days, so they are still healing. There is one large cut that needed a few stitches and one small one with one stitch. The rest were just scrapes. What took the longest was getting the stockings out of the blood and dirt."

Her mom patted her hand. "I'll look at them tomorrow, when Alyssa changes the dressing."

Lily took a deep breath. "I just hope they are healed enough to wear the shoes. I'm glad we didn't go with many sandals. At least this way if I still need bandages they won't show."

"I did bring the boots too, in case you decided to wear those."

"Oh good, I can't wear them with the gown, but they might come in handy with some of the other clothes. I hope all the sightseeing and pre-events aren't walking and standing."

"Maybe we should stop in Denver on the way to the airport and see if we can get you some lower-heeled shoes that would be more comfortable for those early occasions."

Lily nodded. "That might be a very good idea, we can ask the ladies of the family for recommendations. I don't think Drew will mind. He's pretty laid back."

"And fairly smitten with you."

That statement stunned Lily. Smitten? No. Was he?

Her dad groaned. "Elaine, you promised."

"She brought it up."

"Mom, I think you are seeing things. He's been the perfect gentleman."

"Well, of course, he has been. You couldn't remember your own name. Or if you were engaged or married even. But now that you have your memory back and we know the truth about Ronald, you are a free agent. And Drew seems much more like your type than Ronald ever was. Plus, Drew actually pays attention to how you're feeling. None of us noticed you were drooping, but he did."

Well that was true, but she'd also told him she hadn't slept well, so he knew what to look for. Not that she'd ever known anyone that had paid that close attention to her. "Yes, but I've only known him a few days."

"True, but you'll be in each other's pocket for another ten days at least."

That idea sounded very nice, a little on the scary side, but nice just the same. "Moooom."

"I know honey, just take it one day at a time."

Lily looked at her dad and he just rolled his eyes, which made Lily want to grin, but she knew it would only prolong the discussion and that was the very last thing she wanted to do.

CHAPTER 11

*T*he next morning after she'd seen Alyssa and taken a shower, yay, Lily knew she needed to get busy. Her flight had to be changed and she wanted to ensure she could sit by Drew. Plus, he needed a hotel room adjacent to hers. She had to send email to the pageant coordinator to tell them that she would be bringing a bodyguard, so he would need meals and passes for the event.

They sent her a list of instructions for the bodyguards which she forwarded to his email. It also included an itinerary for the pre-events, so she was happy to look that over. She was glad to see that the first day was a boat tour of Ellis Island and other New York attractions.

The second day was Manhattan locations, but even those looked like they would be in double-decker buses. With stops everywhere for photo shoots. Comfortable shoes would definitely help however, because there would be walking involved, especially in Times Square.

The last thing she did was go onto the pageant social media sites. She'd been remiss in her duty as a contestant to keep the buzz going for the pageant. So, she posted and commented, both on the pageant pages and on her personal pages, on all the different platforms, talking about how excited she was, as the count-down for the last week before the pageant events began.

Her sister Rose called. "Oh my God, are you okay? I just heard the news. Mom and dad didn't tell me anything, when they left, other than they were going to meet you in Colorado. And now to find out Ronald was being a sneaky snake. I just can't believe it, I never really liked him much, but I never would have guessed anything like this."

When her sister finally had to stop to drag in a breath, Lily said, "I'm fine. I wasn't about to let that man derail my promise to Olivia."

Rose huffed. "I suppose not. I wish you'd never made that stupid promise in the first place. Then none of this would have happened."

"Yes, I know. How are the munchkins?" Lily held her breath hoping the distraction would work. One never knew about Rose, sometimes she was like a dog with a bone and would not be deterred.

"Sandy is doing great, she loves first grade and her teacher Miss Evelynn, but she doesn't like having to hold hands with that stinky Gerald Brentwood."

Lily laughed, "The little boy here at the ranch was complaining about the very same thing last night, having to hold hands with a little girl named Cindy. He's just in Kindergarten."

Rose chuckled. "So, it seems to be a universal issue at that age."

"Yeah. How's Jimmy?"

Rose sighed. "Keeping his mother hopping, he's got so much energy. Even when I take him to preschool part of the day, he still comes home raring to go. John just shakes his head and says boys will be boys. Which isn't helpful in the least."

Lily knew Rose's husband, John, wasn't nearly as high strung and persnickety as his wife, so until he got worried about little Jimmy's behavior there was probably nothing to be concerned with. She chatted with her sister for a few more minutes, not at all sad when Rose said she had to run.

Later in the day, when school got out, she had a text from her brother, telling her he was sorry to hear about the troubles, but he was certain she had it all handled, and he'd be rooting for her next weekend. Typical seventeen-year-old guy, probably too busy thinking about football practice, or girls, to have a real conversation.

Lily didn't see a lot of Drew, only at meals, and she assumed he was getting his ducks in a row to be able to take the time off to spend with her. They had a lot of texts back and forth as she booked the flights and hotel rooms.

Meals quickly became her favorite times of the day. The whole family came together and there was a lot of talk and laughter. She now understood Alyssa's comment about eating her sad solitary lunch.

Lily liked dinner the best, when all the girlfriends were off work and little Tony was home from school. This was his first year of school and he was having a wonderful time. He was a bright boy and adorable.

She also liked all the girls Drew's siblings were engaged to. Last night after all her drama had been talked about, the topic for dinner was weddings. With three of them coming up in the next few months there was a lot to talk about.

Elaine had jumped right into the discussion, since they'd done a full blown-out wedding for Rose. Her mom had plenty of ideas and suggestions.

No one quite knew what to do or say about the destination wedding to Hawaii, but both Rachel and Adam assured them that they had a great wedding coordinator that was taking care of everything, and all they had to do was show up. She had excellent reviews and recommendations, so they weren't worried.

Lily couldn't wait to see what the topic of conversation would be tonight. It was such a lively family, no telling what they would come up with.

She was surprised when the conversation turned to her visit to New York. She'd caught Drew right before they all sat and had told him that all the arrangements had been made.

"I found out all I need to know about flying with my gun, too. So, we should be good to go. That sightseeing itinerary is going to keep us hopping, especially with them planning to do photo shoots at nearly every stop."

"Right? It's crazy all the things they are cramming into two days."

Emma had clearly overheard them because as soon as they sat down and had filled their plates, she asked, "So tell us what is on the itinerary and where all they are going to take your picture. Have you ever been to New York?"

Lily shook her head. "No, I haven't, which now in retrospect seems rather telling that Ronald never invited me to his home. He always came to see me. I wonder just how much of his sophistication was a big fat lie."

Lily frowned, but then shook it off to answer Emma's first questions. "They have two days of sightseeing. The first day is a boat and harbor tour with photo stops before we get on the boats and there will be a significant stop at the Statue of Liberty, where they will photograph us both as a group and individually. I don't remember the rest of the stops, since that one is the most exciting to me."

Drew rattled off several other photo locations and then waved for her to continue.

"That night will be a fancy reception to meet the mayor and elected officials of New York. Oh, and the first morning, we'll meet all the pageant people at an early reception before the sightseeing. The next night is another reception with our sponsors and the overall sponsors for the pageant."

"Wow lots of eating out. I hope they have decent food for you all, so you don't get all bloated," Summer, Cade's fiancé said. "Sometimes organizers are trying to be so uptown, that they forget all about who they are feeding."

Lily had no idea how Summer knew that, but she certainly did seem to know what she was talking about, and hoped the organizers had run the competitions long enough that they had learned that lesson. She smiled at Summer. "Let's hope they've got that figured out after all the years of running these."

Drew said, "The second day of sightseeing and endless photo sessions, are all around Manhattan."

"Oh yes, sorry I got distracted. They plan to shuttle us around to the different locations. Times Square will be one of the primary photo ops."

Rachel sighed, "I mostly take landscape pictures, but I would love to follow you around and take candids at all those amazing places."

Lily grinned. "That would be so much fun. You and Adam could both come. Oh, and Beau and Alyssa could join us as my official medical team."

Cade spoke up, "Hey what about us?"

Lily tapped a finger to her lip. "Hmm, I can't think of a good reason."

Summer said, "I could do makeup and hair."

Katie nodded and smiled at her friend. "You certainly

could, much better than anyone else. I can't think of a single thing I could do."

Both Cade and Chase spoke at the same time. "Moral support." Then they high-fived each other over the table, and Katie laughed.

Emma said, "I think Tony and I will sit this one out. He would miss school and that would be a disaster."

Tony nodded solemnly. "It would. I would be very sad to miss school just for a boat trip and lots of pictures. I like the boat here in town when we go out fishing, but lots of pictures is so hard to sit still for."

Lily couldn't agree more with Tony's sentiment. "That's very true Tony, it is hard to sit still for pictures. It's much more fun to go to school."

Tony grinned and took a big bite of his chicken leg, while everyone beamed at the little boy.

Lily noticed Drew had grown silent during the exchange, he was clearly in his own world and she wondered what he was thinking.

DREW KNEW they were all teasing about going to New York, but as they talked, he realized he wouldn't mind them going along for extra backup. He couldn't shake the feeling that there was something very bad awaiting them in New York. He'd been trying to ignore the nagging feeling all day, but it just wouldn't go away.

He thought about the cost and logistics of his whole damn family going and realized it wasn't feasible, so he tried to push the ideas aside and join back in the discussion, but they stayed in the back of his mind, nagging at him.

After dinner broke up and everyone went their separate

ways, Drew's dad suggested they have a chat in the office. So, he followed his mom and dad into the room and took a seat.

Travis began the conversation. "I noticed you got quiet while all your siblings were joking about going to New York with you. Tell me what's on your mind."

Drew felt stupid for letting his thoughts show so easily. He was supposed to have a stone face, it was a requirement of the job and he'd done pretty well perfecting his. Obviously not well enough to shield his thoughts from his parents. "It's nothing really. It would be fun for all of us in New York."

Meg rolled her eyes. "Fun had nothing to do with what you were thinking, son. Tell us."

Busted, he needed to work on his poker face. "It really isn't worth talking about." When both of his parents just sat there looking at him, he caved. "All right fine. I just have a nagging feeling of unease about going to New York. Not the actual going but what we might find or get caught up in when we get there."

He stood up and paced. "This thing with Lily just seems off. I mean it's a stupid beauty pageant, it's not like it's an international incident. So, why did they go to so much trouble? That Ronald guy had to find a way to meet Lily and then give her the bums rush. But do it well enough to convince her, she's not an airhead, so he did a good job of convincing her he loved her."

Drew sat back down in the chair. "Did they do this with all the contestants? Some of them? Just Lily? I just can't wrap my mind around it. So, what will they try next? By what Lily said Ronald had mentioned, I don't think 'his bosses' would have been adverse, to more permanent measures."

He sighed and sat forward resting his elbows on his knees. "So, when everyone was teasing about going to New York it got me thinking about how much better we could

SHIRLEY PENICK

protect Lily. With Beau and Adam there we could kind of surround her. And then the twins might be extremely useful if we used their twin-ishness to fool people into thinking there was just one of them, in case there was some reason to have a secret agent."

He ran his hands through his hair. "I know it sounds ridiculous and we probably won't need to do anything at all. Plus, it's completely unfeasible for all of us to go to New York, but it keeps niggling at my mind. I've just got a gut feeling that something bad is waiting."

He looked up and crossed his arms. "See, I told you it was stupid."

His parents exchanged a glance and his dad said. "It's not stupid at all, Drew. We've always taught you to trust your gut. The main problem I can see is that you're going in blind. None of us have any idea what the pageant entails, why someone would care who wins, how it will be run, or what the stakes are."

Meg spoke up. "It could be anything. It could be some mobster whose baby girl wants to win, so he's taking out the competition. It could be that the winner gets some kind of recognition that is a big deal. Maybe it's a sponsor that wants their candidate to win to edge out a competitor sponsoring one of the other girls. Maybe there is an international component that we know nothing about. We can only guess the motivation. But what they did to Lily is not minor, so it wouldn't surprise any of us if they tried something in New York."

Travis nodded. "So, if you want or feel like you need backup, then you take backup with you. We work out the feasibility issues later, safety is the most important thing."

Drew felt a huge relief that his parents were taking this as seriously as he was, but he still didn't want to run off half-cocked. All of them going to New York would be expensive and it would leave the ranch short-handed. So, he didn't want to jump the gun. "All right. Let me think about it some more and see if I can figure out what or who, I would really need."

His dad rubbed a hand over his face. "We're here to help, so do feel free to run your thoughts and ideas by us. And if you feel like you need or even want your siblings nearby to help, you've got them. Don't hesitate. I would rather see you take them with you and not need them than not take them and find yourself in a bind that could have been alleviated."

"Thanks, mom and dad. I'll keep that in mind, we've still got a week. I'm going to see what I can learn." He got up and walked out of the room. He decided to begin with an internet search and see what all this pageant entailed. Who would be at it, what the prizes were, who were the sponsors. Anything he could find out to give him a hint. He knew Drake was running a deeper scan on Ronald Duvall, maybe he would find something to help. Some association that would point them in the right direction.

RONALD STARTLED when his phone rang. His nerves were on high alert and he was debating if he should flee, like he'd done from Colorado. Something was making him jumpy. It wasn't time for the next call from his bosses, but they were calling. Damn, he'd bluffed his way through the first time. He could do it again.

"This is Ronald."

"Is it now?"

The voice on the other end was so cold he nearly got frostbite holding his phone. Hands shaking, he said, "What's up?"

"Funny you should ask. Lily just posted on social media that she would be at the pageant. Care to explain?"

Fuck, he was going to have to dig out. Dammit, he wasn't prepared to run. What was he going to tell them? "Oh, well, I took your advice and decided to give her as a snack to the wild animals. Guess she outwitted them."

"Leaving her as a snack would only work if you'd killed her first, moron. I don't think you have the balls for that. What really happened?"

Shit he was going to have to come clean, surely, they would understand. "She got loose. I went into town to get her some food. I had her shoes and coat and purse with me, I'd tied her to the bed. Somehow, she got loose and ran out into the wilderness barefoot, in winter in Colorado. I figured she was lost or attacked by some animal, so I left."

"You didn't search for her?"

"No. I didn't want to get lost, too."

"You failed me."

Ronald chuckled weakly. "I'll go to the pageant and take care of her."

"No need, we've got people in place for that."

Ronald was relieved he didn't need to do anything else, would they still pay him what they'd promised? He could get out of the country with just half of it. "Oh, great. Well, as long as it's taken care of. Um, I don't suppose you'd pay me a bit of what was promised, just enough to get out of the country."

"Why would I pay you if you failed me?"

Ronald decided to be brave. "Well I do have your phone number. I could forget it with enough money for a plane ticket and a few thousand to keep me going."

There was a knock on his door and he jumped, probably just some nosy neighbor, he would just ignore it.

"I hear you have company, answer the door, Ronald."

"No, it's probably just a neighbor, so what do you say to my proposition?"

"I say you're an idiot. Good bye, Ronald."

Before he could blink his door crashed in. His last thoughts were, "Damn. Not a nosy neighbor."

CHAPTER 12

*T*here was a knock on Lily's door, it was mid-morning, she'd had breakfast earlier and was working on pageant stuff. She'd missed too many days and needed to get ready, there was a lot of things she needed to be ready to discuss. Ronald had distracted her some during her prep months and then she lost her memory, so she wanted to make sure she'd recalled everything.

When she opened the door it was Drew, she was happy to see him, she'd not seen a lot of him, he'd been absent a lot of yesterday. With her trying to get it together for the pageant she hadn't been downstairs much either.

Lily looked carefully at him and was surprised to see him looking worried. He said, "Sheriff Drake called to let everyone know he was coming over and that you and your family, along with mine, needed to hear what he had to say. He'll be here in ten minutes."

Lily didn't like the sound of that, but she told Drew she'd be down in a minute. He went off to find the rest of the people that needed to be there. When she got downstairs, everyone was gathering around the table.

115

When Sheriff Drake walked in Lily could tell something was very, very wrong.

He sat down heavily at the kitchen table. "I regret to inform you, but Ronald Duvall was found dead in his apartment, yesterday morning. Before I came over, I called New York to get the facts, telling them that Ronald Duvall was a person of interest in a situation we had here. Apparently, his landlady had gotten a complaint about loud noises and arguing late at night, two nights ago. She went up to tell Ronald he needed to keep control over his guests. When she arrived, the door was found slightly ajar and the hinges sprung, so she went in and found his body, he'd been shot."

Lily felt all the blood drain from her head. Shot? Yes, she wanted to kick him, but dead? Ronald? Why? But she knew the answer to that, he had failed in his mission to keep her safely tucked away until after the pageant was over. She'd called the hotel for an extra room and had let the pageant officials know she would be bringing a bodyguard, and she'd posted on the pageant social media page. Lily counted back and realized it would have been the same day Ronald was killed. Had he been shot because of her actions? This was a lot more serious than she'd realized.

Everyone at the table was chattering a mile a minute. She couldn't think. Which action had triggered his 'bosses', was it someone in the pageant, or did they have hotel connections or was it the social media post? She had no idea, but she'd clearly let the bad guys know she wasn't out of the running and Ronald had paid the ultimate price.

She wanted to throw up.

Was a pageant really worth all of this? Not in her opinion, but clearly in someone's it was. She wondered again if she should drop out, but she felt the same strong conviction that she shouldn't let these unknown murderers win.

The talk dwindled down and Lily could feel the eyes of the whole group focused on her.

She said, "I really want to run and hide and have nothing to do with this pageant, but I just can't do it. I can't knuckle under to these unknown murdering monsters. What do all of you think?"

Her mom looked up with many emotions flitting through her eyes. "Oh Lily, on one hand I want you safe and sound at home, or even here, where no one knows where you are. But I also agree that these people cannot be allowed to go Scott-free pushing their agenda. They need to be stopped and shown that they can't just do whatever they want. I never really felt Ronald was exactly right for you, but even with all his misdeeds, I don't think he should have paid for it with his life."

Lily couldn't agree more.

Her dad frowned. "Drew and I will be right there with you. I have no intention of letting any harm come to my little girl."

She turned in time to see Drew exchange a look with his dad and mom, who both gave him a slight nod, then he cleared his throat, and everyone gave him their attention.

He quickly glanced at each of his siblings and said, "I know you were all teasing the other night about wanting to go to New York, but if any of you are serious, I wouldn't turn down the backup."

The only people in the room not shocked by this announcement were Drew and his parents, and maybe Grandpa K. The reactions were all different.

Adam and Rachel sat back in their chairs, although she noticed they'd linked hands.

Beau and Alyssa were talking in hushed tones.

Cade looked at Summer and then said, "We're in."

Chase got his phone out and his thumbs flew over the keyboard.

Emma grimaced. "I'm going to have to sit this one out, although I wish I could join you."

Her dad looked at Travis. "Are you sure about this?" Travis just nodded.

Meg said to Lily's mom. "It will be all right. You can't have a dozen Kiplings surrounding the place and not be seen." Lily saw her mom smiling through her tears.

Grandpa K puffed out his chest, clearly proud as he could be of his grandkids.

Drake sat quietly watching the rest of the people at the table.

Lily herself was dumbfounded and couldn't have commented to save her life. Which hopefully wasn't something she needed to be worried about.

After a few minutes Drew cleared his throat again and regained everyone's attention. "So, who is on board?"

As Lily looked around the table she saw determination etched on each face. Each couple affirmed they would be going. Only Emma, Grandpa K and Drew's parents were staying back to work the ranch.

Drew nodded and looked more relieved with each affirmation. "Great, so I've been thinking about it. Rachel and Adam, I want you two to go in as a photographer and assistant. I don't want anyone to know you are with us. Rachel you use your maiden name on your photos and since you guys aren't married yet and I think that's a good idea to perpetuate. You and your camera will see things we can't, especially with your zoom."

Sheriff Drake said, "I think the twins should be one person. That way you can have one be the backup."

Drew grinned at his boss. "Exactly what I was thinking. Since Summer is famous, I think Cade should be the out front one and Chase can be the detective. Summer can go in as Lily's makeup crew, but slowly expand to help all the girls with makeup tips and tricks if she wants to, that way she can gather information from the contestants, and see if any of them know anything. Cade can pretend to stand around being smitten."

"No pretense needed," Cade said with a grin.

Drew tapped his fingers on the table. "I think the four of you can get a room with two queen beds. And see if you can gather together any clothes that you have that match. We are planning to stop in Denver on the way to the airport, so if you need more you can pick up some things. Katie you can be Lily's secretary or maybe for both Summer and Lily. I was looking through the pageant website and some of the girls have a large entourage, so I don't think it will be a problem."

He stopped talking and sighed. "I'm not quite sure how to stage Beau and Alyssa."

Drake didn't seem to have a suggestion either and neither did Travis or anyone else. Alyssa said, "We can think about it."

Drew continued the discussion. "Now, I can and plan to take my gun. Since I'm a police officer I've jumped through the hoops and everything is arranged. But the rest of you can't."

Cade spoke up. "I'll bring my rope and my secret weapon." He grinned at Summer.

Summer grinned right back. "I don't need no stinkin' weapon, my body is good enough."

Drew chuckled. "That's true enough. Rachel's secret weapon is her camera, for both the telephoto and evidence."

Adam said, "I can bring my own camera. I'm not half bad with it. We still have those motion sensors from when those dumbasses were looking for gold. They are small enough to put a couple in with Rachel's equipment. They might come in handy."

Beau and Alyssa said they would bring medical supplies, just in case. And another camera or two they normally used for photographing the stock.

They talked a little longer about ideas and strategy, but since no one knew what they were going up against they really couldn't make too many plans. This was definitely going to be a fly-by-the-seat-of-your-pants kind of operation. Hopefully something would come to light once they got to New York.

Lily was rather astounded by all the ideas and plans they did come up with. She wondered about some of the statements they'd made, like Summer being famous and having a body that was a secret weapon, but now was not the time to ask about that. So, she sat and listened and tried to interject anything she knew about the pageant.

Emma had left earlier saying she was going to look into flight and hotel accommodations. The discussion was running out of steam when Emma came back and handed out sheets of paper to everyone. Apparently, they all now had flights and rooms and a couple of rental cars, just in case.

It had taken Lily a lot longer to get hers and Drew's, Lily decided Emma must be some kind of wiz to be able to book four more sets in such a short time.

DREW FELT a lot more confident with all his siblings backing him up. He'd have gone and protected Lily by himself, but the backup would be great. He didn't really think anything would happen, but if something did go down, the Kipling brothers and their women would be a force to be reckoned with.

He thought about calling his best buddy Zach to see if he could join him, but he remembered he was in Las Vegas at the bull riding finals. He knew his friend would drop everything to join him, if he needed it, but Drew decided his family was enough backup.

They all knew how the others thought and would react, in any given situation, so it would be like a team. Even if there were other security and bodyguards in place, he didn't know them. He knew his siblings and could count on their actions. *Cowboy up!*

When everyone began moving off he decided to ask Lily if they could talk. He wanted to gauge her reaction to the news of Ronald's death and also wanted to talk to her about how they should operate, strategize a bit. Plus, they'd both been so busy he just missed her, plain and simple as that.

"Lily, do you have a minute?"

She stopped and smiled up at him and all his brain cells fried. She had such a great smile. For a moment his mind blanked, but he managed to kickstart it back into gear. *Try not to act like an idiot, Drew.*

He looked down into her joyous face. "Do you want to maybe go outside for our chat?"

"That would be great. I am feeling a little cooped up, although I don't know how far I should be walking."

Alyssa came up from behind them and said, "Not far. Maybe take her in your truck, Drew. She hasn't seen anything of the ranch."

Lily laughed. "That would be fun. Do we have time for a mini tour?"

He hadn't planned on being gone that long, but Lily looked so hopeful, he couldn't turn her down. "Sure, that would be fun."

"Oh goody, I'll go get a jacket, and let my parents know."

Alyssa watched her go, then turned to him. "It will do her

good to think of something else. Maybe take her out to see your land. Show her our house and Beau's and where the twins are building. Now that she's met everyone, clue her in on everything. Summer's TV and cheer. Rachel's books. Take some food with you and don't hurry back. It will both do you a world of good."

He nodded, it did sound like a good idea. He could use some down time and it would be better for her to know everyone's history. Alyssa went over to the fridge and quickly made a bag of snacks and drinks for them to take with them.

Lily didn't take long despite her slow movement. She had on a jean jacket over a sweater of burnt orange. Clearly the woman knew how to layer, which was always a good thing to know in the Colorado mountains and especially when it was early winter. The weather could be bright with sunshine one minute and snowing the next, which Alyssa had discovered the hard way.

He grabbed the bag of goodies Alyssa had put together, his duster, and his keys hanging on the peg by the door. Then he reached up and unlocked the Gun safe and pulled his badge and gun out.

Lily's eyes widened, and he said, "I don't leave home without it. Just part of the job."

She nodded but didn't look convinced. He stuffed it into a saddle bag even though they were taking the truck, and they walked out into the bright morning. It was chilly but not near freezing like the day he'd found her, and the sun was bright, making the sky a brilliant blue.

She followed him to his truck and clambered in, while he stowed the food and saddle bag in the rear seat. They all drove extended cabs, his father thought it was dumb to have a two-passenger vehicle in a family the size of theirs, so there was always room for whoever needed to go along.

"Alyssa suggested I take you on a drive along the eastern side of the ranch, so you can see the other houses, and land." He started the truck and began driving on the newly formed road. They hadn't had anything linking the siblings' land to the main house until all the building began and then it only made sense. It was a one lane unpaved road, but it was well graded and served its purpose.

"The first house is Beau and Alyssa's. Each of us picked a parcel of land a few years ago, and Beau already knew he was going to be the family vet, so he picked the closest to be ready and nearby for emergencies."

He pulled into the short drive and up to the house.

Lily said, "Oh it's so pretty, and way bigger than I expected."

"Alyssa comes from a large family who all live in Washington state, so they wanted a couple of guest rooms even though the main house has plenty. They also plan to have a pack of kids themselves. That whole side on the right is setup to be a hospital ward for any animals that need constant care. They've only used it once, when the old dog that used to sleep in the kitchen passed on."

"Oh, that's sad."

"No not really, the dog was a bazillion years old and couldn't do much anymore, he wasn't a pet, he'd been a working dog who had not been able to continue, so we made him a nice bed in a warm spot to live out his last days, which ended up being a couple of years."

Lily smiled. "In other words, you're a family of softies."

"Can't say that isn't true. Beau has a pet heifer that tangled with a mountain lion as a calf, he nursed Dolly back to health and that started his career as a vet."

"Her name was Dolly?"

"We teased him and called her Dolly, because she was always with him, like a living Doll."

Lily giggled, and he loved the sound.

"We can see if we can introduce you to Dolly, she's old too, and should have been put down, but Beau was having none of that. So, she lives on the land and is the old wise one the other younger mama's look up to."

That statement caused Lily to light up with laughter, and he vowed to find other stories to make her laugh.

As he drove out of the yard he said, "I imagine the vet clinic will be useful as time goes on."

When they got to Adam's house Lily sighed. "Oh, it's gorgeous. I'll bet those huge windows have an excellent view."

"They do. Rachel being the photographer that she is, insisted on putting the garage under the house, to raise the first level up, so she could see the mountains past the trees. In the back there is a view of the river."

"So, you said when we were at the cabin, that Rachel had a book deal."

"I did, she's got a great coffee-table type book of the Chelan valley in eastern Washington. It's where both she and Alyssa are from."

"Oh, right, you did mention they were friends. How did they manage to snag two of your brothers?"

As he turned around to head toward the next location he said, "Alyssa came from a college she was attending over on the front range. She was here to be Beau's intern for the spring. He thought she was Drake's new girlfriend and acted like an ass, because he'd been attracted to her."

"Drake is old enough to be her father."

"Which is why it pissed Beau off and why he was a jerk. When he found out the truth he had a lot of groveling to do. Dolly, poor thing, got caught in a poacher's trap and the two of them worked to get her out of it and taken care of. Beau always says Alyssa fell in love with him because of his bedside manner, which might not be far from the truth."

Lily rolled her eyes. "Men."

"Hey, I'm one of those."

"Yes, and so far, you're doing well. Don't blow it. So how did Rachel and Adam happen?"

"Oh, it's an even better story. Adam was being all pissy toward Beau because Alyssa was so much younger than he was."

"They are only a few years apart, aren't they?"

"Seven, which wasn't a big deal to anyone except Adam. Anyway, Rachel came out early for Alyssa's graduation and to take engagement photos. One look at her and Adam fell hard for a woman *nine* years his junior."

Lily laughed out loud. "Oh, I can imagine the teasing he got about that."

"Well, not until he was over being hell on wheels, about the whole thing." Drew lowered his voice and waggled his head. "I'm the oldest and have a responsibility to set an example for my siblings. I can't go off with this child and be carefree."

Lily was laughing at his depiction of Adam being a stick in the mud. "Stop, you have to stop, I'm going to wet my pants if you keep making me laugh."

He grinned at her and returned to his normal voice and mannerisms. "There's a porta-potty at the next location if you have a need. Anyway, I think dad and mom finally told him to get over himself."

"So, the twin's houses are next. They are in the early stages of building, so they'll be living at the house for a while after they get married. But like I said there is a porta-potty."

She narrowed her eyes at him. "I think I'll be good, as long as you don't keep making me laugh."

Drew tried to give her his most innocent look. "I can

make no guarantees to that. My siblings are kind of on the crazy side."

Lily pointed her finger at him. "And you are taking full advantage of that."

He shrugged and put his pinky to his lips. "Could be."

She chuckled and slugged him. "Stop that, you are no Dr. Evil."

This time he shrugged and poured on the hick accent. "Aw shucks, ma'am, just tellin' you a couple of tales."

She crossed her arms as the laughter increased. "All right, if you are going to keep this up, maybe I *should* use the outhouse."

He pulled into the next drive where a foundation had been prepared and the studs were up, but not much else. There were workers swarming around, but the porta-potty didn't have a line. He flourished his hand toward it. "Your powder room awaits. But wait." He dug around in the glove compartment and handed her a small roll of toilet paper. "Just in case. And I've got water, so you can wash."

She looked skeptical but then sighed. He got out of the truck and walked her over. To guard the door while she was inside.

The foreman came over. "Is there something you need, Drew?"

"Nope, just taking a guest around the ranch and she needed to use the facilities."

"Well, you timed it perfectly then, they just cleaned it out this morning, so it's fresh as a daisy."

Drew chuckled. "Good to know. She won't be too traumatized then."

"We can hope. I better get back to bossing people around. Later."

Lily came out, rubbing her hands together. "They had

hand sanitizer, but I still wouldn't mind rinsing them in water."

"Your wish is my command. I have small bottles of drinking water. Or the gallon I keep in the truck for whatever I might need it for. I even have a roll of paper towels."

"Well aren't you mister handy. The gallon is fine. We might want to drink the others."

When she was clean and dry and back in the truck, he drove down a little further.

Lily said, "You didn't tell me about the twins getting their girls."

"I can start that story, but it might take a bit of telling. Especially for Cade. So, we'll begin with Katie and Chase. Chase, Cade, and Katie have been friends since grade school. Best friends. Hanging out, doing everything together, no romance at all."

Lily's eyebrows rose. "What changed?"

"Alyssa's older brother came for her graduation." He shook his head. "Tim, Alyssa's brother, said something about what a little cutie Katie was, and Chase saw red, or maybe it was green. He was furious. Cade talked him off the ledge, by saying that of course she was pretty, and did Chase really think no one was going to notice that, and scoop her up someday?"

Drew shook his head at his idiot brother. "Apparently that opened Chase's eyes to the beauty that Katie is, and the rest is history. Well, other than the fact that Katie had apparently been into him for years and was more than happy to tempt the boy into a romantic relationship."

Lily clapped her hands, her eyes bright with excitement, which made Drew want to lap her up. "Good for Katie and yay for the Tim guy showing up, to give Chase a little push in the right direction."

"Yeah, Tim and Rachel were clowning around at dinner

one night, talking about Tim buying the mini-golf place in town. That scared the bejeezus out of Chase, so he stepped up his game. Tim had no real interest in moving here, it was all pie in the sky talk, but Chase wasn't putting that to the test."

"This Tim guy sounds like quite the character."

"Oh yeah, he is."

"It would be fun to meet him."

And suddenly Drew had a little more sympathy for what Chase had gone through, because he didn't want Tim Jefferson within a hundred yards of Lily. So, he changed the subject and decided he would think about his reaction later.

CHAPTER 13

*L*ily noticed that Drew had gotten quiet for a moment and the atmosphere had cooled. She wondered what had just happened.

Then Drew said, "So Cade and Summer. Now this one is quite the story. Summer moved here in middle school. She wore huge glasses and baggy overalls, with her hair pulled so tight to her head you couldn't tell what color it was. She was kind of an ugly duckling, that didn't participate in any school activities and didn't really have any friends."

Lily couldn't believe what she was hearing. Summer? An ugly duckling, how was that even possible? And didn't she teach classes for kids after school? Lily was sure that's what she'd said. "What? Are you sure about that?"

"Absolutely. Summer was hiding. But that's the end of the story or maybe the middle. So back to the beginning. Cade had been in an abusive relationship with a woman that we now know is bat-shit crazy. She had something she held over his head to keep him in line and she sabotaged any female he tried to date. Like pushing them down stairs and putting skunks in their new cars type of things."

"That's horrible, how did he finally get away from her?"

"She broke up with him and was 'dating' some guy in Steamboat Springs. Come to find out he was her shrink. Anyway, Cade convinced Summer to pretend to be his girl-friend for the rodeo weekend that was coming up. Even though she feared retaliation from the crazy one she agreed. So, Summer decided if she was going out with Cade, who she'd had a crush on, that she was not going to hide anymore."

"Good for her."

He pulled into the next area where the foundation was being poured, waved his hand and continued the story as he drove out. "As it turns out, she had a darn good reason for hiding. Summer is Heather Sinclair from the TV show *Training up Heather*."

"Are you kidding? Seriously? I thought she looked a little familiar, but Heather? Wow. I did hear something about a scandal, but I was busy doing all this pageant crap and didn't get to hear all of it."

"Long story short, some TV exec had tried to get Summer to sleep with him, and when she wouldn't, he torpedoed the show, then blamed Summer. Summer and her family decided not to face the wrath of the fans, after some pretty nasty stuff went down, and they came here, so Summer could hide."

"Wow, that's crazy. She had to be in her early teens to come here in middle school. What an old pervert."

"Yeah. Then Cade's crazy ex outed her, so Summer was finally old enough and strong enough to tell her story. So, she went to LA and told the truth. And that, as they say, was that."

Lily sat there wide eyed for a couple of minutes. "So, when she said her body was a weapon she was talking about the gymnastics she did on the show?"

"Yes, she has a huge home gym and has kept her body

finely tuned. She could easily take someone down, and not only that, there is always the surprise factor when she starts flipping around. Cade is taking lessons, to learn how to do it, too."

"Wow, that's an amazing story. So that's also why Summer can do makeup and maybe get close to some of the other girls, because she's famous and knows her shit, when it comes to makeup and hair."

"Yep."

She sat there thinking while he waved toward where Emma's house would someday be built and drove on toward what she assumed was his plot of land.

He pulled up and stopped. "Here we are, let's walk in and have a bite to eat while we talk some more."

She wanted to know his story, she was certain there was one, so she got out of the truck while he brought his bag of snacks, duster, a blanket, and his saddle bag. She stretched and followed him into the clearing. It was so peaceful in there surrounded by trees. She could hear a river not too far away and followed him in that direction.

A few yards from the river was an old log, weathered and gray and smooth enough to sit on. That's where he went to sit, he spread the blanket over the tree and pulled another sawed off stump over to set the food on.

"The road is only another mile down if you keep going along the river, which is why I picked this parcel, so I could get out quick, if I was needed for the job." He waved at the food, which included cheese and crackers, grapes, baby carrots, celery, homemade cookies, and bottles of water.

She took a bottle of water and a piece of paper towel to put some of the snacks on. After she'd eaten a couple of grapes she said, "So tell me why you became a cop instead of being a rancher."

Clearly, she'd hit a sore subject because Drew closed up

and she could practically see him withdraw. It was like he was miles away instead of less than a yard.

"Oh, sorry, that was nosy of me. You don't have to answer." She nibbled on a piece of cheese, and hoped he would relax, and go back to chatting.

Finally, after what seemed like forever to Lily he shook his head and looked her in the eye. "No, it's all right. It's been a long time. I had a girlfriend, we'd been best friends since the second grade, when one of the boys had been mean to her. I'd been taught not to use violence to solve problems, so instead I grabbed one of the girls' jump ropes and hog tied him. I'd been watching Adam practicing for a junior rodeo that was coming up, and he'd shown me how to do it."

Lily could imagine a little Drew tying some kid up, so justice would prevail.

"The teacher was not too impressed by my skills, but Monica was, and we became fast friends after that. We just coasted into a relationship as we got older. No lightning bolts or anything, we just went from being friends to being boyfriend and girlfriend. I'd been saving for a promise ring, or if I could get enough for an engagement ring."

Drew took a deep breath and Lily was almost afraid to hear what he was going to say next.

"We went to our senior prom together and had planned to come back and spend the night in one of the cabins. She'd brought her car out to the ranch to use in the morning since we both needed to work the next day. But I'd fixed up the cabin with flowers and candles to make it a special night for both of us. It wasn't our first time, but I wanted it to be extra romantic."

Lily could see his hands had tightened into fists as he forged on. "Monica had been trying to get into a specific college. She was going to study to become a nurse and had her hopes set on the one school. As we were leaving the prom to come back here, Monica's mother texted her. Her mom had opened the mail from that college thinking it would be an acceptance letter. It wasn't, so she texted Monica to tell her."

"Oh, that's so mean, why didn't she wait until morning?"

Drew shook his head. "No one knows the answer to that. When we got here to the ranch I held Monica while she cried. But afterward she didn't want to stay, and she decided to go home. I didn't want to pressure her, but I'd give anything to have that night back and change that. It probably wouldn't have taken much to convince her, but I was being the gentleman."

Lily whispered, "What happened?"

"A drunk driver happened. He was so drunk he never even saw Monica's little car and t-boned her. Even after he hit her he kept his foot on the gas, pushed her off the road and into a mountain. The car was a pancake, Monica died instantly. The drunk driver, when he got close enough to see the mountain, finally stopped his forward momentum and tried to back up, but he was stuck in a ditch and passed out. He never even saw Monica's car."

"Oh, my God, that's horrible."

"It was. I decided that I didn't need a business degree, Adam already had one. I thought if I became a cop I might be able to stop people from drinking and driving and killing others, so I went to the police academy the day after I graduated from high school and got my bachelor's degree in criminology online."

Lily took Drew's hand and uncurled his fingers one by one. She put both her hands around his and held it while he let the horror and pain slowly seep away. She was glad she knew, but sorry to have made him relive it.

"I'm so sorry. Sorry you had to go through that, and sorry I asked, and made you think about it again."

Drew finally relaxed and gave her a small smile. "Like I said, it's been a long time."

Lily figured maybe seven years, which in some ways was a long time and in others it was no time at all. "Thanks for telling me."

～

DREW FELT some of the broken places in his heart heal as Lily held his hand and stroked it with her thumbs. He didn't ever talk about that time. All his family had lived through it, right beside him, and other people didn't ask about his career choice. Being a law enforcement officer tended to keep most people at arm's length.

He hadn't minded telling Lily though, he knew she would understand but not collapse in hysterics. She was empathetic, but not overly so and he liked that. There were still some girls he had gone to high school with, that to this day, looked at him and started to cry. Yes, it had been a tragedy, but life went on, and he'd stuffed the pain and regret down deep enough to function. It was the cowboy way.

He picked back up the snacks he'd laid down when Lily had asked him the question and took a couple of bites. They were quiet for a few minutes while they ate. The silence was companionable and not strained, and Drew was glad for that.

He heard some rustling over to the right of them and looked around Lily to see if Dolly had some to visit. Nope, not Dolly, it was a black bear and right behind her were two cubs. Oh shit, not good.

He took Lily's hand and whispered, "We need to get back to the truck, quietly and without panicking."

Lily followed his gaze and nodded. She gathered up what she could while he got his gun out, just in case. Drew filled his other hand with the blanket and his duster.

They both slowly eased back behind the log, trying not to attract the attention of the bears. The cubs were looking into the bushes, probably to see if there were any berries or insects, while the mother was headed toward the river, to maybe do some fishing. The bears should be going into their den to hibernate at any time, so this was probably one of their last forages and might be why they'd come so far onto the ranch.

When the bears didn't look at them Drew put the gun into the back of his pants and helped Lily carry some of the things they'd brought with them. They continued to move stealthily, but not dawdling, until they got to the truck. Piling everything into the front with them, rather than take the time to put it in the back.

When they, and all their gear were in the truck, Drew could breathe again. "Well, I guess we should curb picnics in the wilderness for a little while until those bears hibernate."

"Yeah, no hiking into the forest or dancing in the meadow for a few days."

He chuckled. "Were you feeling like dancing or hiking?"

"No, but maybe some of the others should be warned."

"We'll do that as soon as we get back."

"I'm glad I used the facilities back at Cade's soon-to-be house, so those bears didn't scare the pee out of me."

Drew laughed and shook his head. "You're a strange woman."

Lily grinned up at him and he wanted to taste that grin. He wanted to cover her sweet lips with his. Instead he started the truck and eased away from the temptation of Lily, and the foraging bears. Now was not the time or place for anything else.

Lily chattered on the way back to the house and Drew let the sound roll over him, while he thought about his reaction to her smile. Did he want to go there with her? Did he want to open his heart again and share it with another person?

He wasn't much into meaningless relationships, he'd tried it once or twice since Monica's death and it had left him flat. So, if he made a move on Lily, it would be for a real relationship and he doubted their lives were compatible.

She lived in Montana for one thing and was a beauty pageant contestant. She wore silk shirts and killer heels and had manicures. She and her mom had talked about finding somewhere for her nails, both hands and feet, to be freshened up on Sunday or Monday to be ready for the event. She lived on a higher plane than he did. He was a cowboy cop, what did he have to offer this lovely lady from the city?

Although he did have to admit, she fit in with his family really well. She didn't put on any airs or look down on them. Even her family fit in and they had never asked about them letting veterinarians look at their daughter's wounds. He'd been surprised by that.

They'd never really talked about her family or where they lived or what they did. He'd tried looking her up online but Smith, even Lily Smith, was too common of a name, there had been lots of them. Too many to weed through.

Drew was certain Lily would have a fun and happy life in Montana, regardless of everything else. She was right now texting on her phone to friends. Probably talking about the hick that took her out where the bears were.

He inwardly shook his head at himself. No, she probably wouldn't be interested in a guy like him, who lived ten hours away on a cattle ranch. He needed to stick to his own kind, not get all uppity with a girl like Lily. He would go to the pageant and keep her safe, and then he would hug her goodbye and come back to Colorado, while she went off to the next level of the pageant, because he couldn't imagine anyone beating her.

CHAPTER 14

 ily, her mom, and Summer went to Denver on Saturday. They'd decided that waiting until they were headed for the plane was not a good time to try to find comfortable shoes, get a mani and pedi, and find a few more matching clothes for the twins. It had been a lot of years since they had dressed similarly and they didn't have any suits or formal attire that they could wear to the many events. So, Summer was armed with a list and their measurements, to shop for them both.

As they got into Alyssa's car, which had enclosed cargo space that the pickups didn't, Summer giggled. "I can't believe they trust me to buy clothes for them. I am so tempted to buy them something ridiculous, just because I can."

Elaine laughed. "But then they would never trust you again."

Summer tapped one finger on her knee. "Maybe I could buy them something frivolous that won't show. Like boxers or t-shirts, oh, or socks. I have to get *something*."

Lily said, "What about a tie that looks normal from afar

137

but if you get up really close it's naked ladies or cartoon characters or something like that. Then it would be seen, but only you and Katie would get close enough to know what it really was."

"Lily, that is a great idea. I don't know where to find something like that, but it would be perfect."

"Look it up on your phone silly, under novelty ties or something along those lines."

"Of course. Let me see what I can find. I'm glad I don't have to drive. You don't think your feet will hurt from driving, do you?"

Lily shrugged, she was so happy to be behind the wheel, even if she couldn't do it for long. "If it gets to be too much we can switch. Mom can drive, or you can. But for right this minute, I'm thrilled to be behind the wheel, it seems like I've been trapped for weeks."

Elaine said, "It's only been eight days. But that can seem like a long time."

"Yeah mom, it does. But here I am driving off for a shopping adventure. Yay!"

Her mom laughed at her and turned on the radio, so they could sing along to it. Her whole life they'd done that whenever they were taking a road trip. This was a short one, just into Denver, so only about two hours of driving.

Summer didn't immediately join in the singing, but Lily wasn't sure if that was because she was glued to her phone finding ways to tease the twins, or not.

Lily thought about maybe buying Drew a little token of appreciation for all he'd done for her. Maybe they would have something at Summer's tie place that would be fun, but also appreciative. Like a tie with guns on it or cows or something.

She still felt bad for the young man who'd lost his best friend and his wife-to-be. What a horrible thing to go through. Lily knew she should have been more upset about Ronald, both being a rat and then dying in such an awful way. She did feel bad for him, but it wasn't devastating, which only indicated to her that she was never really in love with him, and had truly let him talk her into the engagement.

She certainly didn't feel the zing that she sometimes got from Drew. It didn't happen every time they were together but there were definitely moments when there was something there. Something she'd never felt before from any other man and most assuredly, not from Ronald.

She'd wondered for a moment the other day, when they'd been chased off by the bears, if Drew wanted to kiss her. The feeling hadn't lasted long, just a few seconds, but it had felt like he was considering it. She'd have been more than happy to kiss him, and had almost swayed toward him, but then he pulled back and had driven off toward the house.

Her imagination running wild was what she'd determined it was and nothing more. Thinking back over it now, she didn't think so, there had been something in the air, an expectancy. If it happened again she was going to see if she couldn't move things along, maybe just grab his shirt, pull him down for a kiss, and see what would happen.

Lily didn't normally go around grabbing men and kissing them, but she felt like Drew would be the place to start. She laughed at herself, she wasn't sure she would have the guts to do it at all. It might be an impossible task, but at the same time it might be worth it. She just didn't know, but she wanted to find out. So, if Drew didn't make the move, maybe she would pull on her big girl panties and go for it.

She internally rolled her eyes at herself and sang louder to try and drown out her thoughts.

∾

DREW COULDN'T STOP THINKING about the fact that he'd wanted to kiss Lily and had chickened out. He'd not had a strong desire to kiss a woman since the day Monica had died. He'd kissed a few since then, but it had been more their idea than his. But he'd certainly wanted to kiss Lily, he really thought if there hadn't been a mound of crap between them he might have gone for it.

He had no idea if she would have been on board or not. It seemed like there were times where interest showed in her eyes, but he didn't know if that was wishful thinking on his part. Maybe she was just grateful for his help. She'd been in a committed relationship just a week ago.

Yes, the guy had turned out to be a rat, but if she'd been engaged to him, shouldn't she be more upset? Both about the betrayal and also his death? He had to admit that Lily didn't seem very traumatized by either.

Of course, she'd had a whole night to stew about his betrayal, and then flee from him. Maybe she'd sobbed her heart out over it, he shook his head, he just didn't get the impression she'd been that in love with him. It almost seemed like she'd just been going along for the ride. But why?

She'd said something about him pushing her and of course Ronald's whole plan revolved around getting her to trust him enough to go off for a romantic weekend, shortly before the pageant, so maybe he had pushed, and she'd just knuckled under. He didn't see Lily as the type to do that, but maybe between the pageant pressures and then Ronald, she'd had too much stress to fight with him.

He couldn't think of another scenario that fit, at least not one he wanted to consider. Drew turned his focus off of Lily and back toward the computer. He was studying the hotel floor plan and then he was going to go over the sightseeing trips and look over all the locations they planned to stop at.

He wanted to have an idea of all the places Lily might be vulnerable.

Drew wished he had more information about whether any of the other girls had been threatened like Lily. It would give him a better idea of what he was up against. Lily had gotten him access to the social media pages for the pageant, so he could see what the other contestants were saying, but he didn't see anything that was relevant. It was just a lot of rah, rah, so excited, can't wait kinds of posts.

He'd talked a little more with each of his siblings that were going to be there. Making plans, talking over strategies. He gave them each the link to the hotel website and the itinerary for the pageant days. Adam had suggested they find a way to all come together each day and debrief, and he thought that was an excellent idea.

Drew thought maybe in the twins' room would be best, that way no one would see the guys together. They'd talked about Adam and Rachel calling in, since they were not supposed to be all together. But it also seemed ridiculous to go to so much trouble, that they were sneaking around. Chase skulking was going to be enough. Besides, he didn't think anyone was going to be watching their every move, either.

He'd also decided to enlist Emma to watch the show and let him know immediately, if she saw anything wonky. His mom and dad promised to do the same. He didn't know for sure, but he was pretty certain at least the last bit would be shown live. Other pieces were being recorded, but it still didn't hurt to have everyone keeping their eyes open and looking for trouble or oddities.

Grandpa K knocked on the door frame.

Drew looked up and smiled, "Come on in, Grandpa."

"As long as you're not too busy."

"Never too busy for you. Have a seat."

"Don't mind if I do. So, tell me what you've got planned."

Drew decided that organizing his thoughts, by relating them to his grandfather, would be a step in the right direction. It might point out flaws in his logic or holes in his plans. "That's a good idea, Grandpa. I'm not sure I would call them plans exactly. They're more like contingencies and being aware of our surroundings. I don't know whether anyone will really try something once we get to New York, but I mainly need to keep my eyes open. And since there will be almost a dozen pairs of eyes, I'm hoping we can waylay anyone who might have something shifty going on."

Grandpa K nodded but didn't interrupt.

"I hope that Adam and Rachel can get into the locations where the photo shoots are going to take place and scope them out, maybe Beau and Alyssa can go with them so one pair of them can stay while the other pair goes on to the next. Alyssa and Beau aren't great photographers, but they've got eyes and instincts I can trust. So, if they hang back at each location and just watch, have our backs, so to speak, while Rachel and Beau go on ahead to the next stop."

Grandpa K said, "That sounds reasonable. So, you plan to keep Cade, Summer, and Katie with you?"

"If we can work that out, yes. I don't know how much entourage each contestant is allowed, but a photo shoot seems to scream for at least hair and makeup, and maybe even wardrobe. If Cade is the workhorse for the wardrobe, Summer does hair and Katie helps out as needed, it doesn't seem like too many."

"And Chase?"

"Snoop."

The older man guffawed at that. "So that's the first two days. What about the nights?"

"I'm hoping the receptions will be large enough that we

can have everyone there. If not, they can hang around in common areas to keep an eye on people."

"Good, good. If anything is going to happen it would seem like the days leading up to the pageant would be the most likely time. Once it starts it would bring a lot of attention."

Drew nodded. "That's what I was thinking too, but I don't want to let down our guard until we're on the plane heading home."

"Good thinking. You just never know when a snake might bite."

Drake hadn't really thought about that. Since he didn't know the motivation of getting Lily out of the competition. Grandpa K stood to go, so he put that thought on hold for a moment. "Thanks for stopping by. Let me know if you think of anything else I should do or be aware of."

"Will do, Drew. Mighty proud of you standing up for this girl, it's good for an old man to see that his grandkids are all he'd hoped they would be."

Before Drew could comment his grandfather walked out of the room. Drew thought about what he'd just heard and got a little choked up. He could admit that his siblings were fine upstanding people. They'd all had good role models, who'd taught them the value of hard work and being part of a team, a family. If one member of a team or family didn't do their best, the others had to pick up the slack. It was not an easy lesson to teach, but his parents and grandfather had found a way to do so. Drew counted himself lucky to have been born into this family with the values they had.

He turned back to his plans to protect Lily. Time to put those family values to work. Grandpa K had mentioned something he hadn't thought of and that was timing, which led to motive. He got out a pad of paper and a pen and began brainstorming motives.

Drew got a good handful of possible motives down on the paper, before he realized he needed more information. Part of determining motives revolved around the rewards for the pageant. And was there more, what was the next step after the pageant was won. Was there an even bigger event for the winner?

With a sigh, he woke back up his computer and went back to researching, again. He'd not spent so much time on a computer in years, but he was determined not to let one stone be left unturned. Drew wanted every tidbit of information he could find, before they got on that plane headed for New York. He had to keep his girl safe.

His movement and his thoughts stilled. His girl? He let that idea wash through his mind and heart. It didn't feel wrong or intrusive or even unimportant. It felt right.

Of course, he had no clue how Lily might feel about that idea, but maybe when this was all over it would be the right time to find out. Right now, they needed to keep her safe, that was the first priority and he couldn't afford to be distracted thinking about convincing Lily to be his. So, it would wait, it was only a week, there was no rush.

As he turned back to his computer, a warmth spread through his chest at the idea of Lily being his.

CHAPTER 15

*L*ily slept late the next morning. The shopping trip had worn her out. They'd had a wonderful time buying out every store in Denver. Summer had insisted that Lily buy at least three pairs of comfortable shoes, because even though they were comfortable, her feet would be happier in different shoes each day. Summer had also informed her that she planned to bring at least one extra pair along for the sightseeing days.

They bought a few more things Summer had pushed for, in the makeup realm. She'd looked over Lily's supplies before they left and declared that Lily needed a couple of items to round out her look, and some better brushes.

After hitting the shoes and makeup stores it was time to get the twins' clothes. They'd had fun watching the clerks keep asking 'You want two? Exactly the same?'. They hadn't told anyone why they were buying two, so the confusion was amusing.

When they got to the novelty tie store they'd realized it wasn't only novelty ties, but every conceivable type of tie a man could own. Lily had bought her dad one and three for

Drew. One of which had very discreet pigs with holsters and guns on them, one was a western style string tie and one was a very nice plain blue one.

Summer had picked out nearly a dozen for the twins, some were normal, and some were novelty. One set had lassos on them for Chase being a roper, and there was one set that was positively wicked if you took the time to really look at it. Most people wouldn't. Again, the clerk was mystified by her buying two of each type.

Even Lily's mom had gotten Howard some ties, she'd also found a naughty tie that she cackled over nearly all the way back to the ranch. She'd told Lily that she was going to surprise him with that one when they got to New York.

The manicure and pedicure were the last stop and Lily's feet were more than happy to be pampered. The stitches on the big cut were still in so the technician had covered it with a waterproof bandage to keep it clean. Alyssa planned to take the stitches out on Monday, but she'd declared that it was healing nicely. Lily hadn't been troubled by her injury during the shopping craze, it was more fatigue, than anything worrisome.

Lily sat up in bed and decided it was time to greet the world. She wanted to try out each pair of her comfortable shoes to make sure they were still comfortable after an hour or two, rather than the five minutes in the store.

After she was showered and dressed she pulled on her favorite jeans, a t-shirt that had seen better days, and put on her brand-new shoes. She looked ridiculous but that didn't matter, she was with family or at least as close as one could get, after just meeting a whole group of people.

But she did feel like they were family. They were all taking a week off to go with her to New York to protect her, which meant the few not going would have to pick up the slack. A cattle ranch was always busy, and having that many people all leave at the same time, would be a burden. Yet no one had batted an eye when it was suggested.

That showed they had a lot of faith in Drew, and he had a lot of faith in his siblings. She knew her siblings would have her back if she needed it, but they might also try to persuade her not to go at all. Especially her older sister, she'd always thought being in the pageant was a silly idea and that Olivia's request had overstepped the bounds of friendship.

Lily sighed and made a beeline for the kitchen, she was starving, all that shopping yesterday had taken a lot of energy. She might even eat another carb or two to compensate. She grinned to herself, what a lovely excuse.

She found her mom and dad in the kitchen together with Meg and Travis Kipling and Grandpa K. The older adults stopped talking when she walked in. Had they been talking about her?

Lily looked to her mom, who shrugged. "Nothing to worry about, we're just talking everything through. Travis and Meg are pointing out the strengths of each person going to New York, so we'll know who to tap if it's needed."

Lily nodded, the Kipling's had probably also pointed out weaknesses, but her mom was being diplomatic. She wondered what all had been disclosed, it would have been interesting to hear. "I just came for breakfast, all that shopping."

Meg said, "There's plenty of food cooked or you're welcome to have anything in the house, nothing is off-limits. You and Drew brought lots back from what was in the rental cabin. Clearly he'd planned to keep you there for a while."

Lily shivered at the thought. That would have been a nightmare, sitting with a man that had put on a great act and then turned on a dime to a guy that was really quite conceited and a jerk. She'd been so surprised when they'd gotten in the door of the cabin and he'd tied her to the bed and then had taken everything else away from her.

He'd clearly not cared if she was uncomfortable in her dress clothes and not given her the option to change, not even for bed. Which actually had been a bit of relief, since all she'd brought for the weekend trip was a sexy negligee. She'd not have wanted to run out of the cabin and through the woods in that.

What still mystified her was the complete change in his behavior, it was like two completely different people inhabiting the same body. She had to chalk it up to some really great acting. Clearly, he'd been expecting a huge payoff. Instead he'd paid for his deception with his life.

Lily still had trouble wrapping her head around it. Especially the dead part. But also, the plot to keep her out of the pageant. Ronald had never once indicated she should bow out of the pageant, in fact he had encouraged her. Why? She might have listened to him and stopped if he'd tried to talk her out of it. She had been attempting to mold her life to his, which hadn't been easy.

Had he needed to keep her in the pageant to receive the payment for stopping her from it? In other words, if she'd stopped too early would Ronald have lost the payoff from his 'bosses'. She needed to stop thinking about this so much, it only made her head hurt and cause more questions, and even some pain. Lily did not like the idea that she had been so totally hoodwinked, how could she be that gullible? Caught between the two lives of Ronald the rat.

She sighed and finally filled her plate and carried the tea she'd brewed during all her introspection over to the table. "Is it okay if I sit with you?"

Meg smiled and waved to a chair. "Of course, dear. Do join us."

Lily's dad cleared his throat and looked at Travis. "Let's

go out and look at your herd, the beef we had for dinner last night was delicious. I'd like to take a look at what you're doing."

Lily knew her father was earnest in his request, he was always interested in how people ran their ranches, but she also had to question if he wanted to talk to Travis alone. Grandpa K followed them out of the door and into the bright sunshine.

Elaine looked carefully at her daughter. "How are you feeling today?"

"Stupid, actually."

Both ladies looked surprised by her answer. But it was the truth. "I just can't figure out how I was so completely fooled by Ronald. Am I that gullible or stupid?"

Elaine put her hand on her daughter's arm. "Neither honey, he fooled all of us. We didn't really think he fit you, personality wise, but none of us would have ever guessed what he was up to. The only thing you might be is a little too trusting. But then again, so were we."

Meg sighed. "It's hard to be suspicious. Cade was in an abusive relationship for years. None of us liked the woman and we didn't like seeing the changes Cade went through, to try to make her happy, but we never guessed she was as malicious as we discovered she'd been. Not only to Cade but to any woman he looked at. She was very clever about hiding what she was doing. Some of the girls guessed it was her but there was never any evidence."

Lily was shocked at this revelation. Cade was such a great guy, it was hard to picture him kowtowing to some woman. He and Summer were great together. "How'd you find out?"

"When he didn't grovel and try to get her back after breaking up with her, she finally flipped out and everyone saw it. Her mother had her in therapy in another town. After Cade and Summer got engaged, she tried to run Summer down in the street, so the psychologist had her put into a treatment facility. It was either that or go to jail."

"Wow, that's crazy."

"Yes, she was, probably still is. But maybe she'll get the help she needs and move to Boston, or France, or Singapore." Meg grinned up at them.

Elaine said, "One could only hope."

Lily laughed and the atmosphere in the room lifted. She didn't feel nearly as ridiculous as she had been, which she supposed was the point of Meg's tale. But she had to wonder if she'd missed some essentials in her education, like how not to believe everything she was told. Maybe learn to be more cynical.

She finished off her breakfast and put her plate in the dishwasher. "I'm going to walk around a bit, to make sure these are truly comfortable shoes, rather than comfortable in the store and killer in real life."

Both women chuckled at that. Meg said, "How many pairs of shoes does that description fit? Too many to count, all lined up neatly in the closet."

"Exactly, and I would rather know that now, than find out halfway through a tour. Although Summer plans to bring multiple shoes with us. Which I never would have thought to do."

Everyone agreed that they wouldn't have either, and Summer was a godsend. Lily realized that Meg meant that on many different levels. Lily pulled on her jacket and went out into the bright sunshine. The air was frigid, not at all what the sunshine indicated, but they were in the mountains of Colorado, so the cold bright day was a normal occurrence.

She wandered around the yard and down to a small vegetable garden that was clearly finished producing for the year. Beyond that was the corrals and fields. She walked around to the front of the house and was surprised to see an older heifer laying in the sunny parking area.

She walked over to the cow. "You must be Dolly." The animal just looked at her as if to say, 'Duh, who else would you expect in the yard?'

Summer crouched down to give the old gal a scratch between the ears. Dolly seemed to like that.

Drew walked up. "I see you've met Dolly."

"Not formally, but I guessed it was her."

He grinned. "Well let me do the introductions then. Lily Smith please let me introduce you to Dolly Kipling. Dolly, this is Lily, our guest and soon to be pageant winner."

"Don't count your chickens before they're hatched, Drew. I might come in last place."

"Not a chance. You're a sure thing in my book."

"Well, thank you kind sir, but your book doesn't count in the larger scheme of things."

Drew looked into her eyes. "My book, is the only one I care about."

Lily was shocked at the intensity in his eyes. What was he trying to say? She didn't know what to say or do. She wanted to do something, but she didn't know what and that freaked her out. She looked back at Dolly. "I'll bring you a souvenir from New York."

Dolly almost seemed to roll her eyes at her as if to say, 'Clueless human, stop being a chicken.'

Drew chuckled and pulled her up with him. She was close, if she leaned forward just a tiny fraction he'd be within kissing distance. Lily looked into his eyes and saw speculation and desire. She decided to take Dolly's advice and leaned toward him, into his space.

He didn't back off and the look in his eyes became more intense. She lifted up on her toes and pulled him in closer. He moved willingly and lowered his head, so she set her lips on his, in a soft, almost non-kiss. Then she pulled back and saw the storm raging in his eyes, so she went back on her toes for a firmer kiss, and he became an active participant.

Drew took over the kiss and pulled her in closer, wrapping his arms around her waist. The kiss went from tentative to hot in mere seconds. When she opened her lips, his tongue swooped in and she tasted him, as he delved into the soft secret spots of her mouth.

She could have stayed like this, locked in his embrace, his mouth devouring hers, for hours. Apparently, Dolly felt like her mission was accomplished, because she lowed, and stood to wander off. The movement shattered their concentration, and they broke apart, panting, trying to catch their breath.

She touched a hand to her lips, that felt hot and swollen. "Wow."

Drew ran his hands through his hair as he stepped back another step. "I couldn't agree more. But maybe this isn't the best place."

Lily looked around the yard and concurred with that statement. Anyone could drive in or walk around the side of the house. She looked up at him. "As long as we examine it later, I agree."

A slow smile slid over Drew's face. "I could get on board with that."

"Good."

"So, what are you doing out wandering around?"

She pointed at her feet. "Making sure they are comfortable enough to spend a whole day of sightseeing in."

Drew's demeanor changed with the mention of the pageant. "Good. I wanted to talk to you about a few ideas and ask some questions. Do you want to walk and talk?"

She nodded and fell in beside him.

DREW CHASTISED himself for kissing the hell out of Lily in the front yard, not only could anyone have seen them, but he had a job to do, which did not include kissing the girl. He'd seen her from the window and had followed her out, with the intention of talking to her about some precautions he'd been pondering. And, there actually were some questions he wanted to ask.

Then before he knew what was happening she was in his arms and her sweet mouth was on his. Every brain cell had deserted him and all he could think about was devouring that delicious mouth, and the way her warm curves felt against his body. If Dolly hadn't moved, he might have spent the rest of the day in the front yard with his lips glued to Lily's.

His first priority, however, was keeping her safe and that meant he had to keep his head in the game. So, no more kissing, not until he deemed her safe. Then if they still felt the same, they could indulge in examining this… whatever it was. Attraction? Relationship?

He shook himself internally, he had questions and that was more important than dwelling on what was, or wasn't, happening between them. "I'm trying to figure out a motive for why these 'bosses' are trying to keep you out of the contest. It certainly doesn't make sense for them to keep all fifty women out of a contest in order for their favorite to win. So why you? Maybe not only you, but let's look at you specifically. If you didn't show up on Tuesday or Wednesday, would they just leave your spot empty?"

"I have a backup. If she could get there in time, she would take my place."

"All right, that could be a motive. If she wanted to be included, she could have hired someone to get you out."

Lily shook her head. "She's really sweet. I can't see her doing that."

"Maybe not, but we'll put that in the motive possibility pile. If you win what happens next?"

As she spoke she ticked off each statement on her fingers. "My charity wins the prize amount. I win a scholarship to use in promoting my business or cause. There are also lots of minor prizes, for the winner, and also all the contestants. The winner would go on to the international pageant. My sponsors get their names in Pageantry magazine, and wherever my picture ends up, if I'm the winner. That's all I can think of right now."

"That's good. So, a charity wanting you to win could be a motive, or maybe someone that hates your charity, and doesn't want them to win." She sucked in a breath, probably to argue, but he just rolled over the top of her. "Someone that wants the scholarship might have the motivation to go the extra mile to keep you out. And your sponsors getting their name plastered everywhere might also be a reason."

He put his hands in his back pockets. "The problem with most of those is, they would have to eliminate all the girls to know if they were going to win. Just taking you out wouldn't accomplish any of those other things. Except maybe knocking out your non-profit."

"But there might be more than one of us with the same charity. I didn't pick a very specific one."

"I can look into that. But if it's not that then what would someone gain by keeping you away?"

"Which brings it back to my runner-up. But I still can't believe she would do something like this."

"All right let's go just a little bigger, say four or five girls. Is there anything in common between you and a few of the girls? Like is there a regional prize of some type? You're in Montana. Is there a Rocky Mountain region?"

"Well yes there was, at the lower levels of the competition, but that was more setup as a practice pageant to get us ready for the big one."

Drew nodded, "And, of course the state one."

"Right."

Tell me about your sponsors. Did anyone in particular sink a big sum into you, so they would be featured more than others?"

Lily shook her head. "No, but…"

She trailed off and he looked over to see a frown on her forehead and a faraway look in her eyes. He decided to let her think it through before saying anything else.

"One of the girls mentioned that four of us had direct competitors as our sponsors. Do you think one sponsor would arrange for the other three girls to lose, so they were the only one left?"

"It's possible, all that advertising would be amazing. But it's still a long shot. Wouldn't all the girls have to drop out for the advertising to be that useful?"

Lily stopped walking, again deep in thought. "I wonder. If I left the pageant, I know my runner-up doesn't have the same companies backing her. So, my sponsors would be knocked out of the free, nationwide advertising. If the other two or three alternatives don't have the same sponsors either, then by eliminating three contestants the one sponsor would be the only one seen. Even without winning, the sponsors get a lot of promo during the televised event."

"Okay, that leaves us with three decent motives. Let the idea rest for now, sometimes the subconscious is better at this kind of speculation. If you think of anything else, let me know."

"I will. You said earlier that you have some strategies you wanted to talk about, what did you have in mind?"

"Well, we could approach this in a couple of different ways. One way is to declare loud and clear that you hired me to be your bodyguard, because of Ronald, basically the truth. Which leaves it open for anyone else that got hoodwinked or threatened to tell you about it. In some ways, I like that idea."

Lily nodded. "But it kind of makes me look like an idiot, and also could alert whoever is behind this that you are gunning for them."

"Exactly. The second scenario is you threw Ronald over, when you met me, and I insisted to come as your bodyguard and boyfriend. Which would keep the bad guys from knowing we were onto them and also give us cover to be together more. I could play the jealous boyfriend card if anyone got too close."

Lily raised one eyebrow. "That one doesn't make me look stupid and gullible, but it makes me look a little like a 'ho'."

Oh, shit, had he insulted her with that suggestion? He hadn't meant it to sound like she was flighty, let alone a slut. His expression must have shown his concern, because she laughed out loud.

"I was just teasing. I definitely like that idea better. That way if something is up that I need to know about you can take my hand or whisper in my ear and everyone will think we're in love." She stopped speaking and blushed, then stammered, "Not that you need to... um... well..."

This time it was his turn to laugh. "I would be more than happy to act smitten. In fact, it would be a whole lot easier than trying to maintain a professional 'hired gun' attitude."

Lily relaxed, and a shy smile covered her face. "All right let's do that."

CHAPTER 16

*L*ily and Drew arrived in New York safely, and checked into the hotel. Chase, Cade, Rachel and Summer had travelled with them. Chase and Cade were not in matching clothing and Chase was going to stay out of sight, while the rest checked into the hotel, and he would follow them up as soon as they were in the room, and the bell-hop was gone. He'd put on some glasses, a bulky coat, and tourist hat pulled low, so he would not be recognized.

Rachel, Adam, Beau and Alyssa had come in on an earlier flight and had texted that they were checked into their hotel also, which was conveniently located across the street. The two hotels had a walkway between the them on the second floor. They'd been thrilled to hear that was the case, because it made it more likely for all of them to be in both hotels, since each hotel had different restaurants, it would be a natural reason to move back and forth.

Lily checked in with the pageant people and they got their official passes, including the ones for Rachel, Summer, and Cade. When Lily had mentioned that she'd made friends with Summer and would be bringing her along the pageant officials had been more than welcoming. It seemed they'd been great fans of 'Bringing up Heather' and thought the publicity of having her on board would be amazing.

Summer had sighed at the thought of being in the public eye but had not complained or changed her mind about helping. It was what they'd talked about, using her fame to get close to the contestants. Now she would have the chance to get close to whomever she might want.

Drew was thrilled with the idea of her maybe chatting up some of the officials or sponsors or whoever found themselves in her orbit. Since she wasn't a competitor people might be more relaxed around her.

Since they'd not been in town long enough to have learned anything, they did not have a group meeting. Instead they all decided to stay in their rooms and lay low. Drew was unpacking his suitcase, when there was a knock on the connecting door to Lily's room. He unlocked it and opened it to her.

She walked in and sat on his bed, then she got up and walked over to his window to look out of it. Finally, she turned toward him and asked, "Can we leave the doors unlocked? Or even open?"

Drew thought Lily was looking a little nervous or uncertain. "Unlocked absolutely. I was going to finish unpacking and then unlock mine. However, since the doors are right next to the bathrooms we might want to close one for privacy."

Lily looked at his suitcase. "You are notoriously neat, aren't you? I hung up my dresses of course, to try to get the creases out, but left a lot of my stuff in the suitcase."

"I don't like having to deal with a suitcase. I'm happy to use the dresser to hold my things. As far as being notoriously neat, I just like to be able to find everything without having to search for it."

She giggled. "Notoriously neat."

Since her shoulders had relaxed and the tight expression had eased he decided he would be whatever she wanted. "So, what freaked you out?"

She looked chagrined, but said, "I heard someone knock on the door across the hall with room service and was worried someone might try to get in by pretending to be hotel staff. When I knew the delivery person was gone, I put up the do not disturb sign, and then set the night lock."

"In that case, we'll order delivery to my room and you can leave your door locked and not open it for any reason. Or, if someone knocks just call out and I'll come over."

"So other than showering and stuff we can leave the doors open?"

Drew saw the worry had not completely left her eyes. "Yes, of course. We can hang out together in one of the rooms if you want."

"Oh good." She promptly crawled up on his bed, put the pillows behind her back and sat there waiting while he finished unpacking. Apparently, she was there to stay. He wasn't quite sure how he was going to handle that, because she looked damn good on his bed. But he'd decided that anything more between them needed to wait until the pageant was over.

He couldn't help but wonder if she was simply scared or wanted to move things along after the kisses they'd shared a few days ago. Drew wanted to groan in frustration, but he didn't want her to think she was a burden, so he zipped his suitcase shut and put it in the closet.

Now the question was, join her on the bed or sit at the tiny table in the uncomfortable chairs. He took up the menu and flipped through it, not seeing a think as he tried to decide what to do. "Did you want something to eat?"

"Maybe, but I don't think there's any food in that hotel amenities folder. The menu is over here on the bedside table." Her expression held a smirk that indicated she'd seen through his pathetic waffling.

Drew looked at what was in his hand and tried to decide whether to tell her the truth or straight out lie to her face. Truth won, he cleared his throat. "I was trying to decide if I trusted myself to crawl up there on that bed with you."

She patted the covers next to her. "By all means come join me. We can order food later."

"But…"

"No buts, you promised me we could explore those kisses more, when we weren't in the front yard." She looked around pointedly. "Not the front yard. No one is coming to talk to us, and we haven't ordered food, so no one will know."

This time he did groan. "I'm trying to do the right thing here. I need to be on my game, so I can protect you. Kissing you is a major distraction."

Lily nodded. Her gaze turned wicked. "As it should be, and I think you'll notice if someone tries to get me, if we are lip to lip, body to body."

Lust flooded him while his brain tried to refute her logic. Lust won. He couldn't think of a thing against it.

SHE HELD her breath as Drew stood stock still. Clearly, trying to find a way to argue with her statement. Lily practically clapped in relief when he kicked off his cowboy boots. She'd been nervous in her own room, but when he'd opened the door and invited her in, her brain had gone down a completely different path. It had taken her a moment to decide if she wanted to act on it, which had made her even more nervous, although it was a completely different kind of fear.

She'd been shocked to hear what had come out of her mouth, but once it was out there, she'd had no intention of trying to pull it back. She knew beyond a shadow of doubt that Lily Smith wanted to be skin to skin with Drew Kipling.

So, as he climbed onto the bed she laid down and reached out to let him know he wasn't backing out of this, and neither was she.

"Are you sure about this, Lily?"

She whispered, "I am, there's been something between us since the first day we met. I don't know what it is, but I trusted you, completely. Even after I remembered what Ronald had done, I still had complete trust in you, Drew."

Drew said, "It was the badge."

Lily nodded. "That was a factor. But there was something else there also, a kind of knowing."

He held her face and looked into her eyes, she didn't shy away, but held his gaze, letting him see what he would. Then she whispered, "This may be the only time we're alone. Let's make the best of it."

He lowered his lips to hers and she rejoiced in the touch, but more importantly she rejoiced in the promise, within the touch. His hands were warm on her face where he continued to hold it, as his lips swept over hers. Light as a feather, but no feather left an electric shock like his lips did on hers. The tingle started on her mouth and spread throughout her whole body, awakening nerve endings, spreading warmth and desire.

It was lovely and her whole body relaxed and savored, but she wanted more. Greedy thing that she was, she had to have more. So, she wrapped her arms around him and pulled him in closer, while at the same time pressing her lips firmer to his. He took the hint and kissed her more fully, his warm firm mouth pressing to hers. Her body received another jolt of electricity that was all Drew.

She opened her mouth and his tongue swept inside to taste and savor. Lily's tongue dueled with his, sending fresh shivers throughout, to shoot from her fingers and toes when they could not be contained. Her entire being was vibrating with pleasure and desire.

Her fingers were seeking, trying to find their way under his clothes, she wanted skin, she wanted to run her hands over his back and chest, to trace the muscles hidden underneath the fabric. But the clothing thwarted her efforts.

When his mouth left hers to trace a path of fire on her jaw and neck, she fought against the sensations enough to gasp out, "Too many clothes."

He nipped her earlobe and shivers of delight spread outward. Drew pulled back, unbuckled his belt and slipped it through the belt loops, so he could pull the shirttails out of his pants. While Lily watched with an eager gaze, he unbuttoned the shirt, and pulled it off. Her disappointment nearly made her cry, to see he had a t-shirt on underneath.

Her expression must have given away her disappointment because he grinned and pulled the t-shirt off over his head. That was more like it. She reached out to stroke the firm chest and the muscles that defined it. A small scattering of chest hair gave her fingers another level of sensual enjoyment.

He shivered at her touch, and she reveled in her feminine power over this strong self-reliant man. It was a heady feeling.

Drew slowly slipped the buttons loose on her shirt, his eyes never leaving hers. She continued to stroke where ever she could reach, but he was determined and didn't let her derail him. Not that she really wanted to derail him, but she did enjoy when her touches scattered his wits and caused him to pause. It made her want to laugh and sing, that she could disrupt his concentration, with a few simple touches.

He did manage to get her shirt fully unbuttoned and drew it open. His eyes immediately riveted to her lacy mint-colored bra, and he swallowed hard.

"So beautiful, you are so beautiful. That green color, is now my favorite color forever."

She laughed at his adoring gaze and whispered, "Wait until you see the lavender one."

He looked in her eyes with a bemused expression. "I can't imagine ever believing lavender will be my favorite color."

Lily gave him a sultry smile. "We'll see."

"Vixen. As much as I love it, I would like to see that bra on the floor."

"That can be arranged." Lily decided to see if she could shock him again, so she hopped out of bed, dropped the shirt and bra to the floor and shimmied out of her pants.

Oh yeah, she had accomplished her goal, he sat there stone still and let his eyes run over her whole body. She could literally feel the heat of his gaze on her skin.

He swore and then said, "If you don't win this pageant it won't be for lack of beauty, that's for damn sure."

Lily curtsied. "Thank you, kind sir. But I feel kind of lonely being the only one naked."

He moved so fast he was a blur, as he shed the rest of his clothes and then pulled her up against his warm body. She'd barely had any time to feast her eyes on him. Lily wasn't about to complain however, because his warm hard body felt magnificent against her smaller soft one. She wrapped her arms around him, backed toward the bed, and pulled him down with her as she fell back on it.

He chuckled at her antics but didn't complain. Instead he took her mouth with his, in a hot, practically savage, kiss that she exulted in. She ran her hands over his back letting her nails slightly abrade his skin and the kiss got even hotter, until she had no ability to move, as all senses were focused on his mouth on hers.

When they needed to breathe, he broke the kiss and began kissing his way down her neck and shoulder to lick the spot where her pulse pounded. Lily trembled, and warmth flooded her, to pool between her thighs.

Drew continued kissing his way down to her breasts which were begging for his touch. He took one turgid nipple into his mouth to suckle, while his hand caressed and squeezed the other. Heat roared through her from his ministrations, and she held his head to her breast for more. He obliged her, only moving enough to give the other breast the same attention.

When her hold on him slackened, he clearly took that as the cue to continue his assault down her body, which he did. Kissing his way down her ribcage to her belly button that he ringed with his tongue and made her shiver. He grinned up at her before continuing south. She'd never felt comfortable enough with a man to allow them to kiss her down there, but with Drew she had no desire to stop his progression. So, when he reached the apex of her legs she allowed them to fall open in invitation.

He didn't hesitate to accept and soon his mouth was on her most guarded spot. Lily found out quickly that the man had a very talented mouth. Lips and teeth and tongue created a storm of sensations that swamped her body, overwhelmed her mind and sent her flying with an orgasm so strong she wasn't sure all of her would return to earth. Ever.

When her mind reconvened, she found Drew back up next to her watching her expressions with a look of fascination. She wanted to hide from his avid gaze, but he took her chin and kissed her softly. "Don't be embarrassed, watching you enjoy my touch is the most erotic thing I've ever seen."

She whispered back, "That was amazing. I've never felt anything like it."

A slow grin slid across his face. "Even better."

Lily kissed him firmly on his grinning mouth until he was panting. She reached down and took hold of the hard cock that was poking into her leg. "Time for round two?"

His eyes all but rolled back in his head as she stroked him and this time, she grinned.

CHAPTER 17

*D*rew loved her touch and had not been joking when he'd told her how much he loved watching her revel in his ministrations. But he needed to stop this now. He didn't have any protection with him. He'd never planned to indulge in his attraction for Lily. They were from different worlds. But more importantly he was there to protect her, not have sex with her.

He groaned as she stroked him and then took hold of her wrist to stop her movement. He grit his teeth and ground out, "We have to stop."

"No, we don't."

"I don't have any protection."

"I do. I'm on the pill and I also have condoms, there are three in the pocket of my pants and the rest of a box in my suitcase." She squeezed him, and he couldn't breathe for a full minute as he fought his way through the fire that shot through his body. By the time he could function again she'd leaped off the bed, grabbed the condoms and was back, tearing one open with her teeth.

Lily was determined, and he didn't have the strength to

fight her off, and if he was honest, he didn't really want to. So, rather than telling her all the reasons this was a bad idea, none of which he could remember at the time, he laid back and let her roll the condom on, while he gritted his teeth against the pleasure. Before he could move she'd climbed on top of him and had impaled herself.

Drew was shocked at her actions but there was no way in hell he was going to complain as she rode him, giving both of them pleasure. He reached up and caressed her breasts which caused her inner muscles to clamp down on him. So, he did it again and gently squeezed, Lily bucked and clenched him tight.

Dear God, he wasn't going to last five minutes at this rate, but he noticed that Lily's breathing was rough, so it might be possible for him to outlast her. He pinched her nipples and then moved one hand down to stroke her clit while the other kept up the assault on her breasts, which seemed to be very sensitive.

It didn't take but a minute before she arched her back and called out his name. He rolled them both over and pounded into her twice and his own climax was wrenched from him. He groaned out her name as his body exploded in ecstasy and his thoughts vanished in the super nova.

When his brain finally reasserted itself, he realized he was squishing Lily, pressing her down into the mattress. He went to roll off of her, so she could breathe but she stopped him.

"Just another few seconds. I like the feel of you on top of me."

He kissed her forehead. "But you need to breathe, too."

She huffed out a weak breath. "Breathing is highly over-rated."

He chuckled and rolled off of her pulling her with him, so she landed on his chest. She drew a deep breath and then kissed his chin. "I guess breathing *is* kind of a good thing."

They lay together like that for a long time until Drew felt her stomach rumble, his answered the call. "I think we're hungry."

"Yes, all that energy for multiple orgasms, does tend to deplete the caloric reserves."

He laughed at her silliness. "Speak for yourself, multiple orgasm woman. We should order some room service."

"Yes, we should, giver of multiple orgasms man." She rolled over and reached for the menu while he dropped the condom into the trash, shaking his head at her quip.

While she perused the menu, he went into the bath room to wash his face and hands. When he came out he pulled on his jeans and t-shirt.

Lily looked up and said, "Now that's just sad, covering up all those muscles."

"I don't think the room service people would want me answering the door in just my skin."

She giggled and handed him the menu. "Depends on who is delivering."

They ended up ordering enough food for an army. Clearly, they were starving, and Lily had said they had to replenish the stores for later activity. Then she'd looked pointedly at him and had ordered chocolate pudding. He'd nearly swallowed his tongue.

They'd ordered healthy food and just a few carbs, so Lily was happy to eat. The girl had an appetite after sex, that was for certain. She ate like a ranch hand, and even devoured her share of the carbs, which he'd never seen her do before. He didn't want to point it out, but he was curious why she was relaxing her standards.

When she'd practically licked her plate clean she smiled at him and said. "The pageant is in a few days, I don't think I'll gain weight in that length of time, so I finally get to eat like a normal person."

Drew smiled and nodded, but in the back of his mind he wondered if she normally ate like a harvest hand or if it was the sex. He would be very interested to discover that. Since he didn't think they would be indulging in any more sex after tonight, it would be easy to tell.

Lily took one spoonful of the pudding and moaned in appreciation. Then she set the spoon down and dropped his shirt that she'd been wearing to the floor. She picked up the pudding and put it on the bedside table. She crept up on all fours on the bed and glanced over her shoulder.

She waggled her butt at him. "Coming?"

He was instantly hard. He ground out, "No, but you will be, after I swat that sassy ass of yours."

She grinned and waggled again. "Bring it, cowboy."

He was at the bed in an instant and swatted her, hard enough to sting, but not enough to bruise.

She laughed. "Oh! I think I need at least one more on the other cheek. Don't you?"

He groaned and obliged her.

She waggled her butt, that now had two pink hand prints, at him. "Perfect, now lose the clothes, officer."

He wasn't sure he could get the jeans off, he was so hard. He'd never been with a sexually playful woman and it was wrecking him, in the best way possible.

LILY WAS HAVING SO much fun teasing Drew. She'd never trusted a man enough to play with him in the bedroom, and she loved that she could with Drew. It was so freeing. She marveled at the fact that she'd only known him a week, yet felt free and safe with him in a way she never had before.

She'd read some books and had fantasized about trying some things, but had resigned herself to never finding out what it would be like. She might have to change her mind about that, if she and Drew stayed together.

It was too early to think about that of course, they lived in different states, and they didn't really know each other that well. If she won the pageant, she would have to train for the International one. She wasn't sure she really wanted to do the International pageant, but she was still going to give it her all. Lily had made a promise and she never reneged on a promise.

She felt Drew come up behind her, she was still on all fours. He kissed each butt cheek where he'd swatted it and then pulled her legs a little farther apart. Lily thrilled at the idea of having him take her from behind, it was one of the things she'd wanted to try. He slid his hard cock up to her wet entrance and stroked her with it.

"Lily, do you want to stay on your hands and knees?"

She could barely respond she was so aroused. "Yes, I've never tried it this way."

"I haven't either, let me know if… well, if you don't like something."

She nodded, and he slid in just a little. It felt different, but not at all bad. She pushed back a little, so he slid in further. He'd gotten the message, so he kept pushing inside, until he was fully seated. He began stroking her and she loved it.

In a strangled voice he said, "I've heard if you go down on your elbows it's a better sensation."

She did as he suggested, and it did feel different. He kept up the long smooth strokes while he reached around and caressed her breasts. Her whole body clenched in pleasure.

"Faster, Drew, harder."

He was obedient to her verbal directions and soon she was flying. High above the earthly plane. He pounded into her a few more times and then came with a muffled shout. Her name on his lips. They both crashed to the bed, boneless.

CHAPTER 18

*L*ily woke with a big warm man wrapped around her. It was a most excellent way to awaken. He was curled around her back with one hand around her waist. She would have been happy to go back to sleep but this was the first day of sightseeing. She looked to the clock on the nightstand, it was still early enough that they didn't have to rush, but she couldn't go back to sleep either. The chocolate pudding was still there, dried out and uneaten.

She sighed at the waste, she'd wanted to lick it off of Drew, but they'd passed out shortly after the doggy-style sex. That had been fun, she could check two things off her sexual bucket list, well three if she wanted to count the two light smacks to her ass. She decided to wait and see on that one.

Drew mumbled, "What was the sigh for?"

"The chocolate pudding, I didn't get to lick off of you."

She was thrilled when he instantly hardened.

His voice was even rougher when he said, "We can always order more."

She turned in his arms and kissed his chin and then his neck.

Lily reached down and caressed his hardened cock. She gave it a gentle squeeze and then turned to hop out of bed. "Maybe, but we need to get moving this morning."

She nearly made it, before he hauled her back onto the bed, flat on her back, and rolled on top of her. "Not quite so quick, young lady."

She laughed up at him. "Did you need something?"

Drew reached over her to the night stand and took the last condom, ripped it open and rolled it on so quick she almost missed it. He slid inside her. "This will only take a minute, Little Miss Tease."

Lily clenched her inner muscles down on him as he withdrew. "Yeah, we probably have enough time for that."

"You are a vixen," Drew muttered when they could both breathe again, and their thundering heartbeats had begun to slow.

She just smiled and turned to look at the clock. With a large sigh she said, "And now we really do have to get going, we need to be downstairs in an hour and a half. Katie, Summer and your brother will be here in forty-five minutes."

Drew nodded. "Okay you go get showered and I'll order us some breakfast."

"All right make sure you get some carbs, after all the activity last night and this morning I'm going to need some."

Drew bowed gallantly. "As you wish."

Lily laughed, grabbed up her clothes and hurried to her room. When she saw the completely untouched bed she had a short debate with herself, and then went over and ruffled it up, so it looked like she had slept in it. She wasn't ready for the rest of the family to know about her and Drew's nighttime fun.

After a quick shower, where she washed away all traces of Drew and his amorous activity, she pulled out the pantsuit she'd chosen for the first day of sightseeing. She'd noticed a bit of beard burn on her inside thighs and a tiny bit on one breast, she didn't think it was noticeable, but they would need to be careful if they continued the sexual adventure tonight. Maybe she'd have to keep that talented mouth from roving over her body, which was sad, but better than curbing all activity.

She got out the accessories she would use with the outfit, after Summer came to do her hair and makeup. She was ready in a robe with a low collar when she heard a knock, on Drew's door. Apparently, he'd clued in his siblings, to tell them to come to his door rather than Lily's.

DREW STOPPED TRIMMING his beard and stared at his reflection. He'd just had a terrifying thought. What if his beard had marked Lily last night. He ran his hand over it, wondering if it could have scratched her soft skin, his beard was softer than if he shaved every day, but was it soft enough?

He didn't know exactly what the competition involved but if it was a swimsuit or anything else revealing he didn't want to cause her to lose. Well they would just have to stop with the nighttime gymnastics. She probably needed her sleep, anyway. Plus, he wasn't completely convinced they should be having sex in the first place, amazingly wonderful sex though it was.

How he was going to stop the sexy little fireball from leading him around by his dick, he had no idea, but he had to try. He couldn't let his lust, no that wasn't quite right, it was more than lust, desire maybe? Yes desire, he couldn't let his desire for her ruin her chances in this pageant.

With that decision firmly in place he resumed trimming his beard. But his brain continued to nag him about how he was going to keep Lily at arm's length. Finally, he decided to lock that question away for later. He needed to think about her safety, while they were out and about today.

He turned that over in his head as he straightened his room and tried to remove all traces of Lily spending the night. He pulled out the bag from the waste basket in the room with condom evidence in it and tossed the whole thing into the bathroom trash. Shaking his head, he set the non-eaten chocolate pudding on the room service tray and put it outside his door. She'd clearly had wicked plans for tormenting the hell out of him, and he had to admit he'd have been totally on board with whatever she wanted. Which was why he was going to have to put a stop to all of it, so she didn't get the upper hand.

He was relieved when there was a knock on his door, being around other people would help him keep his distance, and head on straight.

He opened the door to find Cade, Summer, and Katie. He grinned at them, "Right on time."

Summer and Katie each kissed him on the cheek, as was their custom, and he waved them toward Lily's room. "Go on over, Lily should be ready for you."

Cade walked in and wandered the room like a caged beast. Drew frowned at his brother. "What's up?"

Cade ran a hand through his hair. "Nothing in particular, I just feel out of sorts. Like something isn't exactly right."

"Chase?"

"He feels the same, we haven't mentioned it to the girls, but Katie's been jumpy, and Summer is quiet."

Drew nodded slowly. "Lily felt nervous in her room last night and spent most of it in mine. She made me promise to leave the connecting door open. Not just unlocked. Open."

Cade sat on the side of the bed. "If it's all of us…"

"Yep, better heed the warning. I'm not sure what else we can do, though."

"Exactly, hard to fight against a shadow, or even prepare, to fight against one." Cade shook his head. "If they make their presence known we'll be on it."

"Damn straight. I haven't talked to Adam or Beau today, have you?"

"Yeah, Rachel called Summer to ask her to bring something. She said they're in place at the first location and Adam and Alyssa are at the second."

There was a knock on the door and Cade tensed. "Just room service, bro. I ordered plenty if you guys want something to munch on."

"We ate earlier but coffee wouldn't go amiss."

Drew answered the door and pulled the rolling cart into the room, after adding a good-sized tip and signing his name to the ticket. "Just FYI, I'm tipping room service well, so they want to deliver to our room."

Cade nodded. "Buying loyalty. Excellent advice. We will too."

Lily called out from the other room. "Did I hear food arrive? I'm starving."

Drew grinned at his brother and pushed the cart into Lily's room. He stopped short when he saw what was going on, Lily was in a short robe that made her legs look longer that he knew they were. She had giant rollers in her hair and Summer was applying makeup. Drew didn't personally think Lily needed any makeup, but didn't voice his opinion.

Summer said, "Let me just finish your eyes and then you can eat while I begin to work on your hair."

Lily squirmed. "Fine, but hurry."

Summer frowned. "Did you forget to eat last night? No, you couldn't have I saw a tray on the floor outside Drew's door that had plenty of plates. The only thing left was a chocolate pudding with only a few bites taken out."

Drew tried not to choke or look at Lily, but he couldn't stop his eyes from meeting hers in the mirror.

Lily gave him a sly look, and then answered Summer. "I just did a strenuous workout this morning, so I need to refuel."

Drew turned his strangled gasp into a cough, and pushed the cart over closer to Lily.

"It smells fantastic. What is it?"

"A little of several things since I wasn't sure what you wanted, but the main dish is a house specialty which is malted waffles."

Lily practically slid out of her chair as her stomach rumbled and she moaned. Drew tensed, she needed to stop with the sex noises or he was going to be demonstrating to everyone in the room what those sounds did to his body. He busied himself with a cup of coffee, willing his hands not to shake.

When Summer was finally happy with Lily's eyes, she had to jump out of the way, so she didn't get mowed down, as Lily rushed to the tray for food.

Katie laughed. "That must have been one hell of a workout."

Drew cleared his throat. "I got enough coffee for everyone, and maybe a few scraps of breakfast if Lily doesn't eat it all."

Lily already had a huge bite of waffle in her mouth, so she just rolled her eyes at him. He grinned at her and loaded up a plate for himself, while the rest of them got coffee. Cade had pulled the two chairs with him from Drew's room, so he went over to sit with his brother.

Once Lily had some food in her stomach, she sat back into the chair and let Summer continue on her hair.

Drew looked around the room to keep his eyes off Lily's legs. There was a pretty aqua pant suit laid out on the bed.

He noticed that Summer had used makeup that would complement the color and bring depth to Lily's eyes. How he knew this, he had no idea, but he could see it nonetheless. The color of her clothes would be easy to keep track of if they got separated, it was a perfect choice.

He signaled to Cade and they went back into his room, so the ladies could finish up.

Cade said, "That outfit should be easy to track. It's an unusual shade of blue."

"Yeah, I was thinking the same thing, aqua isn't a real popular color. She'll stand out, which is both good and bad. We'll be able to keep tabs on her, but so will anyone else."

Cade chuckled. "Aqua? How do you know it's aqua?"

"Police training, we can't go around calling everything blue."

"Seriously? You had to learn color names?"

Drew nodded absently. "Yeah, I hope it doesn't stand out too much. It would be easy to target from a distance."

Cade immediately sobered. "Do you really think someone might take a potshot at her? "

Drew ran his hands through his hair in frustration. "I just don't know. Whoever hired dead Ronald clearly has no issues with killing, and they'd given him permission to use lethal force. He told Lily he wasn't a killer which is the only reason she's still with us. I just can't figure out why anyone would care that much."

"I hear you, it's a fricken beauty pageant. Who really cares who the winner is? Well the girls, of course but still, it seems ridiculous to me."

Drew paced back and forth in the room. "Yeah, the girls care, their families, and their sponsors might care. The pageant people might, but that seems a little bit of a stretch, why would the pageant people want to remove contestants?

We just don't have enough information to go on. Maybe we'll learn more at the meeting this morning."

Cade nodded. "We can only hope. I don't think Lily really cares that much if she wins, she's mostly doing it to honor her friend and the promise she made her."

"I agree and if I think it's getting too dangerous, I will use her friend's love for her to convince her to pull out."

"Good idea."

Katie appeared in the door. "We're ready."

"Great, let's use my door and keep Lily's locked. She's got the do not disturb sign on hers and I'm going to do the same on mine. I'd rather have to reuse my towels and have a messy bed than have someone in here."

Lily walked in right after he finished that statement and Drew lost the ability to speak. She looked amazing, the pantsuit fit her like a glove and showed off all her assets. Her hair was soft curls and the makeup did indeed do something, he didn't know what exactly, but she looked incredible.

Lily clearly noticed he was staring slack-mouthed, because she preened for just a second and then said, "I agree with you, Drew. I don't want anyone in my room or yours, if we keep the connecting doors open and unlocked."

Drew internally shook himself out of the stupor she'd put him in. "You look stunning, Lily."

Cade nodded. "You do, you're going to win for sure."

Lily blushed at the men's compliments. "We'll see about that. Ready to go?"

Thank God he'd gotten all his gear on before Lily arrived because he wasn't sure he would have remembered a damn thing if he hadn't.

"Summer you lead, Katie and Cade flank Lily. I'll bring up the rear."

They left the room in a huddle, but waited while Drew put the 'Do not disturb' sign on the handle and two tiny pieces of tape on both doors. When they got in the elevator Drew was glad to see it was empty. He put Lily, Katie and Cade with their backs against the wall and he took point in front of Summer.

The elevator went straight to the reception floor with no stops and Drew thanked his lucky stars for that. When the doors opened he stepped out and did a quick look around, before gesturing the others out, so he could follow them.

The reception was in a large room with standing tables and a stage in the front of the room. People were milling around, but Summer knew what she was doing and led them to a quiet corner. After a few minutes where they had tried to look casual and probably failed, the event began.

The cheerful pageant official trundled on stage. "Hello and welcome contestants and friends. We are going to commence with a quick introduction. We'll go alphabetically by state and you can each come up on stage with your entourage. Introduce yourself and each member of your group."

Drew and the rest of them watched closely as each state was called out. When they got to Colorado, no one went on stage. Which started a whispered conversation.

The MC finally said, "The Colorado contestant has not shown up and we haven't heard anything from her." He looked around expectantly and then mumbled. "That's very unusual, we've never had a no-show before."

Cade and Drew exchanged a glance. They all moved just a little closer to Lily, Drew saw her shiver, so he placed his hand on the small of her back, she leaned back into it.

She whispered, "I thought I was alone."

"Guess not."

They went through the rest of the states until they got to Montana and the five of them stayed in formation to move to the stage. When they reached the microphone, Summer stepped to the side next to Cade.

Lily took the mic and said in a surprisingly steady voice, "I'm Lily Smith, Ms. Montana, I have with me Katie—my secretary and life organizer, my bodyguard—Drew, and Summer Attwood is helping me with hair and makeup. You might remember Summer from the popular TV show *Training up Heather* and next to her is her fiancé Cade. Summer has mentioned that she would be willing to give makeup pointers to anyone who would like some, as long as it's not everyone at the same time.

Murmurs could be heard throughout the room and Summer gave the crowd a big smile and a small wave. Having effectively taken the limelight away from Lily, they left the podium to return to their corner.

The MC got everyone's attention and the introductions continued. When they got to Ms. Utah, she had a bodyguard with her also. He would see if he could have a chat with the other bodyguard. None of the other girls had a bodyguard, that were introduced as such anyway.

Nothing else out of the ordinary happened until they got to Wyoming. The candidate for that state said that she was the alternative and that the real Ms. Wyoming was in the hospital from a rather severe accident.

Another glance happened between the brothers and they closed rank around Lily once more.

Drew noticed that all the girls with issues so far, were from the Rocky Mountain states. The only one missing was Idaho, he'd not remembered seeing anything unusual in her introduction. New Mexico also had the tail end of the mountains, so it was another possibility, but he didn't remember anything about her introduction either.

Drew texted his parents and asked them to see if they could find out anything about the missing Colorado contestant. Then he texted his boss to ask him to look into the Wyoming accident and the missing Ms. Colorado.

He decided to try to get one of their group close to the Idaho and New Mexico contestants. To see if there was anything unusual about them, when they were up close and personal.

It looked to him like they had a pattern, but why the Rocky Mountain state's contestants were being targeted he had no idea. He hoped they could figure that out before anything else happened.

CHAPTER 19

*L*ily was shaking in her boots, or at least her pretty flats. Colorado, Wyoming, Montana, and Utah contestants looked to have been targeted. What did they all have in common? Ranching, the Rocky Mountains, what else? Clearly it wasn't just her, which in one way was comforting and in another not at all, because it was obvious there was something very bad going on.

Compared to poor Ms. Wyoming, her experience paled in comparison. And where was Ms. Colorado, she hoped and prayed she was okay and just being held captive like Lily had been. What in heavens name was going on? She was going to be glued to Drew every second of every day, he was going to have to pry her off with a crowbar just to pee.

When they started assigning groups to the cars they had, she didn't know if she wanted to be with the other girl with her own bodyguard, too or stay as far away as possible. Would it be safer with two trained men or would they just be a bigger target?

She knew Drew would likely want to talk to the other

bodyguard, to get more information, but that idea kind of scared the crap out of her. Although it didn't look like they were going to have any choice in the matter as they seemed to be assigning cars in alphabetical order, two or three contestants per car.

Lily ended up with Ms. Missouri and Ms. Mississippi. She didn't want to, but she breathed a sigh of relief not to be with the other girls being targeted. As soon as they got in the car the other girls began gushing over Summer, and Lily was perfectly happy to sit back and relax while Summer chatted them up.

Sitting next to Drew's warm body calmed her, even if she could feel his gun at her hip under his duster. It was both a reminder that there might be danger, but also that he was prepared to protect her. Everything seemed to be a double-edged sword and she wasn't sure she liked it one bit. If she hadn't promised Olivia she would be on the next flight back to Montana, but she refused to let fear dictate her life. She was going to see this through. Period.

She was certain that if Olivia knew she was in danger that she would rescind the promise immediately. Lily felt outrage fill her heart, letting someone dictate her life by being evil just didn't sit right with her. She was going to pay attention and see if she couldn't help Drew figure out what was going on, and that meant she needed to get close to Ms. Utah.

She pulled Drew down, so she could whisper in his ear. "So, who besides Ms. Utah?"

He didn't have to ask what she meant. "Idaho and New Mexico."

She nodded to let him know she was on board, with getting close to them.

Katie was sitting on her other side, she got her attention and whispered, "Utah, Idaho, and New Mexico, we need to chat them up. Tell Cade."

Katie squeezed her hand and poked Cade in the shoulder. He turned his head, so Katie could whisper in his ear.

Drew grinned at her and said, "You're one of a kind, sweet Lily."

She snuggled closer to him, happy to have been a help. She wasn't going to cower in some corner and let some jerk take her out of the competition. Nope, she was made of stronger stuff than that. And when fear raised its ugly head again, she was going to remind herself of that. But she wasn't going to turn down the Kipling family's help either.

She wanted to let her mom and dad know too, her dad was good at puzzles and maybe he could help figure it out. They would be arriving tonight, just in time for the gathering to talk about today's observations.

Lily wondered if Adam and Rachel had seen anything yet. Rachel had said she was planning to take pictures of everyone that came close to where she was, and would be using her telephoto lens to get everyone further out. They were going to have a ton of pictures to look through. She didn't know what they might be looking for, but at least it would give them something they could do, besides worry.

When they got to the first stop each contestant was given her sash to wear, Lily wondered if the bad guys already knew her, or whether she was putting on a big fat bullseye. She looked at her sash like it was a snake and then told herself not to be a fool and put it on. At least it would be easy to find the other three they needed to talk to.

She guessed that after those three they might also want to talk to the alternate for Ms. Wyoming, but that was probably further down on the priority list because she probably didn't know a thing.

Since they seemed to be doing everything in alphabetical order, she thought it would probably be easiest to get close to Ms. New Mexico. Everyone seemed to be milling around and not standing in line. They were supposed to be sightseeing, after all.

So, she casually wandered toward Ms. New Mexico and finally saw Adam and Rachel a few yards away. She wanted to laugh at the outfit Adam had on, she'd never seen him in anything besides his cowboy gear, so to see him all dressed in black as a photographer's assistant was amusing.

They weren't supposed to know them though, so she had to keep her surprise and laughter bottled up until later tonight. He didn't look precisely comfortable though. Poor guy. Although she wasn't sure any of them were feeling *comfortable*, this was not an easy thing to do. She squared her shoulders and thought no pain, no gain, and moved up next to Ms. New Mexico.

Lily had to think fast to find a way to engage the woman, she finally decided on shoes. "Your Nina, aren't you? Those shoes are amazing, where did you find them?"

Ms. New Mexico looked at Lily's feet which were in flats, since she could not put too much stress on them while touring. The other woman frowned, but then said, "Yes, Nina is correct, Lily, right?"

Lily nodded but waited for Nina to continue.

"Thanks, we came in early to do some shopping. They *are* cute, but I wonder how my feet will feel about them at the end of the day. You seem to have taken a smarter, if less appealing, approach."

"I have pretty shoes with me for the shoots, but my feet got torn up some last week, so I am trying to be careful with them."

Nina looked a little wary at that statement and gave her 'boyfriend' a quick glance. "Oh, I'm sorry to hear that. I hope they'll be well enough to compete."

"Yes, they are, I'm just going to go easy on them as long as I can."

"That's smart. How did you meet Summer?"

They'd never talked about a story for these kinds of questions, so Lily decided to stick as close to the truth as possible. "My bodyguard knows her. So, when I hired him and told him what I was doing, I guess he mentioned it to her and she wanted to come along. She's great with hair and makeup, but has never been around a pageant, so I thought, why not? Plus, she said it would be fun to meet other contestants and help out where she could."

"So, she's really willing to talk to us other girls? I wondered about that."

"Oh, yes, she's quite social and likes to meet new people. Would you like to talk with her?"

"Sure, but it looks like she's surrounded now, so maybe later."

Lily turned her gaze toward where Nina was looking, and sure enough Summer was surrounded. Cade was frowning, glancing back and forth between Summer and Lily, clearly torn between staying with Summer and helping to guard herself. Drew was close enough to feel the heat from his body and Katie was within a couple of feet, so she didn't think there was anything to worry about.

Lily laughed. "Wow, she really is surrounded, maybe we should make her a schedule. Katie is great with things like that."

Nina's lips curved into a tiny smile. "Might not be a bad idea. I don't know how much free time we're going to have though. They've got our days pretty booked out."

Drew touched her back and she took it to mean he wanted to move. "Yeah, I noticed that too. I'll let Summer know you'd like a few minutes. It was nice chatting with you."

Nina smiled a little larger this time. "Thanks, I'd appreciate that. It was nice talking with you, too."

Drew guided her over near where Summer was holding court and Cade visibly relaxed. Cade said to Drew, "Sorry, I wasn't sure if I should stay with Summer or join you. This is kind of tense, there are so many people around."

Drew nodded. "It is, and we're here primarily to guard Lily, but leaving Summer to fend for herself doesn't seem right either. It's about time for Lily's photos, so let's disengage Summer from the throng and get to the staging area."

Cade turned toward Summer and caught her eye.

She smiled sweetly at the girls. "I need to go help Lily in the staging area, but I'll be happy to talk to the rest of you as we go along. We've got the better part of a week so there's no hurry."

Summer started moving toward Lily and the crowd opened for Summer to join them. When they got to the staging area, Summer sighed. "I had no idea I was going to be so popular. I really am not an expert. I know lots of tricks and tips, but nothing spectacular."

Katie grinned at her friend. "You just keep telling yourself that, so you don't get a big head. Silly girl, you know more than all these others added together."

Summer shrugged. "Let's concentrate on Lily."

Lily changed into her heels while Summer touched up her makeup and fluffed her hair. By the time they'd finished, it was her turn, the only thing bad about that was leaving the other three behind for her time in front of the camera, she felt very alone.

DREW DIDN'T like Lily leaving their protection during the photo shoot. He'd felt she was safe with them all surrounding her, but they couldn't do that during the shoot. He kept his eyes moving over the crowd, not really sure what he was

looking for, just trying to take everything in. Looking for…
something.

Someone out of place, someone too interested, someone
evil looking. He rolled his eyes at himself. Just what would
evil look like? Jack Nicholson in the Shining or Jeffrey
Dahmer? Evil could look like anything.

He simply wanted to get this damn dog and pony show
over with, without Lily getting killed or even hurt. Unfortunately, this was only the first stop of many.

Drew knew he had to use each bit of information he
gained to try to find the whole picture. He began by thinking
about what the look between Ms. New Mexico and her
boyfriend was all about when Lily mentioned her feet being
torn up. Had something happened to Nina? Were they the
instigators? He had no idea, but he was going to make sure
Summer had the chance to chat them up.

He turned to Summer, "Sometime today or this evening,
see if you can have a few minutes alone with Ms. New
Mexico. She had an odd reaction to Lily mentioning her feet
being torn up."

Summer looked to Cade and then nodded. "She'll have
her boyfriend with her, so I'll take Cade with me. I'll see if I
can set up a few minutes after we get back to the hotel."

After the first location went smoothly everything fell into
a rhythm as they went around to the different attractions. He
saw either Adam or Beau with their women and cameras at
each tourist spot, but neither approached him, so he assumed
they hadn't seen anything.

They managed to get close enough to talk to Ms. Idaho at
the Statue of Liberty, but she was so excited to be there that
they didn't get any information about her, or any hint that
she'd had any trouble. They would try again after some of
her excitement about being in New York faded.

Drew couldn't have been more ready to head back to the

hotel when they finally called it a day, they would have two and a half hours before they had to be at the reception, so just enough time to rest for a few minutes and then get dressed up for the next event. He was beginning to think that ranching was far easier than what these contestants were going through.

When they got back to their room he checked to make sure the tape was secure on both doors. Lily had kept the night lock on hers, so no one could get in that way. His tape looked fine, so no one had been in their rooms, however there was a note under Lily's door asking her to call the front desk because they had a delivery for her.

He didn't really like the sound of that, what kind of delivery? Who would send something? Her parents maybe, or his? One of her sponsors? He went into her room while she called and asked the front desk to please take the delivery to his room.

When Drew answered the door, one of the hotel staff handed him a large fruit and snack basket. He tipped the guy and brought it in to set on the table. He handed Lily the card and it said it was from the pageant committee. She was excited to open it, but he still felt uneasy, so he asked her to stand back just in case. She rolled her eyes at him, but did as she was told.

He pulled the cellophane off the basket and heard a slight sound. Lily had heard it too, and her eyes got as big as saucers. "Was that what it sounded like?"

Drew pulled his knife out of his boot. "I hope like hell it wasn't."

She stepped back further as Drew pulled the largest thing he could find out of the basket, a box of chocolates. Sure enough, there was another rattle sound, this time it was louder, more distinct.

He peered into the basket to see if he could see inside, but it was too dark.

He texted Cade to bring ice and hurry. Fortunately, Cade's room wasn't far. Within a few minutes Chase was there with a bag filled with ice and an ice bucket full also, Katie was right behind him.

"Cade sent me. I was bored. What's going on?"

Drew took the ice and put it around the basket. "Rattler in the basket, sent to Lily."

"No shit? Are you trying to put him to sleep or draw him out?"

"Either, got your knife on you?"

Chase nodded. "Hell, yes."

"Get it out. Katie girl?"

Katie was already reaching into her purse. "Absolutely, I don't leave home without it."

Lily had fled to her room, but then she walked back in with a hunting knife that would rival anything they had on them.

Drew was surprised, but not a bit sad to find out there would be someone armed on all four sides of the basket. He looked Lily in the eye. "You know what to do?"

"Yes, I'm from Montana, but I don't really like it."

Drew figured Montana had its share of snakes. He and his brother took opposite sides of the table with Lily and Katie in between. Drew was in front of the hole he'd made and hoped the snake came his way. It didn't take long before he saw movement and then the reptile slid out of the basket. Chase took Katie's place to put both guys on the snake side. As soon as the snake's head hit the table Drew lunged and quickly beheaded the menace. Chase sliced through the body, just a handspan further from the head.

Katie said breathlessly, "Any others?"

Drew nudged the basket and didn't hear anything else moving. So, he pulled out a few other items from the basket. "Nope, just the one I think."

Lily breathed a sigh of relief. "We should empty the basket to make sure."

He nodded. "I agree. Chase and I can do that."

Katie slid her knife back in her purse. "I'll call room service and have them send us up some beers." She looked at Lily. "Unless you prefer wine."

"Beer is good. Whiskey would be better, but we have that damn reception in a while and it's obvious we need to be on our toes."

Drew turned his head slowly towards Lily, the woman was full of surprises. Whiskey? A huge hunting knife in her luggage? What was next? Not that he was against those things and he was glad she hadn't run scared from the snake, but it sure didn't fit his perception of her. "I was hoping that wasn't going to be the case, but it is."

With a grimace Lily asked, "Do you think the food in the basket is poisoned or anything?"

"I doubt it. Everything but the fruit is sealed, and I doubt they took the time to poison it. The snake should have been good enough to knock you out of the running. Even if you quickly got medical care, you wouldn't feel good enough to compete."

Lily nodded. "They didn't count on you being with me, and us all having knives to defend ourselves with."

Katie picked up the card from where Lily had dropped it. "I wonder if all the contestants got baskets."

Chase put his arm around his girl. "That's a darn good question, how can we find out?"

Katie fluttered her eyelashes at him. "I could chat up the hotel staff." Chase frowned.

Lily rolled her eyes at Katie and Chase and their silliness. "We can have Summer ask the ones she'll be talking to."

"I'll text her." Katie got out her phone and sent off a quick text. Within seconds she had a response. "She said no problem. She's meeting Ms. Utah in a few minutes in the lobby."

"Cade's going with her?"

Katie nodded. "We'll sneak Chase back to the room in a bit. Lily, let's go to your room for a while. I don't want to look at that snake or the basket."

Drew dropped the snake pieces into the trash and got a wash cloth from the bathroom to clean the table. Chase cleaned up the ice and dumped it in the bathroom sink to melt. They put the fruit in the fridge and the other food by the TV. Setting the basket outside by the door, hopefully whoever brought the beer would take the basket with them.

When they were done setting the room to rights, Drew looked at his brother. "As long as you're stuck here. Did you find out anything useful today?"

"After you sent me your hypothesis about the girls being targeted all being from the Rocky Mountain states I did some research. I made a table of things they had in common and also things that differed. I didn't really see any patterns, but it's some information to look through."

"Good, we'll do that tonight. Anything else?"

"I walked around the hotel some. Looked over the rooms where everything will be held. Checked out the deets on them. Made a sketch of it all for everyone to take a gander at. Also looked over the sightseeing for tomorrow."

"You were busy." Drew was impressed with his brother's activities.

"You were gone a long time. One thing about the reception tonight?"

"What's that?"

"Well since it's with the mayor and a bunch of other

muckety mucks, they are going to be making everyone go through a metal detector. I'm not certain you'll be able to take your weapon, and for certain, all these knives will never make it through."

"Good to know. Hopefully with heightened security the girls will be safe. I think they'll let me take my gun, I had to get permission from the pageant already, so they know I'm carrying. I'll have my badge with me, so that might help."

"The siblings with cameras are going to come to my room early, so we can look through the pictures. We can tag any we think look interesting."

"Sounds good. Wish we knew what we were looking for."

Chase shrugged. "We'll know it when we see it. At least that's what I'm counting on. Plus, I think with all of us in a room together pouring over the info, maybe lightning will strike with one of us. Lily's parents are coming in before the meeting, right?"

Drew nodded and went to go answer the door, Chase moved out of sight. Drew recognized the delivery person as the same one who had brought the basket, so he took his time signing the check.

"That sure is a nice basket you delivered earlier. I'll bet it took you all day to deliver all of them."

"No not really, there were only a few, not everyone got one. I have to admit we were kind of curious about that."

Drew forced a laugh. "I can imagine. Hopefully, they were all on the same floor."

"Nope, but they never are. Plus, the others were delivered earlier while everyone was out. We couldn't do that with yours because the door was locked and the Do Not Disturb was on."

Drew couldn't think of any way to stall longer, so handed he over the signed check. "Thanks. Do you mind taking the basket with you?"

"Will do."

They all enjoyed a beer as they chatted about inconsequential things. Then it was time to get ready for the reception, so they separated company. Summer, Rachel and one of the twins would be back shortly before they needed to leave the room.

CHAPTER 20

*L*ily washed off her makeup, glad that the reception was over. It had been uneventful, but she'd had trouble relaxing and had been jumpy. She'd had to work hard to chat with the dignitaries and pageant staff. She wished she could just relax, but they still had to go meet with everyone to talk about everything they'd learned today.

There was no way she was staying in that room by herself and she knew Drew needed to be in on the discussion, so she would pull on some sweats and sneakers and go with him. She hoped no one would recognize her. Summer had brought some huge glasses with her that Lily was going to wear. They were clear glass and Lily assumed they were the glasses Drew said she'd worn to hide behind. Lily had a scarf to cover her hair, how Drew was going to look any different she had no idea, but he'd told her not to worry.

When she walked into his room she laughed out loud. Drew was dressed in the rattiest pair of sweats she'd ever seen and nearly decrepit high-top tennis shoes. He had a baseball hat on backward and carried a gym bag. He'd done something to make his short beard look almost like it was black.

"You look like a bum, you might get us tossed out of this hotel walking around like that."

He shrugged and shuffled over to her, making her want to hoot with laughter. He normally had a strong loose hipped gait that made it look like he was in charge, but also that he didn't have anything to prove. This time he'd stuck his butt out, hunched over, and shuffled his feet.

He snorted and then wheezed out, "I have no idea what you're talking about, missy."

She couldn't stop her shout of laughter, he'd pitched his voice higher than normal and given it a nasally sound. "You cannot talk like that, I'm going to fall down laughing."

"It's not nice to laugh at the way people talk."

She decided to give him some of his own medicine, so she dug her finger in her nose, and said with a pronounced lisp, "Tho, we thould probably thtart toward Chatheth room, it might take uth thome time to get there."

Drew grinned, "I'm ready if you are, missy."

"Let'th go."

They teased and laughed all the way down the hall to where the meeting was to be held. It was good to laugh, she'd been so tense all day. They didn't even see anyone in the hall, so the disguises hadn't been necessary, but Lily was glad they'd done it, because it had lightened her mood and given her the energy for what was next.

When they knocked on the door Cade answered, and he'd rolled his eyes at his brother. "I see you broke out Dufus, for the occasion."

Lily laughed and they walked in the door. "You mean he's done this before?"

"It's his favorite. Did he shuffle all the way down the hall with his ass sticking out?"

She nodded and took off the glasses and scarf she'd donned. "We were both trying to make the other one laugh. I think he won, I couldn't help it, he's so good at it."

Chase walked over and slapped his brother on the back. "He's had practice."

Lily's phone pinged. "Mom and Dad will be here in five minutes."

Drew looked around the room. "That will be everyone then. Did you find anyone on the pictures?"

Rachel said, "Maybe, no one that really stands out, just normal looking people, but we got some repeats, not with the pageant."

Drew said, "Let's see them. You do realize they aren't going to look like Cruella de Vil, right?"

Rachel elbowed Drew. "Of course, silly. So, there is this guy. He shows up in about half the locations and then we don't see him at all toward the end of the trip."

"Anyone else?"

"Yeah, this lady with the two kids and I assume, husband, they all look like they're having a good time until this older woman comes on the scene and starts talking to them. The guy says a few words and then gets all sullen and walks off. Once the guy left, the older woman got out wipes and began scrubbing on the kids, who don't look happy at all about that. We didn't see them again after that stop."

"Looks like a mother-in-law bossing around the couple, and the guy is a chickenshit that won't stand up for his wife."

"Could be her own mom," Beau said.

Lily didn't think so, but wasn't entirely sure why.

Alyssa shook her head. "No if it was, she'd tell her mom to back off. I would, even with my step-mom. Harder to do that with a mother-in-law."

Yeah, that sounded right to Lily.

Alyssa said, "We got one other, but the person is so far

away it's hard to see him or maybe her, but I'm going with him. His face is always behind a camera. But he was at every stop, in both our pictures and Rachels, seems a little too coincidental to me."

"I agree. Rachel did you zoom in on him?"

"Yeah but it didn't do me any good. His, or her, camera really shielded his face and you can see he's got a hat on low and non-descript clothes."

"Why can't villains look like villains, like they do in Disney movies. No question that Cruella de Vil or Ursula are the villains. Even Cinderella's step-mother clearly looks evil," Lily complained.

Drew laughed. "I wish that was true, Lily, so much easier to know to arrest the big octopus. Instead of some guy with a camera."

Cade opened the door when a knock sounded, and Lily's parents walked in.

"Mom, Dad, so happy to see you," she hugged both her parents. "Did you have a good flight?"

"It was fine, I would rather be in my own truck however, we got the dumbest little rental car. We could barely get our suitcase in," her dad complained.

Elaine rolled her eyes at her husband. "Howard don't be a putz, it's easier to park than your enormous truck, and it was too far to drive."

She turned, and stage whispered to the rest of them. "It *was* hard to get the luggage in. I can't imagine trying to haul groceries with that."

They all laughed and settled in to continue.

Drew quickly caught her parents up with all that had happened since arriving in New York.

Howard said, "Rocky Mountain states, huh? That's rather curious isn't it."

While Elaine shrieked, "A rattlesnake? Seriously? What is

wrong with these people? What if that got loose in the hotel? Do they even have anti-venom in New York City? Thank God the four of you know what you're doing around those things. Now that just pisses me off."

Mama-bear was on a roll, Lily knew it could go on for days. If they did find out who the culprit was, her mother would be giving them a talking to that would make their ears ring for years, hopefully while they were behind bars.

"Elaine, stop, everyone is fine."

Her mom put her hands on her hips. "Unless there was more than one, what if the other girls got a snake and didn't know what to do. There could be others roaming the halls."

Lily hadn't thought about that. Her mom was right, it could be a disaster. They needed to let the pageant people and maybe the hotel security know, asap. She looked at Drew who had apparently realized the same thing.

DAMMIT, what if Lily's mom was right and there were more damn snakes in the hotel? It hadn't occurred to him. Drew looked at Lily and she'd clearly come to the same realization he had. "I'll call the front desk, you call the number they gave you for pageant emergencies. I doubt they had anything like this in mind."

He told Adam, "Keep the discussion going, we need to figure out who these assholes are. We'll go talk to security in our hotel room and be back once they've gone."

Adam fist bumped his brother, "You got it, hope you're back soon.

Lily and Drew hightailed it back to their room as soon as they'd made the calls. There was no joking around this time. They'd barely gotten the door open when a half dozen people showed up.

The head of hotel security, a Mr. Clark said, "Tell me what happened."

Drew quickly related the basket story.

Mr. Clark looked at his second-in-command. "We got another call about a rattler. The people killed it the same as you did. Any idea what's going on?"

Drew and Lily quickly went over what had happened to her prior to coming to the pageant.

When they were finished Drew said, "I think you should check the other contestants from the Rocky Mountain states. Was the other snake in Ms. Utah, Ms. Idaho or Ms. New Mexico's room? Did she have a basket, too?"

The head of security talked it over with the security for the pageant and it was quickly discovered that the snake had been in Ms. New Mexico's room and yes, they had seen a basket of goodies in the room when they had responded to the call. Although the occupants didn't know the snake had come from the basket. They'd stated when they'd gotten back from the sightseeing trip they'd found it curled up on the floor near the heater.

"I think you better check on Ms. Utah, Ms. Idaho, and Ms. Wyoming just to be safe."

Mr. Clark said, "We'll check with the delivery service, they will have a log of everyone who got a basket. That way if your hunch is wrong, we won't miss one."

"If you wouldn't mind letting me know I would appreciate it. I am a police officer, well a sheriff, but I got my degree and passed the academy, so I would be happy to help."

Mr. Clark looked at Drew for a long moment then nodded. "I think I can do that. And you'll let us know what you discover."

It wasn't a question, but he answered it anyway. "I will, indeed."

The pageant security head ran a hand around the back of

his neck. "So now we know why Ms. Colorado didn't show. Has anyone put in a missing person on her?"

Drew folded his arms. "My boss did, when they said she hadn't shown up."

The man shuffled from foot to foot. "Good, good. It never occurred to me. I'm used to keeping fans back, and helping the girls keep track of their things, nothing like this. I'm going to need to get the pageant officials in on this. We'll need to decide what we should do."

Drew said, "If I could make a suggestion?"

"By all means."

"Get some more trained security in here but don't pull the plug, these people need to be stopped and brought to justice. They've killed at least one person, put another in the hospital, and a third is missing. We need to catch them."

Mr. Clark nodded. "I agree, they brought dangerous animals into my hotel, endangering my guests, they need to pay."

Drew asked, "Can we all convene in the morning to talk this out?"

Mr. Clark said, "I think that's an excellent idea. Seven? I'll find us a board room that's not being used." He looked at Drew. "You said Ms. Utah has a bodyguard and you think Ms. New Mexico's boyfriend might be doing the same?"

"Yes."

"When I check their rooms, I'll invite them along."

Drew didn't think there was anything wrong with that, as long as one of them were not the perps. Even if they were, maybe they could flush them out. "Sounds reasonable, although it would leave the contestants vulnerable."

He flashed his glance at Lily. "Good point. What do you plan to do about that?"

Drew grinned with a sly expression. "I brought back-up."

Mr. Clark rubbed his chin. "Sworn in back-up?"

"Nope, family."

Mr. Clark looked around the room where Drew's cowboy hat, boots, hunting knife, and duster were in evidence. "Cowboys? Will they help if we need them?"

"Ranchers. Absolutely."

"I'll be in touch."

CHAPTER 21

*D*rew needed to get down the hall to see what the others had come up with. He now had the head of security's cell number, so if they'd discovered anything they could let him know. He'd also given Mr. Clark his brother's cell numbers, just in case. He was so proud of Lily, all during the security conversation she'd been engaged. He'd taken lead, but she filled in when it was appropriate.

When they'd asked to see the snake, she hadn't hesitated, but had pulled it from the trash, she was clearly made of sterner stuff than he'd realized. Katie wouldn't have touched it unless there was no other choice, and even then, she would have tried to use the ice tongs or a towel or something.

It was a small snake, as far as that went, they wouldn't have been able to use too large of one in the baskets without it being seen. Smaller rattlers were sometimes the most deadly. She'd handed the snake to Mr. Clark and said that they'd cut off maybe six inches. The pageant security had practically passed out and even the indomitable Mr. Clark had looked a little green holding the snake.

They'd found a bag to put it, and the other pieces in, not

SHIRLEY PENICK

wanting to scare the maids, which he'd not even thought of.
It might have scared them half to death. Especially if they
moved the bag enough to set off the rattle. Much better to
have security take it.

He hoped like hell they could find any others that might
have been brought in. It could be a matter of life and death if
someone got bitten and they didn't know what to do or
didn't have any anti-venom in the city. He had no idea what
kind of snakes lived in New York, but he doubted many of
them would be in the downtown area.

He and Lily got back to the room to find a lively conversation going on about who might be behind all of this. The
group quieted when they joined them.

Cade was the first to ask, "What did they say?"

"There was another snake in Ms. New Mexico's room. We
told them our theories and they are going to go check in the
rooms of the rest of the ones we suspect are being targeted.
They're also going to look up who had a basket delivery, in
case we're dead wrong."

Alyssa said, "My gut tells me we're not wrong, but I'd be
glad to know there aren't random snakes roaming the halls."

Katie and Summer both shivered.

Beau looked at Alyssa and then back to Drew. "We have
some anti-venom in the med kit."

Alyssa nodded. "Of course, we do. I hadn't thought about
it. We've got enough for a couple of cattle, we always keep it
on hand. That amount would work for a number of people.
Good thinking, honey."

Drew pulled out his phone and texted the information to
Mr. Clark, who immediately acknowledged him.

"I gave the hotel security officer your cell numbers. He
asked if you would be willing to help, if needed. I told him
yes. The pageant security is pretty worthless, they're not
prepared for anything on this scope. I urged them to find

some who would be better. We're having a meet-and-greet tomorrow at seven. I was thinking the girls and Chase could gather together in my and Lily's room and the rest of us guys could meet with the security detail."

Drew held up a hand. "Before you ladies say anything, it has nothing whatsoever to do with your capability to kick ass. I just don't want all of us in the same room at the same time. Plus, I want to keep the twins a secret a little longer."

The ladies shot looks at each other and Alyssa said, "We can live with that."

Drew relaxed and asked Adam, "So, what did I miss?"

Adam quickly filled him in on what they'd done in his absence, and the ideas they had for tomorrow. Drew couldn't see anything wrong with what they'd said.

Lily was shooting her father puzzled looks, but he didn't notice, he was studying something on Chase's computer. Drew asked, "Mr. Smith, what is it that has you so intrigued?"

Howard looked up. "I can't quite put my finger on it, but something is tugging at me as I look over the lists Chase made of the Rocky Mountain contestants and their similarities and differences. Can I get a paper copy to take with me?"

Lily smiled at her father. "He can send you the file, daddy."

"I know Lily-bug, but I want to be able to write on them."

Chase pulled some papers from a bag. "I know how you feel, sir. I like paper too. So, I printed some off. Who else wants a copy?"

Several of them did, including Drew. Chase had plenty of copies of both that, and the maps he'd made of the hotel and the sightseeing route for tomorrow. Drew decided to look at the lists tomorrow but had Chase plug his computer into the TV so they could all look at the maps together.

There was a lot of good information Chase had gathered,

but Drew decided to see if he could get a more detailed map of the hotel tomorrow morning at the strategy meeting.

Before they broke up for the night he asked Rachel and Alyssa to send him the photos of the people they'd seen in common on the pictures. And he asked Chase to send him an electronic copy of the contestant lists. He wanted to share those, tomorrow morning, with whatever security was gathered.

Mr. Clark might be able to use the pictures to see if any of those people showed up on the hotel security feed.

LILY WAS EXHAUSTED by the time they got back to their room. The day had taken a toll on her. She'd had to be on and perky all day and then the rattlesnake had freaked her out more than she'd let on. She knew she could have killed it, but she was glad the guys had done it. And when Katie had been squeamish about it, Lily hadn't hesitated to leave the room and let the men deal with the mess.

She didn't like the fact that they were still in danger, whoever it was that Ronald was working for, were not nice people. They clearly didn't care if there were rattlers roaming the halls. She hoped like hell someone could figure out what was going on and stop these madmen.

Lily quickly got ready for bed and joined Drew in his room. No way in hell was she sleeping alone. When she got to his room he was studying the lists Chase had given him. She knew he might want to stay up longer, but she needed his warmth, her blood felt like it was ice water.

"Come to bed Drew, you need sleep before you meet with everyone tomorrow."

"I need to figure out who is trying to hurt you, Lily. Go ahead to bed, I'll join you in a while." He waved his hand vaguely toward the bed, not taking his gaze from the papers.

Lily got behind him, wrapped her arms around him, and laid her head on his back. "No, Drew, please come to bed. I need you to help me feel safe."

He must have noticed the tremble in her voice because he put the papers down and turned in her arms. "I'm going to keep you safe, Lily."

"I know, but I just feel cold. You could warm me up. I have more condoms." She held out her hand to show him.

"Oh, Lily you don't have to bribe me with sex."

She looked up through her lashes at him. "No bribery. I just think I'll sleep better if we indulge. Don't you think?"

He laughed a strangled laugh. "It would relax us, and warm you up. It's been kind of a tense day."

She gave him a sultry smile and started pulling at his sweats. He'd already taken off his high tops, so it didn't take her long to get him undressed. When she dropped the hotel robe to the floor she saw him swallow. It was very gratifying to see he liked the skimpy negligee.

"You are so gorgeous and I'm very glad that Ronald never got to see you in this. Nothing, no amount of money is worth this sight."

She thrilled at his words. "I'm happy to be showing it to you, too. Ronald and I never totally clicked like you and I do. It was always a chore to be intimate with him."

Drew put his fingers to her lips. "Let's not talk about the not so dearly departed."

She kissed his fingers and smiled. "Excellent idea."

Lily let Drew wrap his arms around her and pull her in close to kiss her. She quickly engaged, but as they tasted each other she inched him ever so slowly toward the bed. Lips and tongue began the dance, and she wanted to continue it with him on his back, and her on top.

She wanted to set the pace and ride him. He'd taken the reins before in their love making, but now it was her turn, again. When she got him to the bed she nudged him down and followed. She rose up and straddled him so her hot core was almost where she wanted it, but first she tossed all but one condom on the bedside table and then tore open the last one. She took her time rolling it on him, teasing him as much as he could stand, without him trying to usurp her.

When she had them both fully protected, she rose up and slid down along his hot length, and he slid right into her wet channel, filling her gloriously. She arched her back and he slid in a tiny bit further and groaned.

Lily smiled at the sexy sound and leaned forward so her breasts dangled above him. He took the hint and filled his hands, flicking his thumbs over her straining nipples. The sensations shot more warmth between her legs and she started to ride. Slowly at first, tensing her inner muscles, as she pulled up, squeezing him and making him hiss with pleasure.

His hands moved to her hips to encourage her to move faster and that suited her just fine, so she complied with his unspoken request. Faster and harder she went pleasuring herself and him at the same time. He used one hand to tweak one nipple and then the other and she felt her release gathering, so she rode harder, wanting him to join her when she came.

Drew rose up to meet her as she came down and his expression was tense, so she knew he was as close as she was. Her orgasm swamped her, and she tensed her muscles as tight as she could, so he followed her into the abyss. His cock pumped inside her as her muscles milked him of his seed. When the tension eased she lay down atop him, sweaty and spent.

Their hearts galloped in tandem and their breathing was

rough. She reached back and pulled the sheets over the top of them, not yet ready to separate from their intimate coupling. He pulled her chin up so he could cover his mouth with hers. Kissing her softly, slowly like they had all night. She reveled in the touch, in the gentleness after their wild ride. Wishing they could stay like this forever in the sanctity of his room.

The world was waiting outside their door, where danger was lurking. But for now, she was relaxed, warm, and protected. Safe, she was safe.

CHAPTER 22

$\mathcal{D}$rew woke to the alarm he'd set on his phone, grateful they'd gotten a good night's sleep. Mr. Clark had texted him last night, while Lily was sending him to nirvana, to say they'd found one more basket that hadn't been opened, the snake was peacefully sleeping. It was now also in pieces and had been removed from the room. The staff had said that was all the baskets they had been delivered, so Mr. Clark had decided not to go to the other two contestants' rooms and bother them.

Lily was wrapped around him, sleeping deeply. He'd been concerned that maybe she was too keyed up to sleep but the bout of sex had used them both up and they'd slept well. Today was another day, and he had a meeting to be at in an hour. He needed a shower and coffee.

He didn't want to wake Lily, but she would need to get dressed, so when the ladies and Chase descended she was ready. He thought the gentlest way to wake her would be with the smell of coffee, so he started some up in the tiny coffee maker in his room. He wondered if he should brew some in her tiny coffee pot too, but then decided to shower first and fill the second pot once he was dressed.

When he emerged from the shower she was sitting up in his bed, a cup of coffee in her hands. Her hair was a rat's nest, from his hands last night, and she had on the hotel robe, her eyes sleepy and her lips curved in a Madonna-like smile. He leaned down to kiss her. She tasted like coffee and sexy woman.

"Good morning lovely lady, I see the coffee called out to you."

"It did, I almost came to join you in the shower, but I couldn't get beyond the coffee. If you'd woken me, we could have had morning sex in the shower."

Drew swallowed hard at the seduction in her voice and turned to pour his own coffee. "Maybe next time when we don't have hordes of people about to come into our room."

She quickly looked at the bedside clock, then relaxed. "Plenty of time to get dressed."

"Only because we didn't have morning sex in the shower."

She laughed, and the sound shimmered through him, igniting every nerve. "That's probably true."

He came back to the bed with his coffee and kissed her nose. "Definitely true. When I get you all wet and soapy in the shower, it's not going to be a quick encounter. It will be a long, slow, slippery, experience, and then we'll have to start over to get clean. We definitely would not be ready for guests any time soon."

She shivered. "I'm going to hold you to that."

He grinned at her. "Good."

She looked at her almost empty coffee cup. "That tiny pot is not nearly enough coffee."

"I was going to brew some in yours too, but you distracted me. Here you take the last in this one and I'll start some in your pot. That should tide us over until the family arrives. They are going to hit the coffee shop downstairs and bring food and more coffee with them."

Lily watched him pour the last of the pot into her cup with a greedy expression. "Excellent, even half of two of those tiny pots in these miniscule cups are not going to get me going. Although I did sleep well, did you?"

"Yep, like the dead. Your relaxation techniques worked like a charm."

A slow smile slid across her face and lit up her eyes. "Happy to be of service."

Desire slid through him, hot, and sharp, and demanding. "Now, you stop that. Come on let's go to your room. The coffee can brew while you shower. We won't have a lot of time after the briefing before the next sightseeing trip around Manhattan."

"All right. I suppose that's true. I'd much rather spend the day in here with you, than go traipse around being a tourist. We could think of new ways to 'relax'. Handcuffs might be fun."

Drew groaned as the vision of Lily stretched out on the bed unable to move while he enjoyed every inch of her body, filled his thoughts. "Lily, I beg you, stop. I have to go meet with a whole ton of security people, and I don't want to be hard as a rock when I do."

The woman had the gall to look him over and lick her lips. "I could help with that."

He groaned. "No, we don't have time, now get your sexy ass into the shower."

She stood and stretched, a long sensuous movement that had his eyes crossing in lust, then she started for the door. Before she reached it she looked back over her shoulder and said, "And if I don't, what are you going to do? Spank me?"

Dear God, the woman had him on a razor's edge. Then she turned off the sexy like it was a switch and grinned at him standing there swamped in lust. "Coffee, you were going to make coffee."

She skipped out of the door like a little girl, and he dragged the ragged scraps of his control back around him. Lord have mercy the woman was dangerous with a capital D. Then again, she'd given him some ideas for when this damn mess was over, maybe they could spend a few days trying out her ideas before they had to go back to their real lives.

He went to make coffee when he heard her shower come on, the idea of going back to their lives weighing heavily on his heart, he was going to miss her like crazy. He was totally certain of that, and not sure how he would be able to let her go. He had to remind himself, they were from totally different planets. He was a cowboy cop and she was a princess. He shook his head at the foolish thought, but it didn't go away, she was high class, beautiful, and not for the likes of him.

Although she did seem pretty familiar with a hunting knife, and she'd made no bones about running out of the woods barefoot or picking up snakes. Maybe she had a side that was more down to earth. But no, he had to be strong, she wouldn't be happy on a cattle ranch, she was meant for the bright lights of a city, even if it was in Montana.

When the coffee was brewing, he went back to his room to gather what he needed to take with him to the security meeting. He straightened his sheets and pulled the blankets over the top. Shoved the condom evidence deep in the larger trash can and took Lily's negligee to her room. He didn't need to advertise to his family that the two of them were intimate.

When everything was ready, he went over and poured himself another cup of coffee. Lily had opened the bathroom door and he could hear the hair dryer. They didn't have much time before they had to face the day. The pageant would commence in earnest tomorrow, and he wondered if the powers of evil would stop then, or if their attempts would grow more desperate.

Regardless, time was of the essence, they needed to stop these people before someone else got hurt or killed. He was determined it would not be Lily, but he was ready to protect all the girls.

He heard Lily's hair dryer turn off and noticed she was humming. He smiled at the tuneless sound, the girl wasn't a great singer, it made her seem more real, less perfect.

There was a knock at the door and he looked out the peephole to see Katie wave. He opened the door and they all trooped in bringing a wave of coffee and pastry scents with them. His stomach growled as the sugary, yeasty smell enveloped him.

They set everything down on the counter by the TV since his table would barely hold two cups of coffee.

Rachel stuck her head into Lily's door. "We have coffee and very bad for you, pastries, come have some."

He heard Lily cheer, "Yay! I'll be right there."

They all dug in and Lily pushed her way through to grab an enormous cheese Danish. She took one bite and moaned in pleasure. "I haven't had anything naughty like this, since I joined this damn pageant. The days of eating kale and salad and no carbs are over."

Summer said, "But what if you win and then have to go on to the International pageant?"

Lily's mouth dropped open. "Oh no! I don't think I can do this for another six months. I can't win. Someone else has to! Darn it Summer, why did you have to say that?"

Lily looked at her treat in horror.

Finally, she took another bite and smiled. "I refuse to win. I will not give up this delicious cheese Danish. I *am* going to eat every bite and lick my fingers. Then I'm going to drink that enormous coffee, to the very last drop. I don't care. I refuse to care. If I win, I'll decide what to do after that."

Drew watched her gobble her Danish with glee, she was not feeling any guilt, that was for darn sure. He was glad, she was determined to do well in the pageant, but it clearly wasn't her whole life. She seemed to love food and although she'd been eating very healthy when he found her, it was obvious that was for a very specific reason.

He liked her discipline but was glad to see she also liked to enjoy herself. He hoped all the coffee and sugar didn't upset her stomach after so long of not indulging. She'd had coffee for a couple of days now and had relaxed her eating a little bit at a time since they got to New York, so he hoped she would be fine.

He looked at the time and then at his brothers. "We need to get a move on. Chase, ladies, we'll be back soon with the new plans."

LILY WATCHED as the guys trooped out of the door on their way to the security meeting. She didn't mind staying back, she'd seen enough last night, and it had made her tense and worried, so letting the men handle it was just fine with her. She wasn't created to be a cop, that was for darn sure. She could hold her own if she needed to, but she was okay with letting someone else run the show.

Summer looked at her and said, "We need to get you camera ready, let's get cracking."

Alyssa asked, "Can we watch? I'm not much of a makeup person, but it would be fun to see the magic happen."

Summer shrugged. "Fine with me."

Lily had no qualms about them watching, so if Summer

was good with it, so was she. "Come on over, we'll have a makeup party."

Chase grinned and gave an exaggerated shudder. "I think I'll pass, I don't want to have to turn in my man card."

Katie laughed and punched him on the shoulder. "As if." Then she looked over and said in a sultry voice. "I'll just stay here and keep my guy company. Since I got to watch yesterday, and Summer's already taught me some tricks."

Chase's eyebrows had shot up. "You're going to keep me company?"

"Yes. I'll give you something to think about the rest of the day, until we get back."

Lily smirked, realizing Chase was going to be getting the same treatment she'd given to Drew earlier. The other women gave Katie verbal encouragement and some catcalls. Chase had the ability to look both nervous and excited at the same time.

Summer put Lily in the chair she'd used yesterday and laid all her 'tools of beauty' on the little table. Alyssa and Rachel sat in chairs where they could easily see what Summer was doing, without getting in the way. Lily had laid the outfit she was planning to wear today out on the bed, so all she needed to do was let Summer work her magic.

While Summer buzzed around her, explaining what she was doing to the other girls, Lily thought about what it would be like to have Drew as 'her guy'. She decided that she wouldn't mind that a bit, and began thinking about her life, and if maybe she was ready for some changes. Of course, she didn't know if Drew was at all interested in that, but it wouldn't hurt for her to think about it. Would it?

CHAPTER 23

The security summit, as Drew was calling it, lasted two hours. Mr. Clark had called in all of the hotel security staff, some private security, and the New York City police. As the meeting progressed he found out they'd even talked about bringing in the Feds, with the intrastate connections it would make sense.

The bodyguard for Ms. Utah had said she'd pulled him in after an attempted kidnapping, and the boyfriend of Ms. New Mexico related a similar story. Although he admitted that they'd not thought it had anything to do with the pageant and thought she'd been targeted by the sex trade, with them living so close to the Mexican border. They'd both been relieved to find out it was about the pageant.

They'd gone over all the information Drew had gathered and made lots more copies of the photos and Chase's lists. No one had scoffed at his methods or thought processes. On the contrary, they'd all been very attentive and had thanked him for sharing what he'd learned.

Drew was relieved that the girls were going to be better protected as they traveled around the city. There would be an obvious police escort and also several undercover officers travelling with the group and keeping a close watch on the Rocky Mountain states' contestants. The New York City police also like the idea of the cameras and were going to have four officers working the photo shoot areas like Adam and Beau had done yesterday with their ladies.

They also talked about security for the reception being held with the sponsors and pageant officials. They planned for a debrief after the reception, and another strategy meeting in the morning, before the pageant events started.

The brothers walked back to Drew's room in relative silence, not wanting to talk about anything until they were safely in his room where they could speak freely without any chance of being overheard.

When they got to his room, he was glad to see Lily ready, and looking so gorgeous he wanted to worship at her feet. Today she had on a red dress that swirled around her knees and pretty red shoes that were flats, he assumed Summer had the sexy shoes Lily would change into for the actual photo shoots.

Lily's parents had joined the group and Drew was exceptionally glad he'd hid the evidence of their sexual encounters. He had to admit that they were probably more concerned about her safety, than they would be about her amorous activities, but still.

Howard immediately asked how the security meeting went, which confirmed the thought Drew had just had. Lily's parents visibly relaxed as he told them all about what was being done to keep all the contestants safe, with a special eye towards the girls from the Rocky Mountain states.

Drew said, "The only one that doesn't seem to be a target so far is Ms. Idaho, so there was talk of having a security officer join the maids when they cleaned the room, just to see what they could see."

Lily shook her head. "Oh, she's such a nice girl. I can't even imagine her doing something like this."

Chase shrugged. "Maybe it's someone associated with her, and not actually her, doing it."

Howard shot Chase a quick glance. "There is something about the sponsor list that I keep looking at. I still haven't put my finger on it, but something about it seems odd."

"There will be a reception tonight with the sponsors, contestants, and pageant officials, maybe you'll get an inkling about it then, daddy."

"Well I'm going to keep that list in my hands until then. Maybe it will hit me."

Rachel looked at her phone and then at Adam. "We've got the first photo op, let's go get in place."

Adam nodded, and they said their goodbyes. Beau and Alyssa decided the same thing and left on their heels. Drew gave Chase a look and the two of them convened to a corner, so Drew could give his brother some more information and talk about what Chase might want to do while he was at the hotel that day. Howard joined the discussion, since he and Elaine were also unknowns at this time.

Drew decided the older couple could visit some of the sightseeing locations, just to be another pair of eyes. But they didn't need to go to all of them, so they were free to pick and choose and then return back to the hotel whenever they wanted to. He didn't want them to be too obviously interested in the pageant group so that they weren't targeted by the extra security.

Once Lily's parents had their 'assignment' they left to go get ready to be out of the hotel for a few hours at least. Chase would hang out in the room for a while until he was certain all the contestants were out of the hotel then he would commence his surveillance. The five in Lily's entourage would leave together and join up with the other contestants to be assigned tour groups.

There had been a lively discussion, during the security meeting, on whether to keep all the Rocky Mountain girls in one group or spread them out. It was finally decided that it would look too odd to have them all in one group surrounded by security, so they were splitting them up. They wanted to catch the people threatening the girls, not just scare them off.

Drew wanted to catch them too, but not at the risk of Lily's safety. So, he planned to stick to her like glue, and so did Cade.

LILY HAD WANTED to see Manhattan before all the trouble began but now she would much rather stay in the hotel room with Drew where there was little threat of danger. She knew the whole time they were out running around the city; she would be on alert.

She wished this darn pageant was over, so she could settle back down to being her own self, and not have to be constantly watchful. Of course, that would also mean she wouldn't be with Drew, which was beginning to feel less and less attractive to her. She really enjoyed his company. He was efficient and careful to keep her safe without being a dick about it.

During down time he was funny, and they enjoyed the same things. The sex was off the charts, she'd never been so free with a man, or so playful. He could play her body like a finely-tuned instrument. His family was exceptional, coming out like this to protect her when they'd only known her a few days. They'd all put their lives on hold without batting an eye.

Her family was wonderful too, and she loved them, but she doubted they would have been so giving.

Lily sighed as they got to the room where they were all meeting to go off sightseeing and doing photo shoots.

Drew whispered in her ear, "What was the sigh for?"

"Just another day of being treated like cattle, go here, get a picture taken, go there, look at the sight, then on to the next place and more pictures. I'm ready to move on past this stage."

Drew chuckled and then mooed in her ear. She elbowed him as they shuffled forward to take their place. The first part of the excursion was on a double decker bus, where they would tour the outskirts, and then come back for a walking tour and the photo shoots would begin in earnest. Each small group had a slightly different pattern, so they weren't all in one place at one time, but they would hit every location.

When they got on the tour bus she tried to be friendly to everyone. Usually it wasn't a problem, but today she was just not feeling like her sweet self. They had decided, while they were waiting, to sit in the lower section of the bus, so they were not quite so exposed. All the other girls had made a beeline for the roof to see better, so it left them relatively alone on the bottom level.

When they got to the Brooklyn Bridge, they were all glued to the windows.

Lily whispered to Drew, "All right, this sight makes it worth it."

Drew agreed with her, but still let out a tiny moo.

Central Park was also amazing, it was such a huge park. They did have a photo shoot in the park at an iconic location. She saw Alyssa and Beau off in the distance taking pictures. She wanted to wave, but had to stop herself, they weren't supposed to know each other.

When they trooped back on the bus, Ms. Oregon asked

them if they wanted to trade and ride on top. Lily thanked her for her offer but told her they were just fine on the lower level.

The Empire State Building was a fun stop and they got their pictures taken there also. Her mom and dad were there, playing tourist. Looking out over the city with the machines made for that, and taking lots of pictures with their phones. It was fun to see them enjoying themselves or at least pretending to.

After they got back to their seats, Lily hoped there weren't too many more photo ops, she was getting tired of getting on and off the bus, she was not a glutton for punishment like some people.

When they got to Times Square, Lily was perfectly happy to leave the bus behind and start the walking tour, although she hadn't realized how many people would be crammed into the area.

When they'd gotten off the bus, she'd noticed a couple of guys give Drew a look and then one went next to Cade in the front and one went by Drew behind her. She was now surrounded by six people. She was glad to be encircled by her entourage, because that meant someone would have to go to great lengths to get to her.

They moved through the crowd as a block and people had to flow around them. Some people glared at them for not breaking apart, but they just continued as they were. People would just have to glare.

She heard the man next to Drew murmur something, but she couldn't hear what was said, about the same time the man next to Cade nodded to the left and they steered in that direction. She wasn't sure where they were headed, but if Drew and Cade were okay with it, then so was she. Lily had to assume they were part of the security detail that had been put in force.

They went into the lobby of a different hotel and over to a quiet corner. The guy that was with Drew said, "We wanted to let you know that Ms. Utah was nearly hit with a pressure syringe earlier. Her bodyguard stopped the attack and we have the perp in custody, but he's not talking. The contents of the syringe would not have killed her, but it would have made her very sick. She would not have been able to compete."

The other guy that was walking with Cade said, "We'll need to stay alert, in case there are more people out there with syringes, he only had three on him, so we don't know if that means there's a second guy out there, or if there are only three contestants being targeted at this time. We're going to keep you surrounded while you finish the tour and photo shoots."

The first guy rubbed the back of his neck. "The police officials have decided to call in the Feds, so we don't know what will happen when they come in. They might go right over our heads and take control, or they might come in as more feet on the ground and let us handle it as we planned. We won't know more until later tonight."

Drew said, "Even if they go over our heads and change things up, it will still put more eyes and ears on the situation, and that can't be a bad thing. At least in my opinion."

Lily nodded and then said, "I'm glad Ms. Utah wasn't hurt. She must have a great bodyguard. Of course, so do I. I have a whole six-pack of them."

The first guy chuckled. "Yeah, her bodyguard is some kind of martial arts master. He had the dickhead with the syringe disarmed and in a strangle hold before the perp got within a foot of Ms. Utah. She's a little shook up, but continued right on with the tour. Her bodyguard was glued to her side, and she's got a couple of plain clothed officers with her, also."

Cade said, "We should probably get back out there. We don't want to hold anything up and cause a commotion."

They got back in formation and walked in lock step out onto the busy streets of Manhattan. Fortunately, there were no more incidents of trouble.

.

CHAPTER 24

$\mathcal{D}$rew was getting all dressed up for the reception that evening. He'd decided to go all cowboy cop, for the night's entertainment. His boots were polished, his hat was brushed, he'd put on his best string tie, and he wore his badge and gun.

Chase had reported that there was some discussion among the staff setting up the reception about the seating arrangements, but he hadn't been able to find out what it was about. Drew didn't want to take any chances, so he was dressing to the hilt. He just hoped his full-on cowboy cop gear didn't embarrass Lily. He looked good, but he was still shouting at the top of his lungs, 'hick'.

When Lily was ready she joined him in her room. His heart virtually stopped when she walked in, she was so gorgeous. She wore a long sheath dress in deep blue that hugged her curves and dipped low both in front and in back. His mouth went dry as he took in her magnificence. She had what looked like diamonds in her ears, and in a necklace that dipped tantalizingly low toward the shadowy area between her breasts. He stood stone still, not moving a muscle, barely breathing, because he wanted to take her in his arms, kiss her senseless and then strip that delicious dress off of her, so he could worship her body for hours.

She looked up shyly. "Do I look okay?"

"Okay? No, you don't look okay. You look amazing. Magnificent. You put the stars to shame. Lily, my God if we didn't have to be downstairs in fifteen minutes... well let's just say it would take hours to do what I want to do."

Her smile lit up the room. "You look pretty spectacular yourself."

"Not too much hick?"

A confused look crossed her face and she said, "Not in the least ,you look hot, cowboy, and I kind of feel the same way you do, that if we don't get out of this room right now ,we won't be making it to the reception at all."

Drew grinned and held out his arm. "Then let us depart, lovely lady."

"Without the entourage?"

"We'll grab them on the way to the elevator."

"Is Chase coming tonight?"

"Yes, I'm having them dress similar though, to confuse the issue. Give us a little advantage by having them take a some of the focus."

Lily laughed. "It will be fun to watch the reactions."

Before they got to the elevator the other two couples had joined them. Drew inwardly winced when the twins were dressed in their country finery, too. She was going to go screaming into the wind, being surrounded by all of them in their hats and boots. He had no idea what Beau and Adam would be dressed like, but he wouldn't be a bit surprised if all five of them were full country. Poor girl, he just hoped she wasn't embarrassed, they were going to draw attention, and with any luck it wouldn't be too much.

LILY SMILED at the others when they met up in the hall on the way to the elevator. Chase and Cade were dressed identically but Lily could still tell them apart, by the way they moved and their expressions. They'd gone full out cowboy too, just like Drew. She was surrounded by the most handsome ranchers ever, and their ladies were no slouches. The six of them were sure to turn heads. And if the rest of them all showed up in full western gear, whoever the bad guys were would know they weren't going to have a chance to get to Lily.

When they got to the reception area and checked in, she noticed her parents were already confirmed, so they must be in the room. She whispered to Drew that they should find them first, before they did anything else.

Lily didn't have to worry about that because she spotted her father immediately at the bar. Lily said, "Daddy is in line at the bar," so they all headed that direction.

Drew said, "I don't see him."

Lily scoffed, "He's next in line."

By the time they reached the bar her dad turned out of line and he smiled.

DREW THOUGHT HE WAS DREAMING. Lily's father was dressed almost identically to himself, minus the badge and gun. The man was country from the top of his Stetson to the tips of his Tecova's. What in the hell was that all about? Drew was so confused he couldn't speak. No one bought those kinds of clothes for a one-time event. Why was Lily's father in western gear? Sure, he was from Montana, but that didn't mean everyone dressed like a rancher.

233

Lily hugged her father, "Looking good, daddy. I was wondering when you would break out your ranching duds."

"Lily-bug, I didn't have a reason to wear my boots until tonight, all that running around town, boots aren't meant for walking, they're made for riding."

Lily laughed and turned to kiss her mom. "You had to force him not to wear them, didn't you?"

"I might have applied some subtle pressure." Elaine's eyes twinkled.

Just then Adam walked up. "Mr. Smith, I see you're representing the ranch tonight. Hoping to sell some of that delightful horseflesh you raise?"

Drew turned to look at his oldest brother. Horseflesh? Lily's dad? And then it struck him like a thunderbolt. The Singing S ranch, known for it's top of the line quarter horses. Lily was a rancher's daughter, just like he was a rancher's son. She wasn't a city girl at all. Then all the puzzle pieces clicked together, no wonder she wasn't afraid to face the weather, rather than a dangerous man. She knew what the weather was like, she'd been born and raised in the Montana Rockies, she could read the sky the same as he could.

That put an entirely different spin on things. His heart raced with the possibilities. But he couldn't go off half-cocked, he was going to have to think long and hard about what he really wanted. Now was not the time for deep introspection, he was there to keep Lily safe, so he needed to keep his mind on the job.

~

LILY NOTICED Drew had gotten really quiet and still. She looked around to see what had caused his behavior and didn't see anything out of the ordinary. Her dad and mom left to take the drinks back to their table. She touched Drew's arm and he jolted. "What's wrong?"

He shook his head and smiled. "Nothing, I was just think-ing. Let's get some drinks and go meet your sponsors. That's the point of this shindig isn't it?"

Drew was holding something back, but he obviously wasn't going to tell her what he was thinking about, so she decided not to push it. Maybe after the reception he would tell her what it was. She got a club soda and he got a beer, the rest of his family got drinks and stationed themselves around the room to keep an eye on everything. Cade and Summer stayed with them as they went to go mingle with the spon-sors and pageant officials, some of which she had met, but others were new to her.

Lily decided this had to be the most tedious of all the events. Meeting all these people, gushing about their contri-bution. She moved almost like an automaton from person to person, smiling, saying the same words over and over, it was not a barrel of laughs. There were a lot of photographers in the room, so when Rachel stayed near them, photographing everyone, including her meets-and-greets with her sponsors, no one even noticed.

When she'd done the full circle, the waiters brought out the food and Lily was happy to get a plate and sit at the table they were assigned to. It wasn't food she was used to, but she was hungry, so she ate it. She noticed one of her sponsors and some other men gather in one corner, each of the men had a shot of whiskey and at some command they lifted their drinks, looked fiercely at each other, and then slammed them down in one gulp.

She'd seen this type of behavior before, but these men didn't look like they were friends. In fact, they looked competitive or angry. She couldn't remember which company her sponsor was from, she would have to look at her list and see if she could figure it out. But before she could do so, the men parted company and joined the rest of the group at the tables, so she shrugged it off.

One of the pageant officials took a mic and thanked everyone for attending and sponsoring the girls and the pageant. He asked various people to say a few words. Mentioned that the bar would be open another hour and then invited people to enjoy themselves. Soft music filled the room as people continued to mingle. When some of the other contestants began leaving the room, they decided they could make their escape, they still wanted a family debrief, and Drew would be going to meet with security for a short exchange of information.

It would be at least a couple more hours before they would get back to their room, where they could batten down the hatches and relax their watchfulness. But Lily could at least change out of her killer heels before they all met in the twins' room. She was glad that her feet were holding up fine for the short periods in the heels. She would be wearing them a lot more over the contest weekend, which would start in the morning.

Tomorrow were the interviews. Both for the contest and also to produce snippets to be used during the televised portion. The idea was to talk about their pet projects and the charities they represented. The pageant wanted to evaluate the poise and intelligence of each candidate. The winner needed to be able to think on her feet and present a good image to the public, even when things didn't go her way.

The competition was much more than physical beauty. And since the winner would go to the international competition, they needed to select a person who would represent the United States in the best light. It would be a busy and maybe even grueling day. Drew planned to stay by her side, it surprised her how much the idea of him being with her gave her peace and strength.

She'd planned to do this for over a year, and knew it might be challenging. Never in her wildest dreams had she imagined needing a bodyguard and even more importantly would feel reassured by his presence. But that's exactly how she felt.

When they got near to their room, Drew asked, "Do you want to change into your flats?"

She nodded, and they turned toward his room, telling Cade and Summer, they would be down in a few minutes. Before he allowed her to go in he checked the tape he put on the door every time they left. She pulled out the room card to scan it.

"Wait, the tape is torn." He looked at the other piece, both had been compromised. They walked back to her room and found it compromised also. "They wouldn't be able to get in your door, with the night lock on it, but someone clearly tried."

Lily was frightened by the news, they had the Do Not Disturb signs on both doors.

"I'm going to take you down to the twins' room and call security."

As he speed walked Lily down the hall to his brothers' room he quickly called Mr. Clark and relayed the information. He said he would be there in moments and hung up to dispatch other officers to the other contestants' rooms.

Lily was getting damn tired of whoever this was, that would not let this go. Whatever could be so important to constantly try to stop just a few girls from being in the pageant? It didn't make sense. While they waited for word from Drew, the rest of them went over the photos that had been taken during the sightseeing.

Since the syringe attack had happened in Manhattan they

concentrated their focus on that area, but it was too crowded with people to be able to pick out anyone in particular. One of the people from yesterday had been spotted in one picture, but that could have been a coincidence.

Drew still hadn't returned so they began going through the photos Rachel had taken at the reception. When they got to the photo with the sponsor that she'd seen with the other men she asked her father, "Daddy, who is that sponsor?"

"That's Conrad, from Conrad fertilizer. Why do you ask?"

"I just noticed him having a shot with some of the other girl's sponsors, they looked kind of grumpy or something. Not like they were enjoying their shot."

Howard's eyebrows rose. "Well that sounds odd, Conrad is a great guy, laid back and always has a smile. He's got a great product too, we use it exclusively on our fields. Which is probably why he sponsored you, and of course the publicity is great. It's not free but it's a whole lot cheaper than a TV commercial."

Rachel scrolled through some of her pictures. "I did notice them gather in the corner for a shot and I agree it didn't look like they were having much fun. At least not after one guy showed up. Before the 'bad egg' arrived, they were smiling and laughing having what looked like a nice chat, after that, they all got quiet and looked practically angry. I'm not sure I got a picture of the whole group."

Rachel finally found one photo and showed it to the group. "Here it is. This was taken after the shot, and as they were disbursing."

Howard said, "I recognize the guy with Conrad. He's also in the fertilizer business. I'm not sure about the others."

When a knock sounded chase opened it to admit Drew, and boy did he look pissed. He turned toward Lily with a look of sorrow.

"What happened, Drew?"

"Vandalism. Your room is a mess, your clothes are in shreds, your shoes destroyed. Makeup trashed."

"My clothes?" Lily was shocked to hear what he had to say. Why would anyone trash all her clothes? It was ridiculous.

"Yes. But only your pageant clothes. Your sweats and sneakers are fine, but all your nice clothes are ruined."

Her pageant clothes. Well at least that made sense, someone was still trying to keep her from competing. Tomorrow was supposed to be office attire, she had a great little suit to wear. Well, she'd had one, before the reception. It was a pinstriped navy-blue business suit with a jacket that flared at the hip. She'd loved that suit. Now what was she going to wear?

Those assholes. She'd deliberately picked clothes that she might be able to wear in the future and now all her hard work was in shreds. The hits just kept coming. Why could these people just leave them alone? She wanted to kick something.

Summer pulled out her itinerary. "Business attire. I didn't really bring any business attire. Did any of you?"

Rachel nodded. "I did, just in case I needed to put it on to get in good with the photography team. Adam and I will go get it, maybe it will work, we are close to the same size."

Summer asked, "What size shoes does everyone wear? I have plenty of makeup, so that's not an issue."

When they decided that Katie had feet the closest in size, she marched over to the closet and started dragging out all her heels.

Lily was feeling overwhelmed by the girl's generosity. "But I can't take your clothes."

Alyssa said, "You aren't taking them, you're borrowing them, or really, we are loaning them. We refuse to let you bear the brunt of these jerks' shenanigans."

Beau asked, "What about the other contestants?"

Drew said, "Pretty much the same as Lily for Ms. New Mexico. Nothing for Ms. Utah or the others. Mr. Clark didn't know what to think about that. It's possible there were people on those other floors and they couldn't get in the rooms, or maybe they just ran out of time."

Lily asked, "What is Ms. New Mexico going to do?"

Drew chuckled. "Apparently, she had not completely emptied her suitcase, so while they did shred her clothes, and trash her shoes, they were the ones she'd worn to the photo shoots, not her pageant clothes. She'd sent her suit for tomorrow down to be pressed. They returned it while security was still there."

Lily clapped her hands. "That's awesome, so they haven't succeeded with knocking out any of the rest of us. I'll bet this bad guy feels like we are the bane of his existence. I love it."

Drew grinned at her and she felt a flutter deep inside. He turned back to the group. "I've only got about a half an hour, tell me the highlights of today's watch."

Unfortunately, there hadn't been anything really happen other than the pressure syringe, so they assumed that had been the only planned attack except for the clothes shredding.

Drew and Beau went off to the security meeting and Lily remembered she'd not told Drew about the sponsor shot-taking incident. She would tell him when he came back to get her. In the mean-time she needed to find a suitable outfit for tomorrow's interview. Her mom and dad left to return to their rooms.

Lily and the girls worked to find her an adequate replacement for tomorrow. It wasn't as cute as Lily's suit had been, but it would work. Once they had that worked out they talked about the rest of the clothes needed to finish out the pageant.

240

By the time Drew came back for Lily, she was exhausted. She barely managed to drag herself to his room. Fortunately, he carried all the clothes and shoes for tomorrow. She washed her face, stripped out of her clothes and fell into bed. She didn't even want to see what her closet looked like. She was asleep before Drew could join her in bed. Talking could wait until tomorrow.

CHAPTER 25

*L*ily was startled out of sleep by her phone ringing. It was her dad's ringtone, was there a problem with one of the horses? As she grabbed her phone her mind registered where she was, not on the ranch, or even in Montana, at the pageant, in a hotel with Drew wrapped around her. As she pushed answer she noticed it was four o'clock in the morning, why in the hell was her father calling at this time of day?

She had one moment of panic, thinking the people after her, had gotten to her parents. "Daddy, what's wrong?"

Her father's voice was excited, not scared. "I figured it out Lily-bug! I think, no, I know who's after you and why."

"That's awesome, daddy, you do know it's four a.m., don't you?" Drew stirred next to her

"Oh, I didn't even look at the clock. Sorry, but I couldn't wait to let you know. It's right there in Chase's lists. After I thought about it, I went out to Facebook and verified what I was thinking."

"Okay daddy, let me put you on speaker so Drew can hear too."

"Drew is with you, at four o'clock in the morning?"

Lily rolled her eyes, even though no one could see her, it was still dark in the room. "Oh, now you notice the time. Yes daddy, you woke him too."

Drew turned on the light and sat up, pulling the blankets up over the two of them. Like her father could see them. Lily rolled her eyes at him too, and turned her phone to speaker.

Lily heard her mother say, "Howard, who are you calling in the middle of the night?"

"Lily, I know who is after her."

"And that news couldn't wait two hours."

"I didn't notice the time."

"Oh, Howard."

Lily said, "All right daddy, now that everyone is up, tell us what you discovered."

"Am I on speaker? I put you on speaker too."

Drew answered, "Yes sir, good morning to both of you."

Elaine said a little too brightly, "Good morning, Drew."

Lily thought she heard her father harrumph and mutter something about having a talk with that boy. And then he gasped like her mom had elbowed him.

"All right then. So, you all know I've been pouring over Chase's lists, until I have them practically memorized. And then when Lily mentioned Conrad and the other fertilizer baron's all in a corner having what looked like a not so friendly drink I began to wonder about that. What if it had something to do with the girls?"

She heard her mother gasp and her dad continued speaking, "So when I woke up a little while ago, to use the facilities, it came to me. Each one of the Rocky Mountain contestants has one of the fertilizer kings as a sponsor."

"Daddy, are you talking about the guys you call the 'Shit Barons'? But I thought there were only five of them?" Drew chuckled at the name her father used for the men.

"That's right Lily-bug, there was only five of them, until just recently and a new guy came on the scene. The new guy has been trying to gain a foothold. The Shit Barons' haven't let him into their inner circle, and have made no bones about thinking his product is inferior, and that he is untrustworthy."

"But…"

"No, let me finish. So, I went out on social media and a couple of the guys had posted that they'd been forced to have a drink with the young whippersnapper, who had boasted that his product was going to be getting a lot of coverage in a few days. The Shit Barons just blew him off, he's bragged before. But just think about it, if all the girls that have the other guys as sponsors somehow got knocked out of the pageant, then they wouldn't get any advertising. As it is Colorado and Wyoming aren't here. Which is why it didn't register at first because there were only four men drinking instead of five or now six."

"Daddy, are you seriously trying to tell me that I was kidnapped, almost bitten by a snake, might have been shot with a syringe, and had my clothes ripped to shreds, over manure?" With each word her voice had gotten shriller as she had gotten madder.

"Yep, Lily-bug that's pretty much the bottom line. I think the new guy is pulling the stunts to be the only one to get publicity during the pageant."

Drew took her hand which was ice-cold with fury. "So, Mr. Smith, which contestant is the new guy sponsoring."

"Ms. Idaho, which is why she's had no problems. Wyoming and Colorado are no longer a threat so it's just Lily, Ms. Utah and Ms. New Mexico that need to be protected. If he was still boasting last night, I have no doubt that he will work to derail the three of you or die trying."

Drew said in a tight low voice. "It will be the latter. Now

that we know who to look for, we will leave no stone unturned. I'll let Mr. Clark know so he can round everyone up, what is the new guys name and company?"

Her dad chuckled. "His name is Bubba Pampers and his company is Pamper's Organic Fertilizer."

Lily laughed out loud. "You're kidding."

"Nope, not at all. Kind of appropriate if you ask me. I think they call him Baby Pooper, behind his back" She could just imagine the twinkle in her father's eye.

"Oh Howard, you're like a six-year-old boy." Lily could hear the laughter in her mother's voice, even as she scolded.

Her dad yawned. "Well now that I've related my news, I'm going back to sleep, and maybe now my mind will let me rest."

They said their goodbyes. But now Lily was wide awake, and she was certain she wouldn't be able to go back to sleep. She looked at Drew, "Fertilizer? Really? What is wrong with people?"

Drew nodded and pulled her close to wrap his arm around her. "I couldn't agree more. It really is ridiculous. And to think they also committed murder, put Ms. Wyoming in the hospital, and God only knows what's happened to Ms. Colorado."

Lily shuddered. "I hope they will both be all right. How could someone be so ruthless, doesn't he know he'll get caught and go to jail? Then what good will his stupid business be?'

"Some people think they will never be caught, or they're willing to live on the edge, it's some kind of thrill to see what they can get away with."

"Well, I think it's stupid."

"I guess I don't have to worry about you taking up a life of crime then."

He kissed her shoulder and Lily felt warmth spread

outward. "So, since daddy woke us up before even the chickens, how about we put this extra time to good use."

Drew nuzzled her neck and took her earlobe in his mouth. After teasing it for a moment, that shot even more heat through her body, he whispered in her ear, "What did you have in mind?"

She reached one hand down to find him warm and stiff. "Exactly what you've already begun."

"Excellent." Then he pulled them down under the covers and began to play her body like he designed it and knew all of its intricacies. She was perfectly happy to let him.

DREW GRINNED as he tried to disengage the Lily octopus that was wrapped around him. They'd spent a very fine hour enjoying the delights of the flesh, but now he needed to get moving. He needed to be up and dressed in time for the security meeting. He had news to share. But first he wanted to text Mr. Clark to let him know it should be an all-hands-on-deck meeting. And he wanted to text his brothers and let them know about the revelation also. Plus a few minutes online, to find a picture of the guy wouldn't go amiss.

"Lily sweetheart, I need to get up. We still have to capture Baby Pooper."

Lily squeezed him tight and kissed the middle of his chest and then let him go. As he got out of the bed, he felt a little bereft without her wrapped around him. He told himself not to be a dumb ass, but the feeling stayed. He quickly glanced at the clock and calculated.

"Do you want to join me in the shower?"

She popped up like one of those whack-a-mole things. "Really? You wouldn't mind?"

"Not at all, we have time, as long as we don't get too carried away."

She jumped out of bed and scurried toward her room. "Just let me get my robe and a few things."

By the time she got back, her arms loaded with crap, he'd sent text messages to Mr. Clark and his brothers.

He waved his hand toward her arms. "What *is* all that?"

"Um, shampoo, rinse out conditioner, spray in conditioner, shower gel, facial scrub and masque, toning serum, moisturizer and body lotion. Oh, wait. I forgot deodorant."

She dropped the arm load on the bed and rushed back to her room. He started hauling all her crap into the bathroom. She came back with the deodorant and her bath robe, just as he sat the last item on the sink. She began arranging everything. Half of it went in the shower and half stayed on the sink.

By the time she was going to get finished, they weren't going to have time to shower, let alone have a little fun.

She hung her robe on the back of the door next to his, and then turned with her hands on her hips, her lovely tits still swaying with the movement. "Well what are you waiting for? Get in the shower, Drew."

He chuckled and complied. They managed to get each other somewhat clean, and had a lot of fun doing it. He left before she had a chance to use all the various beauty products. When she finally came out of the bathroom, all rosy and sexy he wanted to pull her back into bed, but they'd run out of time. He'd found a picture of Bubba Pamper and had texted it to both his brothers, and Mr. Clark, so he could make copies for the others.

He went over and kissed Lily hard, just as a knock came on their door. He opened it and let in the female portion of his family, gave Lily a wave, and joined his brothers in the hall.

They all began firing questions at him. "I'll explain it all in five minutes, but I'll start by saying it was Lily's dad that figured it out."

Adam said, "Of course it was. I copied dad on what you sent and all I got back was a text saying, 'Obviously, makes perfect sense'."

Drew chuckled.

When he got to the meeting and explained all, the police and security called it a lucky break, but Drew knew it was more than that. It was an expertise that came with age, and knowledge of the key players. But regardless of how they got it, everyone was relieved to have a place to look.

Now all they had to do was find a way to get real evidence, rather than what they had, which was circumstantial at best. At worst it was pure speculation. They talked about the best way to handle it and decided they didn't have enough to bring the guy in for questioning, so they would begin with surveillance, and once they saw anything they could use as evidence, they would snap him up.

Drew was a little disappointed that the guy was going to be left out there to continue to threaten the girls, but at least now that they knew who to watch they wouldn't be spread so thin. They needed to guard the three girls and keep a watch on Baby Pooper himself and his associates.

When they got back to Drew's room the girls had Lily all dolled up for the interview portion of the pageant. Lily had clued the girls in on who the 'bad guy' was and they were all laughing about Bubba Pamper aka Baby Pooper.

The girls and their entourage would be kept in a room offstage, so they couldn't hear the other contestant's interviews. Once they had given their interview they went to another room to wait until everyone had finished and then there would be a meal served. The girls would have a lot of down time waiting both before and after their interview. Lily had planned on reading but now that she had Drew's family to chat with, that would be much more fun.

CHAPTER 26

*I*t was time for Lily's interview, she was excited to be able to tell all about why she had joined the pageant, and why she had chosen to champion her cause, and charity. Drew smiled at her enthusiasm as he walked out of the room by her side.

A pageant aide was standing outside the door. "Ms. Montana?"

Lily smiled at the woman. "That's me."

"Here is a bottle of water for you to have a drink before you get to the stage, then this nice gentleman can hold it for you."

"Oh, thanks so much, I am feeling a bit parched." Lily took the bottle and started to unscrew the lid, when Drew grabbed it out of her hand.

"Wait." He squeezed the bottle and water shot out of a tiny hole.

The pageant aide looked surprised. "Why is it leaking?"

Drew didn't answer. "Where did you get this?"

"Oh, her sponsor gave it to me. He wanted to give one to

all his girls. I have the other two here for the other contestants."

Lily and Drew exchanged a look. "Which two women?"

She looked at a note. "Let me check to make sure. Yes, just as I thought, Ms. New Mexico and Ms. Utah."

Drew's heart sped up. Maybe he had the evidence they needed right there in his hand. "Do you know who the man was, could you pick him out?"

"Oh, that's easy, he's sitting in the center of about row ten. I saw him sit there right after he gave me the bottles."

"Can you point him out to me?" Drew asked.

"Sure, that guy right there with the blue suit and string tie."

Drew spoke into the radio that he'd been given to keep in touch with security. "We've got some evidence on the suspect, at the contestant's room." He looked at the aide whose eyes had widened as he spoke. "Would you be willing to tell the police what happened?"

"Um sure, is something wrong?"

"Possibly."

The aide's eyes widened. "Did I do something wrong?"

Lily put her hand on the woman's arm. "No, you didn't do anything wrong, but you can help by telling the police what happened."

Drew heard the announcement that they would be taking a short break and saw the guy grin, and then cover his mouth with his hand, he obviously thought something had happened to Lily.

As soon as the security and police converged on them, Drew handed them the water bottle he held, and explained what had happened. He signaled his family to move into the auditorium but stay towards the back in case the guy figured out what was going on.

He conferred with the others and they decided how they

wanted to handle it, and split off into multiple directions. The New York City police took all three water bottles to have a tox screen run on them, as well as fingerprints on the two no one had touched. All three bottles did have tiny holes in them that a syringe might have made.

Drew got in position in the back of the auditorium. The hotel security walked out from backstage with the pageant aide, his hand was gripping her upper arm and they marched down the stairs on stage left. Bubba Pamper looked toward them and then got up quickly hurrying down the opposite side of his row.

There was a police officer at the end of the row and he called out for him to halt, but Baby Pooper sprayed what looked like mace into the officer's eyes and kept moving. Cade had been further up in the auditorium and began following the guy as he sprayed everyone he got near.

There was practically a cloud of mace in the air. Summer walked in the back of the auditorium and Drew about had heart failure since she was in the man's direct path. But Cade pulled his rope seemingly out of thin air and spun it at the man. Cade caught the perp around the elbows which caused him to drop the mace.

Summer flipped toward him and swept his feet out from under him. Drew was right on her tail and he grabbed a spare power cord, lying next to the other cables and cords running between the stage and TV cameras, and hog tied the man with it in seconds.

The three exchanged high fives, and Cade said with a smirk, "Team Roping at its finest."

The rest of the security and police officer team surrounded them to take the man in custody. Even without knowing what might be in the tainted water bottles, he'd maced a half dozen people, several of which were police officers and the dumb ass had also gotten the Federal agent. So, he was going to jail, which would give them plenty of time to find evidence for the rest of the crimes.

As they were hauling him out Lily walked up, and Baby Pooper sputtered, "What are you? A fucking cat, with nine lives? Just what does it take to take you down? That damn Ronald couldn't manage it, and the snake failed, and..."

The dumb ass finally realized what he'd just said and clamped his mouth shut tight, but the damage was done. He'd just blurted out his guilt in front of a dozen witnesses, including a TV camera that had kept recording during his entire, aborted, flight for freedom.

Drew shook his head, the guy really sucked at being a criminal. He caught Mr. Clark's eye and could read the same thought in his gaze. Drew saluted Mr. Clark and then pulled Lily into his arms. "I think you're safe now."

Lily laid her head on his shoulder and then looked up. "But you're going to stay with me until the end, right?"

"Absolutely, nowhere else I'd rather be than protecting my favorite beauty queen."

LILY WAS THRILLED that the danger was finally over. They'd given everyone an hour to reconvene to finish the interviews, during which they aired out the room. After her interview was over, the pageant officials allowed her and Drew to go to the police department to give their statements, rather than sit cloistered in the other contestant room.

The pageant officials had not mentioned to any of the other contestants anything that had gone on in the auditorium, other than to alert the other bodyguards that the threat had been neutralized and the man taken into custody. They'd told the contestants that the delay was due to an air circulation problem.

Lily gave her statement with as much detail as she could remember, and she had to repeat several times what the guy had shouted at her as he was being escorted outside. But now it was done, and they had the evening off, so the whole Kipling family and her's gathered in the revolving restaurant of the Marriot Marquess to celebrate. And celebrate they did, with good food and plenty of drinks.

There was still two days of competition before the big finale on Sunday night, where they would crown the winner. Lily was beginning to hope that she would not win, which was counter-productive, and she tried to push the thought away. But in her heart of hearts she knew she just wanted to be done with it all.

She shook herself out of her thoughts and reengaged with the celebration in the revolving restaurant. But before she could even say a word her phone buzzed. It was her sister who sent her a clip of the capture of Baby Pooper. Lily laughed as she watched it and heard Cade say something about team roping. When she looked up just about everyone else had their phone out, probably watching the same clip.

Except Drew, who was texting. When she lifted an eyebrow at him.

He said quietly, "My best friend is giving me holy hell, for not calling him to help."

Lily chuckled, then said to the group, "I think this calls for a toast. To the best team ropers in the country."

When they all drank she said, "You know every male in the country is going to want a rope now, and every girl is going to want to learn Summer's moves." She looked at Drew. "I can't imagine how many kids are going to be grabbing every cord in the house to try to hog tie everything from the dog to their siblings."

Howard said, "You Kipling's have single-handedly created a generation of monsters."

255

Cade shook his head. "Nope, just a few cowboys. Maybe we'll get some country music created in our honor."

Chase rolled his eyes at his twin. "You are a certifiable nut case."

"If I'm one, then so are you." The joshing began in earnest then.

Lily tuned them out and took Drew's hand into hers to hold under the table. Drew seemed content to let his siblings tease each other while he held Lily's hand.

When it got to be late enough to escape the merriment, Lily said, "I'm going to bed. There's still a lot more things to do this weekend and I need my beauty sleep."

Drew and her parents got up to leave too, while the rest of the Kipling's waived them off. Lily saw her dad stop by the Maître D and told him to put their tab on his credit card, as long as they wanted to party.

Drew spoke up as they left the restaurant. "You didn't need to do that, Mr. Smith."

Her dad put his arm around Drew. "You and your family saved my little girl and I appreciate it. It's the least I could do to say thanks. Maybe I'll send down a new pony or two for your string."

When Drew started to deny the need her father looked him in the eye and said, "My daughter's wellbeing is much more precious than a couple of horses. You didn't know her from Adam, and that didn't stop any of you from coming to her aid. And before you say anything, I know that's just the cowboy way, but it still doesn't change the facts."

"Very well, thanks. I think Adam was going to be asking you about a couple of new horses. How about you let us buy a couple and you can throw in an extra?"

Howard laughed. "You've got yourself a deal."

CHAPTER 27

*L*ily hoped the rest of the pageant would pass by peacefully. She and Drew continued to sleep in his bed, even though it was now safe for her to return to her own. She had a nightmare where she was a cat, and there was a big pile of baby poop that kept trying to smother her, but after she and Drew laughed about the dream she settled into a peaceful sleep.

The only real concern she had was what would happen after the pageant was over. If she won, she would have to continue down the path toward the international contest. If she lost she could return home and get back out on the ranch with her horse.

But if she was honest with herself, which she always tried to be, where she really wanted to go was back to the Rockin' K to be near Drew. The problem was they really hadn't known each other that long and she wondered if she was rushing her fences. So, as she walked through the rest of the competitions she thought about it, a lot.

The final night of the pageant, the part that would be shown all across America and possibly even other countries arrived. Lily and the Kipling girls had gone out during a short break to find a new dress for Lily to wear. Since New York was one of the shopping capitals of the world, it wasn't hard to find something, they even had a seamstress on staff that could make any alterations needed.

Lily and the girls were all together for the final dressing and primping session. Summer had given her a heavier night time look that was kind of mysterious and sexy. It wasn't really for the pageant, but she wanted to wow Drew. Summer had been on board with the idea and had gone all out.

When she was ready, she let the rest of the girls go into Drew's room to witness his reaction. It was all she'd hoped it would be. He'd turned to see her walk into the room, his jaw dropped, his pupils dilated, and he almost dropped his phone, but Chase caught it in time.

The girls all grinned at her and she sauntered over to Drew, put one finger under his chin and shut his mouth. That seemed to shake him out of his stupor, because he muttered, "Lily, you are stunning."

She smiled up at him. "Well, thank you, kind sir."

"No, I mean it. You're... words fail me. You're always beautiful, but tonight there's just something..."

He stammered to a halt and his ears turned pink, when he saw everyone watching him, Lily blushed herself and then stepped up and gave him a light kiss. "I couldn't ask for a better compliment. Just ignore the uninvited spectators."

"Hey, we were to, invited." Cade whined.

Lily laughed and stepped back. "All right, let's get this show on the road."

She took Drew's arm and led the way down the hall. She whispered, "Don't worry, we won't have any company when you take the dress off of me."

He whispered back, "I can hardly wait."

"Me, too." She thought about the look she'd seen in his eyes and knew that even if she won the pageant, it wouldn't compare to the thrill of his expression when she'd walked into the room.

They met her parents at the prearranged location and her mom and dad fussed over her.

"Lily-bug you look so beautiful, you are going to put the other girls to shame."

"Oh daddy, you're biased."

Elaine said, "Nonsense, you do look amazing, sweetheart."

"Thanks mom. Summer went to town."

Summer shook her head. "Just enhancing the beauty already there."

Lily laughed. "Okay, I can see I'm outnumbered in this, so I'll just bask in everyone's adoration."

They all laughed and continued on their trek to the final area. Her mom and dad and all Drew's family planned to sit together to watch the final taping of the show. Summer and Drew were allowed backstage with her, but no one else.

Lily knew, that now that the fear was gone, she would have been fine by herself, but she didn't mind Summer being there to make sure everything was perfect. And having her guy with her made it better all the way around. Wait, her guy?

She realized that she thought of Drew that way, but she had no idea if he thought about her the same. She wasn't sure she was brave enough to come right out and ask him. She'd never been the one to instigate a romance. But this with Drew seemed bigger than a simple romance, and that kind of scared her even more.

With the last few minutes of the pageant bearing down on her, she didn't have any time to think about it. She had to put her whole mind to the next couple of hours as they completed the final competition. There would be plenty of slack time in between events, where they would insert the commercials and the previously taped segments. But she still needed to keep her brain on the pageant and not on the hunky cowboy cop, that she wasn't quite sure she wanted to live without.

⁓

DREW WAS glad they were letting him stay with Lily. Sure, the menace had been removed, but he still wanted to be near her, if only just to spend the time together. Their return to the real world was fast approaching and he wasn't all that excited about it. He'd never felt the kinship with another woman like he did with Lily.

She seemed to know what he was feeling and wanting, even before he did. Her presence calmed him when he was tense, and uplifted him when he was down. They were like two puzzle pieces that fit together. He'd always thought people that said things like that were idiots. Never believing that he needed anyone to complete him. But she'd proven him wrong. Drew felt more together when he was with her.

He didn't want to walk away from her tomorrow when they got on the plane, but they hadn't known each other long enough to do anything differently. He stood in the prep room and watched Summer flit around Lily, smoothing a single hair, pulling the dress down in back, fluffing on a bit of powder and touching up her lipstick. The last of which made Drew want to kiss those lips and mess them up again.

Suddenly his phone buzzed with an incoming text, from the police sargent that had taken Bubba Pamper into custody. He turned away from the room to read it. It said, "Beware, person of interest is watching the clock, with glee on his face. Suspect something else might be planned."

Immediately following that was another text from Mr.

Clark telling Drew to meet him in the hall outside the girl's room. Drew looked for Ms. Utah's bodyguard, but he wasn't in the room and neither was Ms. New Mexico's boyfriend.

Shit, he didn't want to leave the girls unprotected even to go out into the hall. But he didn't want them all freaking out by having security bust in the door. He told Lily and Summer he needed to step out into the hall for a sec. and tried to warn Summer to keep an eye on Lily with just a look. He didn't know if he succeeded, but she had to guess he meant something by it.

Drew stepped into the hall as Mr. Clark came into view. "Did you get that text?"

"Yes, did you text my brothers to meet us here?"

"I did. Any ideas what might be going down?"

Drew thought back to everything he knew but had no ideas. "I can't think of a thing. But the guy was all about publicity, so I would guess whatever it is will be on camera and live. I don't know what he has to gain by it though, if he's going to jail."

Mr. Clark shook his head, "A last hurrah of some kind."

His brothers rounded the corner and skidded to a stop. Adam asked, "What's going on?"

Drew frowned. "You got the same texts we did, any ideas?"

Chase rubbed his chin and all the Kipling's turned toward him, of all the brothers Chase thought the longest before he acted. Drew asked, "What?"

"Well he did say something as he was being led out. I was in the hall outside the auditorium, you know, as a final backup."

Drew tried not to be impatient, but he wanted Chase to get to it. Chase now had the attention of Mr. Clark and the other two security officers that had shown up.

"He said something about running out of room. I don't

know what he meant by it, but he said the pageant would be running out of room."

Drew demanded, "What does that mean?"

Chase shrugged, "I have no idea, how could the pageant run out of room? Like on stage? Or on TV? I don't know but that's what he said."

Mr. Clark nodded slowly. "It's the best clue we have. Can two of you go back in and keep an eye on the contestants? They'll be called out in five minutes. Stay with them, but out of the view of the camera."

Drew looked at his brothers. Beau had a first aid kit with him and he was certain Adam would have a throwing knife or two hidden on his person. "Beau and Adam, stay with the girls. We'll take the twins with us."

Mr. Clark said, "Let's assume it's physical room and take a look at the stage and the stage dressings for the different parts needed to finish out tonight. But if anyone thinks of another idea, don't hesitate to speak up, we're going on very little information."

He led the way and the rest of the men followed, Drew and his brothers bringing up the rear. Drew noticed the twins had their heads together and he didn't disturb them, their two heads equaled about four in times like these, since they were so connected, a few words and thoughts went a long way.

They entered the backstage area, where the stage dressings were kept when not in use. They spread out and carefully looked over each one to make sure nothing looked out of the ordinary. The stage hands didn't like them poking around, but Mr. Clark let them know that he had the authority to do as he thought was necessary, so the hands went off to one side and grumbled about rent-a-cops putting on airs.

They didn't find anything amiss, so they moved toward

the stage itself, they had to stay out of view, while at the same time examine the area. The girls had been called on stage and were going through some kind of introductions. Drew wondered about when their sponsors would be mentioned, since that seemed to be the focus of their perp's attention.

He texted his sister who would be glued to the TV, to ask her to text him immediately, when they started talking about sponsors for the girls. Since they always seemed to go in alphabetical order Drew was fairly certain that whatever might happen would be after Ms. Idaho's sponsors were mentioned.

The twins came up to him and Cade said, "What if he's going to do something weird like fill the stage with fertilizer or shit or something?"

"How would he do that?"

"We don't know but we were thinking maybe we should go outside and look around. We aren't doing any good here."

"All right go ahead, but keep in touch if you find anything." He nodded toward Adam and Beau who were standing just offstage. "Tell them, too."

The twins took off at a jog, stopping only long enough to clue Adam and Beau in. Drew let their idea sink in and tried to think like the idiot they'd captured. If he wanted publicity at all costs and he owned a fertilizer factory, how would he disrupt the pageant to get his name out. He thought the twins' idea of filling the stage with fertilizer would work very well. It would be publicity all right, not good publicity, but the guy had to be a little batshit crazy to go to the lengths that he had, so anything was possible.

There was a couple of small back doors to the stage, but it would take a dump truck or something like that, to fill up the stage with anything. The twins would find those quickly, and he kind of doubted that the city of New York would let dump trucks filled with fertilizer just hang out in the alley, near a major hotel like they were in.

How else could the guy do it? Drew looked up to see if there was a skylight or anything above them. He didn't see a skylight just the swags and curtains that could be raised and lowered. He turned his back on the bright lights of the stage and looked above them again. Some of the draping's up there looked a little heavy.

Was it possible that Baby Pooper had somehow gotten a stage full of fertilizer up there? He saw movement out of the corner of his eye. Someone was climbing up the ladders that went up to the catwalks. He tried to catch Mr. Clark's attention, but he wasn't looking in Drew's direction. Rather than taking the time to text, he quickly followed the man climbing skyward.

When he was halfway up he remembered the voice to text app. He rarely used it, but now would be perfect, they were having a break on stage, so he could talk. He accessed it and told the security team what he suspected. Then he continued his climb skyward.

He saw one of the security officers run forward to talk to the pageant officials and hoped they got the girls to safety. Maybe they could fill in the time with more of the previously taped sections.

After that, Drew kept his eyes on the man he'd followed. He wished he had Cade's rope on him. He wasn't as good with one as his brother, but he could hold his own. When he got up to the catwalk he saw some rope hanging on a hook. Drew grabbed it and took it with him. It was about the right weight, polyester braid. He thought it might work, if he could tie the hondo quick enough.

Not having enough time to tie a proper stopper knot in the end, he tied a quick one that should work for this one time. He kept moving as he tied, and he knew Cade would chide him on the sloppiness of it, but he got the hondo loop tied, good enough to thread the other end through.

The other guy glanced back and saw Drew following him, and started moving quicker toward some of the same types of rope he had in his hands. They were tied to the catwalk and seemed to be straining under the weight. Drew didn't know if the catwalks were sturdy enough for all the pressure those huge bags would be putting on them. Now that he was close enough, he could see the weight and size of the bags lifted high above the stage. He could also detect the scent of fertilizer.

Mr. Clark appeared on the other side of the stage, but Drew was closer to the guy, who had begun to untie one of the knots. He was close enough to stop the guy, if he didn't miss, so rather than waste more time he circled the rope above his head letting out enough to capture the man and let it fly. His aim was true, and he pulled back on the rope to eliminate the slack. He continued to tug, to get the man away from the area securing the giant bags of fertilizer, but the knot the other guy had been working on was slipping. Drew hollered at Mr. Clark who made a lunge for it and managed to grab it before it wrenched free from the catwalk. Chase, who had come up the ladder, at the back of the stage, hurried over to help Mr. Clark re-secure the rope keeping the fertilizer from crashing down.

When his hands were free, Mr. Clark signaled the security officer still on the stage, that it was safe to continue the program. The man Drew had roped started to protest, so rather than have the guy continue to disrupt the pageant, Drew used his own tie to gag the man with, glad he hadn't worn a string tie tonight. He carefully perp-walked the guy to the ladder. Seeing another security officer below he let up on the rope to give the guy his hands to climb down the ladder, but warned him in a harsh whisper that if he tried anything foolish he was going to tighten the rope and hang the guy from the catwalk until the pageant was over in an hour and a half.

The man turned pale and nodded. He didn't cause any trouble getting down the ladder. Drew happily handed over the dumb-shit to the security officer after tightening the slack once more to keep him secured. The security officer looked at the rope holding the man like it was a snake.

Drew rolled his eyes at the guy, as Cade walked up and slapped him on the back. He whispered in his ear, "Mighty fine roping little brother, but your hondo could use some work."

Drew chuckled and whispered back, "Fine if you think you can do better on the run, forty feet above the floor on a rickety catwalk, go for it."

"Heck, I don't think it's more than thirty feet above the floor, and let's hope it isn't too rickety, so it keeps holding those huge bags of shit off the stage."

Drew laughed, "For sure. God what a mess that would have made, and some of the girls could have been hurt."

Cade nudged Drew with his shoulder. "Another cowboy with a rope saves the day."

Mr. Clark walked up then. "Could one of you show me how to use one of those things? They seem to come in pretty handy."

Cade and Drew both grinned at him.

CHAPTER 28

*T*here were no more issues, and an hour and a half later Ms. USA was crowned. It wasn't Lily. Drew was disappointed for her. She was third runner up, but unless something crazy happened to the others she wouldn't be entering the international competition.

She walked off stage and straight into his arms. "It's over."

"I'm sorry you didn't win."

"I'm not. This has been a crazy ride and I'm glad it's over. The first thing I want is a pizza and beer. Or maybe tacos and a margarita, with a side of nachos and guacamole. Or a big fat juicy burger and a mountain of fries, oh and a chocolate milkshake."

"Whoa, go easy there home-girl, I doubt your stomach can take all of that so quick, after eating no carbs for a year."

"I've been having a few carbs this week."

"Yeah, but nothing like you're describing."

"Fine, party pooper, then let's go have wild and crazy sex."

Drew about swallowed his tongue as her father spoke from behind him. "Great job, Lily-bug. I'm sorry, but not sorry, you didn't win. I didn't really want you going off to

God knows where for the next competition. This one has been enough to give me gray hair."

They turned toward her parents who both gave her a hug. "I agree with you, daddy, I'll be happy to stay home and go back to eating like a normal person."

Howard chuckled. "That is one perk of not winning I guess. So, what did you decide on? Pizza? Or Tacos?"

"You forgot a fat juicy burger with a mound of fries and chocolate milkshake," Elaine said.

Her dad laughed, and Drew hoped he hadn't heard her last suggestion.

Elaine nudged her husband. "Let's go find someplace to indulge in at least one of those, and Drew can tell us what was going on behind the scenes, when they moved all you girls off stage, and his brothers disappeared like smoke."

Rachel said, "Excellent idea. There is supposed to be one of the best New York style pizza joints, one block over, let's go there."

Drew asked Lily, "Do you want to change first?"

"Nope, they'll just have to take me in my dress."

Alyssa said, "Yay, let's go. I'm starving for food, and information."

Drew looked at his sister-in-law. "Impatient much?"

"Hey, be nice to me, I'm eating for two."

Dead silence reigned for about three seconds and then there were whoops of joy, enough to draw attention to the group.

Alyssa looked at Beau. "Oops."

Beau laughed and kissed her nose. "It's okay sweetheart, although mom and dad are going to be disappointed to find out last."

Cade chimed in, "And Grandpa K and Emma and Tony. Not to mention *your* whole family."

Rachel frowned. "But most importantly your best friend."

Alyssa grabbed Rachel in a bear hug. "I was going to tell you first, after Beau of course, but then I just blurted it out."

"When did you take the test?" Rachel demanded.

"This morning, my stomach's been a little queasy."

Rachel gave Alyssa another hug. "Oh, well if you've only known a few hours, I'll give you a pass this time."

"We have been kind of busy," Alyssa said waving toward Lily.

Alyssa put her hands on her hips and turned toward the family. "Now none of you rat me out before we get home to tell the rest of them."

Her phone buzzed. Beau's phone buzzed. The twins turned their phones toward Alyssa, then said in unison, "Too late."

Alyssa groaned. Beau said, "Come on let's get to the restaurant and we can text or call them back while we wait for pizza."

Cade said to Alyssa, "At least we didn't tell your family."

Alyssa's phone dinged this time, which was her parents' text sound. She hung her head. "Well someone did."

Cade grabbed one hand and Chase the other and they dragged Alyssa along. "Come on, pizza awaits."

LILY SMILED as she and Drew followed his family. They were a happy bunch and so close. She wouldn't mind being a part of that. She'd felt her phone vibrate a couple of times once she got her tiny purse back from Summer, it was most likely her siblings texting her in support, but they were nothing like Drew's huge family. They loved her, she knew that, but their ages were more spread out, so the closeness was also spread out.

Her mom came up next to her and took her hand. "They've got a wonderful family."

"They do, but so do we."

"That's true, but with them it seems the more really is the merrier. And with Rose being so much older and dear William younger, you three don't have the same camaraderie."

Lily sighed. "I guess that's true, we span fifteen years for the three of us and I think Drew said there's nine years between Adam and Emma, with six of them crammed into those years. Meg and Travis were busy."

"True. You would have had another couple of siblings, if I hadn't miscarried."

"We had the number in our family that we were supposed to have, and think how much fun it will be to meet the other two someday in the afterlife."

Elaine squeezed her hand. "It will be wonderful."

Lily hoped she hadn't upset her mom with the talk about more siblings. She never really thought about the miscarried babies much, but she was certain it was much more on her mom's mind, especially being around large close families like the Kiplings. She been thinking about maybe her and Drew staying together to see if their relationship held, but after this talk with her mom, she knew if she left to live in Colorado, her mom and dad would both miss her.

She didn't live at home, she had a small apartment in town near her job where she worked at horse sanctuary for older horses, but she went home several times a week and helped out with the horses on weekends and anytime there was a need. So, she just needed to let the idea of her and Drew drift away. There were other great guys out there that didn't live three states away. She hadn't found them yet, but she knew they were out there.

The pizza place was all it was cracked up to be, it was fun

and crowded and had great food. They ordered a half dozen pizzas of all varieties. When the servers could hardly fit all of them on the table, they decided they'd gone a little overboard.

But Cade spoke up, "It will be just the right amount to have for breakfast in the morning."

Alyssa said, "No breakfast pizza for me."

Cade rubbed his hands together in glee. "More for me."

Chase rolled his eyes at his twin and the rest of them laughed.

The beer flowed, and they managed to put a pretty good-sized dent in the pizza. There was still plenty for breakfast, but not at all what Lily had thought would be left, when the pizzas had first been brought out.

As they got up to leave Lily groaned. "I should have had a salad and less pizza."

Drew looked at her in mock horror. "What? Desecrate that amazing pizza with salad? You need to have your mouth washed out with soap for even saying such a thing."

Rachel grinned at her. "You'll walk it off on the way back to the hotel."

Drew glanced at her parents starting for the door and waggled his eyebrows at her. "And some other activity when we get back to the room."

Lily felt her face heat and whispered, "You stop that."

Drew laughed and said, "Packing, we still have to pack up everything."

"I don't have a lot to pack, most of mine got shredded."

Drew made sure all his siblings were far enough away not to overhear and waggled his eyebrows at her again. "Hmm, guess you'll have to sleep naked."

Lily punched him in the stomach with their box of left-over pizza. "Stop it, they're going to get suspicious if we don't get out there. Try to keep your mind out of the gutter."

"No gutter, just thinking of the best game plan for the evening. There were lots of things you wanted to try, as I recall."

This time her face flamed with heat and she squirmed. Drew took the pizza in one hand and grabbed her hand with the other and began pulling her quickly out the door. They caught up with everyone in an instant. He would have kept dragging her right past them, but she pulled back and made him stay in the rear, she didn't want anyone getting any ideas why the two of them were blasting past the rest of the crowd.

When they got to the hotel the woman at the desk and the concierge both noted their appearance and asked them to wait for just a moment. There was a small lounge area to the right and the whole group of them were asked to wait. Drew sighed dramatically, and Lily laughed.

They milled around for only a minute or two before Mr. Clark came in with two other men. One had been part of the pageant officials and the other they had seen occasionally.

Mr. Clark cleared his throat, to get everyone's attention. "I've got the hotel owner Mr. Abramson and the head of the pageant Mr. Kline with me, they would like to say a few words."

Before the others spoke, Mr. Clark introduced the different family members to the two men.

Mr. Kline said, "We wish to thank you for saving the pageant. If it hadn't been for all of you working together the pageant would have been ruined by one man, for his own personal gain. Just so you know, now that the pageant is over, Ms. Colorado was released. She's back home, upset naturally, with a few minor injuries, and a little dehydrated, but she will be fine."

Lily sighed with relief.

Mr. Abramson took his turn next. "Our hotel chain and this hotel, in particular, would like to thank you for working hard to keep our guests safe. Your report of the snake helped to ensure the safety of our guests. And the apprehension of the man on the catwalks, saved us a lot of cleanup and damage. The hotel chain would like to give each one of you a lifetime card entitling you to stay for half price at any one of our hotels worldwide, at any time, for the rest of your lives. I am sweetening that a bit more, by giving each of you a lifetime free pass at this particular hotel. Anytime you want to come to New York, your stay will be on the house."

Lily was surprised when he handed out what looked like gold-plated cards to each person in their group. She didn't think she'd done anything to deserve such treatment, she'd been more victim than anything else.

Mr. Kline spoke one last time. "Lily, thank you so much for being in our pageant and thank you for bringing this group with you. We'd like to set up a scholarship in your name."

Lily gasped. It was such an honor, but she wanted the honor to go where it belonged. "Would you mind changing that to the Olivia Johnson scholarship. That was my best friend, who passed away, before she could fulfill her dream of participating in a pageant, and begged me to go in her place. Without that deathbed promise, I wouldn't have been here at all."

Mr. Kline looked a little taken aback and then slowly nodded. "That is certainly doable and a lovely story to go along with it. Thank you, my dear."

Mr. Abramson said as almost an afterthought. "Lily we've given you and the other contestant that lost her clothes a prepaid Visa to replace what you lost. We are still investigating how our security or staff may have been in on that, deliberate or not. Everyone's stay at this hotel for the pageant has been taken care of. But we didn't find a couple of the rooms in our system."

Drew said, "I had them book across the street in that hotel that connects. Just to keep suspicion down while we were trying to figure out what was going on."

Mr. Abramson frowned, then nodded, "That was probably wise. We'll get those rooms taken care of also. Were they under the Kipling name?"

Adam shook his head. "One is, Beau Kipling, but the other is under Rachel's name, Rachel Reardon."

Mr. Clark and Mr. Abramson both snapped their gaze to Rachel, who was standing next to Adam.

Mr. Abramson said, "The photographer?"

Rachel nodded shyly. Mr. Abramson nearly clapped his hands with excitement. Lily almost laughed out loud. The man had been nice, but very stoic, until that exact moment. "I love your photography. I would like to replace some of the old, tired, artwork in the hotel with some of yours. Do you have an agent?"

Rachel reached into her purse and drew out a card. "Thank you, please feel free to contact her."

Mr. Abramson grinned and took the card. "You'll have to come back when we get them installed."

Rachel didn't look too excited by that, but she nodded graciously.

They all shook hands and the three men walked off with Mr. Abramson gushing, on and on, over Rachel's photography.

Howard said, "I don't know if we'll ever use these cards, but it was mighty nice of them to hand them out."

Elaine looked at her husband. "Oh, I think we can find ways to use them on occasion. There is one of their hotels in Billings, and several in Hawaii."

Rachel looked at the card in her hand and then back at Adam. "Is this hotel chain the one we have booked in January?"

Adam looked at the card and then pulled out his phone. "It is indeed. Well, that is a mighty nice coincidence. If they actually honor it."

Drew punched his brother on the arm. "They'll honor it. Don't be so pessimistic."

Adam grinned. "That will save us a shit ton of money."

Drew nodded. "Yep and if they really buy some of Rachel's pictures for this hotel, you're going to have more money than you'll need. You can become a kept man."

"Yeah, right up until dad kicks me in the ass, and tells me to get to work."

They all laughed and went their separate ways.

CHAPTER 29

*L*ily and Drew walked hand in hand up to their room. The twins and their ladies had decided to go into the bar and have a drink before heading up to their room. With their weddings coming up in December they wanted to talk about possible honeymoon locations, now that they had half price stays at one of the largest hotel chains in the world.

Lily was glad to finally be alone with Drew. She'd enjoyed the celebration, but the time to be with him was slipping through her fingers, and she couldn't stop it. She refused to be sad about it though, she was determined to wring every last drop of enjoyment out of being with him, before they parted ways and went back to their real lives.

When they got to his room they both looked around for a moment as if trying to decide what the next step was.

Lily said, "So maybe I'm going out on a limb here, but you did promise to help me out of my dress, many hours ago."

Drew pulled her into his arms and kissed her forehead. "I did. But a lot has happened since then. You did a good thing asking to have that scholarship put into Olivia's name."

She drew in a ragged breath. "I had to; it was *her* dream. I hope she'll look down from heaven and smile when some lucky girl is given that scholarship."

Drew ran one hand up and down her back in a soothing motion. "I'm sure she will. She might be a little horrified by what you went through to fulfill your promise to her, however."

Lily chuckled, "For sure, but it all worked out in the end and now we have lifetime discounts. I know my mom is going to be dragging daddy around a lot more than she's ever done in the past. She's always wanted to travel and not just to horse shows."

"Yeah, I did get that idea, do you suppose she's in their room looking at where all they have hotels?"

"It's entirely possible. But let's move on to the main course here, cowboy. You made some promises earlier, I plan to hold you to."

"It would be my pleasure, lovely lady." He pulled the zipper on her dress down slowly, oh so slowly, one click at a time. The sound echoed in the silent room. With each click the tension in both of them built, until she was ready to go up in flames from the mere thought of what was about to happen between them.

When he finally had it completely unzipped, the dress fell to the floor in a silky heap, the fabric sliding over her body causing nerve endings to stand up and take notice. He looked down at the sexy lace bra she had on and the fire lit in his eyes.

"You are so gorgeous, Lily. It's almost more than a man can take."

She thrilled at his words but was impatient for more action, so she reached behind her and unsnapped the bra and let it fall to the floor. His hands slowly eased up from her waist, to her breasts and he took them in his hands weighing them and gently squeezing them. Her nipples furled and begged for his touch. He didn't hesitate to answer their call, first with his fingers and then with his mouth.

When she was squirming from the pleasure of his hands and mouth on her, he went down on his knees and slowly rolled her panty hose down her body, caressing her as he did so. She stepped out of them and the sky-high heels she'd worn. He caressed, then kissed, each foot as it was freed, and her knees wobbled.

Drew steadied her. And from his kneeling position looked up into her eyes. As their gaze met she saw a look of satisfaction form. Slowly he looked down her body, his gaze making her skin heat and tingle in anticipation. He gently pulled her panties down and then he licked her, and her legs turned to jelly.

He deftly turned her, so she was sitting on the bed and then he pulled her legs apart to look at the very core of her. The man hummed in appreciation, and then put her legs over his shoulders and feasted.

She was still quivering from all the attention he'd given her most secret place, when he turned her on the bed and started dropping his clothes. Lily didn't even have the energy to watch as the gorgeous man stripped at lightning speed. She heard him tear open a packet, and did manage to rouse herself enough to watch him roll a condom on his engorged cock.

Drew saw her watching and smiled. "Mind if I join you?"

Lily patted the bed and opened her legs in invitation. "That would be most welcome."

He crawled on the bed and made himself at home between her legs. Drew pleasured her with long smooth strokes. She wrapped her legs around his waist, so he would slide in deeper. Lily would be happy to stay this way forever, but she knew their time was coming to an end, so she tried to imprint the feelings he was giving her into her DNA, so she could recall them in the long lonely months after they parted company.

She knew for a fact it was going to take her a long time to get over the cowboy cop currently loving her, he was going to be a hard act to follow, for any other man that wanted to come into her life. There was no way she would have been gullible enough for Ronald to prey upon if she'd met Drew first. He'd just set the bar too high for anyone else to meet.

Wordlessly urging him to pick up the speed, she squeezed his ass, and raised up to meet each stroke. He complied with her non-verbal request and the two of them raced up to the pinnacle and kept flying as the joy broke over them. So, in tune with each other that it was almost a spiritual connection.

Lily rolled her eyes at the melodrama of her thoughts, but couldn't exactly deny them completely either. She held him tight as he pressed her into the mattress, not letting him roll off of her too quickly. She loved the feel of him, the weight, the strength, the warmth. When she loosened her hold, he rolled them both to their sides and gently kissed her lips.

"God, Lily, you are amazing. I don't want this night to ever end."

"I don't either. We've only known each other a couple of weeks, but you've ruined me for any other man."

"Not to be possessive or anything, but I hate the thought of you being with another man."

"No more than I hate the idea of you with another woman. But..." She let the sentence trail off not wanting to talk about all the reasons this would never work.

He sighed. "Yeah, but."

"Let's not think about tomorrow. We still have tonight."

"I know. I just wish..."

Lily put her hand over his mouth. "Shh don't say it. Just love me."

"I do, Lily. I really do."

"I love you too, Drew. And that's all we need for tonight."

They stayed face to face for a long time, talking, laughing, sharing secrets, essentially trying to cram a lifetime into a few short hours. Both of them determined that it would be enough, and both of them were certain they were only fooling themselves.

They made love one last time before falling asleep wrapped in each other's arms, their legs tangled together, her head on his chest where she could hear his heart beat. And if there was a tear or two shed, neither one of them acknowledged it.

DREW WOKE THE NEXT MORNING, his heart heavy. Lily was wrapped around him like cling wrap, her hair in his face, the covers completely wrapped around her to the point he was sure to catch frostbite. He had maybe three square-inches of the pillow for his head, they were so far over on his side of the bed. Drew knew he would be happy to wake up with her exactly like this every night for the rest of their lives. But it wasn't meant to be.

Their lives were miles apart. She had a good job she loved, and her family all lived close to their Montana ranch. Lily loved her sister's kids and he loved his nephew, and knew he would feel the same about the baby Alyssa and Beau would have soon. His big family was firmly ensconced in Colorado and he had his job where he was slowly climbing the ladder. Drake had mentioned retiring in a few years, and had mentioned that Drew would have a shot at the next rung of the ladder when that happened.

They were close enough to get together on occasion, but would that really be fair to either of them? No, it would not, which is why he was determined to smile, and let the love of his life board a plane headed away from him. Hell would freeze over before he made it more difficult for Lily. Drew held her tight as she slept on, they had some time this morning before they had to get moving. He thought about waking her up to take her to breakfast, but he would much rather just hold her close.

She woke slowly a little while later and looked up at him. He smiled down at her. She kissed his chest. "What are you thinking about?"

He couldn't tell her the truth about the sadness he was feeling, so he said, "You, and what a bed and blanket hog you are."

She snuggled into the blankets more. "That's the price of sleeping with me. I steal the blankets because you're naturally warm, so you don't need them."

He raised one eyebrow. "And the bed hog?"

He could see her trying to come up with a reason. "My blankets take up a lot of room. You still have plenty of space."

"I have one inch on the other side of me and maybe three inches of pillow."

She looked up at where his head was. "I think you have at least four and a half."

He laughed and tickled her. "You are a scamp."

"I know, but a fun one."

"Indeed. Now do you want to order room service, or do you want cold pizza?"

"Oh, room service, pancakes with syrup and bacon and lots of coffee with cream and sugar. I'll eat the pizza... later."

Drew wondered if the hesitation had been to avoid mentioning the airplane that would separate them. He sure as hell was planning to avoid the mention of it. Their last few hours together was not going to be spent sad, if he had anything to say about it. He hoped Lily felt the same way.

"All right. I'll order us room service. I could brew a pot of coffee in the tiny machine."

"I think it's more of a shot than a pot, but I'll take what I can get."

He laughed and slid off his side of the bed, trying not to land on the floor in a heap. It was touch and go for a moment. Drew could feel Lily's gaze on him as he ordered food and filled the miniscule coffee pot. He pulled a pair of jeans out of his bag and dragged them on, commando. Guessing they might fool around a little more after they ate.

Lily whined, "That's no fun, you got dressed."

"I don't want to scare the room service person."

"But you put my eye candy away," she said with a pouty face.

"Only for a few minutes, silly girl."

"Promise?"

"You want me to promise to walk around and have breakfast in the nude?"

The crazy woman nodded happily. "Yes."

"You're a little on the crazy side, you know that don't you?"

Lily shook her head. "Just enjoying the view, while I still can." She looked stricken for a moment, so he preened for her, making his muscles stand out and striking poses until she laughed at his antics.

She shooed him toward the door when someone knocked. "All right Adonis, answer the door." Then she scampered into the bathroom.

They didn't eat in the nude and for that he was grateful, he wasn't sure he could keep his hands off of her if they'd tried it. She'd come out of the bathroom after he'd signed the ticket, and had on the hotel robe, she'd left in his bathroom the previous day. She'd pulled her hair into a pony tail and had washed her face.

While they ate they carefully avoided the elephant in the room of their departure in a few hours. Once they'd slaked that hunger, they made love for the last time with an intensity that shocked him.

Wrung out from the pleasure they laid on the bed as their bodies cooled and their hearts slowed. Drew wanted to howl in frustration but kept his feelings on a tight rein. When he got home this evening he was going to take his horse on a furious run. He hoped it would blow some of the pain away. He knew his horse would love it.

When he and Lily could finally move, they had a slippery fun shower, which got more water on the floor than down the drain. And he wasn't sure if either one of them were clean, but they were both smiling, when they got out to dry off.

Without acknowledging what they were doing, they parted company to get dressed and pack. It didn't take either of them long. Lily's suitcase was essentially empty, with all her pageant clothes destroyed, all she had was her regular clothes, and the one dress she'd bought for the last night. She'd already returned the outfits borrowed from his family. Before they left the room, they kissed long and slow, holding each other tight.

Then they walked out to join their families and the real world. Part of his heart was left in that room.

CHAPTER 30

*L*ily was glad the ride to the airport was a little crazy. The hotel had ordered them a stretch limo that they could all fit in. A limo was pretty common on the streets of New York, but theirs was long enough to turn heads. They had a marvelous time trying to guess what people were thinking. A few people even stopped to check their phone, they joked about them searching to see what big star was in town, when in reality, it was just a bunch of cowboys from Colorado and Montana.

When the limo pulled up to the airport they had red carpet treatment, but they could see the confusion on the faces of the airport employees when no one famous got out of the vehicle. They even had escorts through security where they didn't have to remove their shoes and belts and take their laptops out of their bags. They all grinned at each other at the ease of passage, at a normally packed airport, with huge long lines at every station.

They were taken to the airline lounge where there were free drinks and snacks. Lily's mom whispered, "I had no idea any of this even existed."

285

Lily whispered back, "I didn't either."

Since they'd planned on standing in all those lines, they had at least an hour to hang out in the lounge before they needed to go to their gates. By some cosmic coincidence their flights left at almost the same time, but from different ends of the concourse. So, when the time came there were hugs all around and promises to see each other again sometime in the future. Drew gave Lily a kiss on her forehead, and she knew it was because if they shared a real kiss, they might not ever stop.

Lily walked next to her mom with her father leading the way. He could always manage to clear a path through any crowd, so they were happy to follow in his wake.

Elaine said, "Drew is a fine man."

Lily sighed and tried not to start sobbing. "He is, but he lives so far away. We both have our jobs and families."

"It's only a ten-hour drive. We could come visit any time."

"I would miss you and Rose's babies. And my job."

"There is always facetime for the babies. And a job is just a job."

"Oh mama, I wish there was some way."

"There is always a way, if you want it bad enough."

Lily didn't respond but continued to think it over as they walked through the busy airport. When they got to the gate her father looked for some empty chairs. But Lily couldn't sit, she looked back the long way they had come and then down at her parents.

"I can't go. I can't let him leave."

Her mom nodded. "I know, go."

She rushed over to kiss her dad on his forehead and her mom on the cheek. "I'll call." Then she grabbed her carry on, that held most of the clothes, and put her purse on cross-body, and turned to go.

"Lily-bug?"

Lily didn't turn back. She heard her mom say, "Let her go, Howard. Drew's the one."

"The one, one?"

"Yes."

Her father bellowed, "Good luck, Lily-bug."

She raised a hand in acknowledgement and picked up speed. *Hurry, hurry, hurry.* Her thoughts chanted with each step. *Don't leave, Drew, I'm coming, wait for me.* She sent that thought toward him.

There was a clock, dammit he should be boarding now, and she wasn't quite halfway. *No, no, no, don't leave me, Drew.* She tried to run faster but her bag kept crashing into everything, she couldn't leave it, airport security got very cranky about things like that.

She skidded to a halt as an airport vehicle pulled in front of her, stopping to let some older people off at their gate. She looked back at the clock. It was too late, he had to be boarding. She sighed in defeat, her breath bellowing from her mad dash through the airport, she wanted to cry and scream and kick things. But instead she just stood there while the older people gathered their luggage and the cart moved off.

She looked up and saw a mirage. Drew was standing on the other side of where the cart had been, looking down at the floor. Not believing her eyes she whispered, "Drew?"

His head snapped up, and a slow smile slid across his previously distraught features.

DREW COULDN'T BELIEVE what he was seeing. Lily stood on the other side of where the cart had been, which had stopped his mad dash through the terminal toward her gate. He'd wanted to throw something when they'd blocked his path, but he'd already known he'd waited too long.

He'd walked morosely to his gate, and had been waiting for them to call out preboarding, when Adam had sauntered up and said, "Are you really going to walk away from her?"

"I have to, we live in different states."

"Didn't stop me and Rachel."

"Lily has a job she loves and her family…"

Adam shrugged, "So, you move to Montana."

"My job…"

"Oh, I didn't realize there wasn't any sheriff departments in Montana."

Drew was not in the mood for Adam's sarcasm. "Of course, there are, stop being an asshole."

"I'm certain Drake would give you a fine recommendation, to another department in Montana."

Was it really that easy? He tried to think over the pounding of his heart. He wasn't licensed in another state. "I would have to take tests."

"So?"

"Fuck, you're right. It's just a fricken job." He slapped his brother on the back. "Tell mom and dad I'll call." And then he'd taken off running, like his ass was on fire. But it hadn't been enough. He'd run out of time and then the cart had blocked his path.

Except, there she was staring at him, like she'd seen a ghost. Her pony tail was falling out. He didn't know if it was tears or sweat on her face. Her shirt had come untucked, and was rucked up around her purse strap. She was beautiful, so damn beautiful. He probably stunk like a mule, from his own run through the airport, but when he opened his arms she walked right into them.

"I couldn't do it. I couldn't let you go," she sobbed.

"I couldn't either, you're my life."

"I'll move to Colorado."

"I'll move to Montana."

He laughed and squeezed her tight. "We could live in Casper and split the difference."

She grinned up at him. "That would make it a five-plus-hour drive in either direction to see everyone."

"We could trade off major holidays, between the two families."

"But, your pretty land."

He shrugged, "We'll build us a getaway house on it. For vacations and stuff."

"We could build another on daddy's land. For vacations and stuff."

"We could."

Lily asked, "Do you really think it would work?"

"We'll make it work. I'm not living without you, Lily. I meant what I said, you're my life, my heart, my one and only. I love you and I'm not letting you go. I don't give a flying fuck that we've only known each other a couple of weeks."

"Oh good. I'm not living without you either. I love you too, and I don't care if it's only been a dozen days either. You're already in my heart."

They stood in the middle of the airport holding each other, not moving. His chin rested on the top of her head and her head was on his chest.

Finally, after a long time, Lily pulled back. "We missed our flights."

Drew grimaced, "We sure did. Want to go back to the pageant hotel?"

Lily shook her head, "No. I'm kind of over that place."

Drew let out the breath he was holding. "Good, I feel the same way. Want to escape somewhere for a few days?"

Lily looked at him through her eyelashes. "We could go check out Casper, see if we really want to live there."

He nodded. "I've not been to your ranch, either. Or met your siblings."

"No, you haven't and that would be fun, but let's take a few days for ourselves first, and really talk about what we want to do. Where we want to live."

"I can do that. What about your job?"

"I took a leave of absence for the pageant and don't have a firm return date. I wasn't going to go back this week, anyway. Will Drake be okay with you taking a few more days?"

"I've been on the clock all week. I can easily take a few more days."

"So, Casper?"

He wondered if the airline had a flight into Casper, it wasn't a super busy destination. With probably only one or two flights a day. "Let's go see what they have available."

They walked back to the ticket counter, hand in hand, not really caring where they went, as long as it was together.

CHAPTER 31

*L*ily was excited when the airline did have a flight into Casper, with only one stop, so they went there to explore the city. It was a larger city than either of them had ever lived in. She wasn't sure she would want to live somewhere that populated.

She said, "Casper is so big compared to my town and yours, do you think we could be happy here?"

"I will be happy wherever you are, but I agree it isn't the small town we're used to. But there are plenty of smaller towns around it. We wouldn't have to live in Casper proper. In fact, when we're ready to leave let's rent a car and drive up to your area, we can look at the little towns on the way north."

Lily felt a lot better about that idea, the idea of living in a city even as large as Casper did not appeal. "That sounds like fun."

"Great. I'll call the rental car people and see where we can drop the car in Montana. Then we can use yours after that."

"All right, then can we just take some days to chill before

we head north. Since it doesn't look like either of us is that excited to live here?"

"Absolutely."

They spent several days holed up in their hotel room, enjoying each other and talking about their hopes and dreams, and what they really cared about. When they were ready to move on and do more exploring they left the hotel. They had looked around some in Casper for jobs, but neither one of them had been too excited about that, so they hadn't wasted a lot of time. The only thing they did look into was the sheriff's department since that was a county wide operation.

They stopped and looked around all the small towns on the drive north, and as they entered each new county they stopped to make inquiries at the sheriff's department. Some of the areas looked nice, but no lightning struck.

Lily was careful to keep a record of each town, what kinds of businesses they had and notes on the law enforcement. She thought maybe they simply needed to look over all the options and then one of them would feel right.

When they got to Montana they didn't stop any longer but drove straight through to her parent's house. Her mom had Lily's childhood room prepared for them to stay in. Howard on the other hand didn't look too pleased at that idea.

Drew asked her father if he could have a private word with him, so they went off to her dad's office.

Lily asked her mom, "Should Drew and I stay in Livingston, in my apartment?"

Elaine shook her head. "I don't think that will be necessary. I think Drew will let your father know he has nothing to fear from the two of you being together."

Her mother's prediction was correct. When the two men came back from the talk—that had obviously included some whiskey—her father was much more relaxed and happy about Drew visiting them.

That night Lily asked Drew what had happened during the talk.

"Nothing really," Drew said, "First I poured him a drink and took one for myself, then I asked him if I could marry you. He consented to that idea and we drank to a successful marriage."

Drew sent her an uneasy look. "I explained that my siblings had snatched up the next two months with their weddings, so you and I would have to wait until at least February. Apparently, my dad had mentioned that to him, so he wasn't at all surprised. So when would you like to get married?"

Lily wasn't quite ready to commit to a date yet. She wanted to decide on a place to live before she went down that path. "I want to think about that a little longer, if that's all right with you."

He took her hand and squeezed. "That's fine with me. It's all been rather sudden. But let's not wait too long."

Her heart warmed at his desire to commit to spending his life with her. Her face must have shown how she felt because he rolled her onto the bed and kissed her for long minutes. The kisses turned hotter and they ended up naked and breathless.

As they drifted off to sleep wrapped up in each other's arms, she reveled in having Drew in her childhood room. He looked good among her memories and mementos. It made her happy to add him into her life.

Lily's mom arranged for a dinner the next day, where Drew could meet her family. She wasn't apprehensive about him meeting them. Her sister would be polite, her brother friendly, but her family did not have the same dynamic his did.

When Rose charged in the door and grabbed Lily into a bear hug and squeezed her so hard she thought a rib might crack, Lily was so surprised she could have been knocked over with a feather.

Rose finally released her and put her hands on her hips. Then she shook one finger at Lily. "Don't you ever scare the crap out of me like that again, Lily. My heart can't take it. I'm sorry if this hurts your feelings, but I prayed really hard that you wouldn't win that stupid pageant and have to go on to the international competition. I just couldn't imagine going through that fear again."

Rose's eyes filled with tears and she hugged Lily again in another bone crushing embrace. Lily was surprised at the vehemence of Rose's words and actions. She'd always been so cool headed and relaxed.

Lily patted her sister's back. "It's okay, big sis. I'm fine, and perfectly happy not to go on to the next pageant level."

Rose pulled back and released her stranglehold on Lily. "Good, because I love you and can't lose you."

"I love you too, Rose. Where are John and the kids?"

"Oh, I left him to bring in the munchkins. I needed to see you immediately, he wasn't even parked when I jumped out of the car." She shrugged as if she always jumped out of a moving vehicle. "So where is this new man of yours? I swear Lily, engaged to two different men within a month, what are you thinking?"

"I'm thinking Drew is amazing. Now he's right over there waiting to meet you."

Rose turned the direction she'd indicated and took a long look at Drew. She turned back and whispered, "Rancher?"

Lily grinned and nodded. "Cattle, and he's also a sheriff's deputy."

"A cop? Well good, he'll keep you safe then."

"He already has."

"Well he's a damn sight better than Ronald the weasel."

"I like Ronald the rat, and I couldn't agree more, now come meet my man."

To Lily's surprise Rose was nearly as enthusiastic to meet Drew as she had been to see Lily. Then John came in with the kids and there was the normal family chaos that involves small children. Drew got down on the floor to meet and then play with her niece and nephew. Something Ronald wouldn't have been caught dead doing.

Her brother came in a little while later, he'd been on a road trip with the football team, and had just gotten back in town in time for dinner.

William grabbed her and swung her around. "Glad you're home, sis. So, introduce me to the big bad roper who saved you from that Pamper guy. If it was me, I would have changed my name, who wants to be named the same as a diaper company?"

Lily laughed and introduced her brother to Drew.

William looked Drew in the eye and shook his hand. "Thanks for taking care of my sister. You're going to keep doing that, right?"

Drew nodded. "Yes, I am, from now on she's my first priority."

"Good, then welcome to the family."

The meal was pleasant and delicious. They all hashed over the idea of where Drew and Lily might settle. They talked about the pros and cons for each state. In the end no one thought a ten-hour drive was a big deal, which helped both Lily and Drew to relax.

They looked around town there, too, and visited Lily's job. Where her coworkers congratulated her on completing the pageant. She told her boss she wasn't ready to come back. Her boss took one long look at Drew and told her to take her time. She also said that they would miss her if she decided not to return, but maybe she could start up another branch of the sanctuary wherever she landed. Lily hugged everyone and said her goodbyes. Next, they went to her little apartment.

Drew and Lily both knew that even if they decided to live in Montana, there was no way they would want to live in her tiny apartment, so they packed up her belongings and put them in storage. Cleaned the apartment and turned in the keys. The manager said she'd just had someone looking for a place just like it, so they would let Lily out of her lease, with only a two hundred dollar turn-over fee.

The last stop was the cemetery. Drew went with her to visit Olivia's grave, Lily laid her pageant sash on it, along with a bouquet of her friend's favorite flowers. Drew gave her time alone, while he waited on a nearby bench.

When she was finished talking to the best friend of her past, she went to go join her best friend of the future. Drew pulled her into his arms where he held her tight.

Lily gasped. "Do you smell that?"

"Sure do." He looked around. "Not sure where it's coming from."

"It's Olivia's favorite scent."

"I don't remember it being that strong in the car, when we had the flowers in there."

"It's not from the flowers. That's the smell of lilacs."

Drew frowned. "But they only bloom in the spring."

Lily had tears on her cheeks and she could barely whisper, "Exactly. I think it's Olivia, blessing us and our love. Maybe saying farewell."

Drew wiped the tears off her face and kissed her nose. "I would have liked Olivia."

She nodded as more tears fell. "Yes, you would have."

THEY LEFT the next day to drive down to Colorado. Lily had insisted, that to make an informed decision they needed to take a good long look around his home town, also. She hadn't been anywhere except for the ranch.

On the drive down, they paid attention to the towns south of Casper, just in case they wanted to live around that area. There were two different ways to get to his home, one was down interstate twenty-five that went through Denver, but there was also a back way that—according to the mapping software—shaved an hour off the drive, so they decided to look that over. It was a smaller road but went through the national forest, or near it, so it was a prettier drive.

His family gave them a warm welcome, and he was happy to show off his home state. He drove her to the small towns near his home and would have liked to take her into the National Park, but it was too late in the season and the road was closed due to snowfall. He noticed there had been some snow while he was gone. Not a lot at the ranch but up on Trail Ridge Road it was most likely significantly heavier.

They took things slow and looked at possible job openings around the area. He talked to Drake about possibly moving. Drake was disappointed but wished him well and told him to take the time he needed to make the best decision. Drake also told Drew, that he would give him a stellar recommendation, if he decided to move on.

Travis also took him aside to tell him if he needed to live somewhere else to be with Lily, they would miss him fiercely, but they all wanted him to be happy. If that was living somewhere else, then they would be glad for him.

Drew was glad for their support, but they still hadn't decided where they wanted to live. One day as they were walking through town they turned down a street Lily hadn't seen before.

"Oh, look at that pretty church. Can we go in and look at it?"

"Sure, it should be open this time of day." He steered her toward the steps and they went inside.

Lily sighed when they walked into the sanctuary. It had one whole side of the church that was huge windows that held an amazing view of the lake and mountains behind it.

"It's amazing. Can we get married here? It's plenty large enough for both our families, and even some people from both our towns that would want to come."

"Yeah, I can see that. Let's talk to the receptionist and see what dates they have available."

They decided to get married on Valentine's day, surprisingly, it was one of the dates open due to a recent cancellation. With choosing February it was early enough that they wouldn't have to worry about calving or foaling season.

Once they made that decision, they decided to live in Colorado until their wedding. The twins and their sweethearts were getting married in December. Adam and Rachel were having a destination wedding in Hawaii in January. And then their wedding would be in February. So, it made the most sense to stay in Colorado until then. Which also gave them the time to decide about a permanent location. With that settled they breathed a sigh of relief and made plans to go back to Montana to get more of Lily's clothes.

A few days later Lily insisted it was time for him to visit Monica's grave.

Drew frowned. "I don't need to visit Monica's grave."

"I think you do. It would give you closure."

"That's silly, she's been gone for years. I don't need closure."

But Lily didn't let up. Drew didn't really want to visit it, but he gave into Lily's insistence. She promised to go with him to the cemetery. He bought a bouquet of Monica's favorite flowers that had to be shipped in from Denver.

When they got to the cemetery Lily walked over to the grave and looked at it for a long moment. She turned and squeezed his arm. "I'm going to go sit on that bench over there and give you a couple of minutes. Say your goodbyes, Drew."

He shook his head as she walked away, he didn't really feel this was necessary, but she'd felt better after they'd gone to Olivia's grave, so he supposed it wouldn't hurt. He knelt down and laid the flowers carefully on her grave, and a sense of peace settled over his heart. He remembered the life he'd had with Monica and all they had shared. Then he glanced over to Lily and envisioned his future. Lily was right, he *had* needed to say a final farewell to his first love, now that he'd found his final love.

He also realized he could finally let Monica rest, since he had managed to save Lily, even when he hadn't been able to do the same for Monica. That release also set him free from his need to be a sheriff, he still might *want* to be one, but he didn't *have* to be one, he didn't have anything to prove. He was glad he'd come to say goodbye.

He could almost feel Monica ruffle his hair as she had when they were together. It had become—over the years— her way of saying goodbye. She'd not done it the night she died, she'd been too sad and had forgone her silly tradition. It had always bothered him. Not consciously, but it had been there in his heart. So, to feel her do it today—even if it was really just the wind—healed something deep inside.

Then he stood to walk over to Lily, he was ready to face the future with his new love, and knew Monica was laughing and happy for him.

Lily walked into his arms, she belonged there, and regardless of where they decided to live, he knew he would be taking home with him. Lily was his future, his love, his home.

The End
If you enjoyed this story, please leave a review on Amazon, Bookbub, or Goodreads.
Thanks so much!

Taming Adam: Burlap and Barbed Wire #2
Adam and Rachel's story

Tempting Chase: Burlap and Barbed Wire #3
Chase and Katie's story

Roping Cade: Burlap and Barbed Wire #4
Cade and Summer's story

Trusting Drew: Burlap and Barbed Wire #5
Drew and Lily's story

HELLUVA ENGINEER SERIES

Helluva Engineer
Steve and Patsy's story

ABOUT THE AUTHOR

What does a geeky math nerd know about writing romance?

That's a darn good question. As a former techy I've done everything from computer programming to international trainer. Prior to college I had lots of different jobs and activities that were so diverse, I was an anomaly.

None of that qualifies me for writing novels. But I have some darn good stories to tell and a lot of imagination.

I have lived in Colorado, Hawaii and currently reside in Washington. Going from two states with 340 days of sun to a state with 340 days of clouds, I had to do something to perk me up. And that's when I started this new adventure called author. Joining the Romance Writers of America and two local chapters, helped me learn the craft quickly and has been a ton of fun.

My family consists of two grown children, their spouses, two adorable grand-daughters, and one grand dog. My favorite activity is playing with my grand-daughters!

When the girls can't play with their amazing grandmother, my interests are reading and writing, yay! I started reading at a young age with the Nancy Drew mysteries and have continued to be an avid reader my whole life. My favorite reading material is romance, but occasionally if other stories creep into my to-be-read pile, I don't kick them out.

Some of the strange jobs I have held are a carnation grower's worker, a trap club puller, a pizza hut waitress, a software engineer, an international trainer, and a business program manager. I took welding, drafting and upholstery in high school, a long time ago, when girls didn't take those classes, so I have an eclectic bunch of knowledge and experience.

And for something really unusual... I once had a raccoon as a pet.

Join with me as I tell my stories, weaving real tidbits from my life in with imaginary ones. You'll have to guess which is which. It will be a hoot!

~

To sign up for Shirley's New Release Newsletter,
send email to shirleypenick@outlook.com,
subject newsletter.

Made in the USA
Middletown, DE
27 May 2019